WHEN WE WERE YOUNG

MICHELE BROUDER

This is a work of fiction. Names, characters, places and incidents are either a product of the author's imagination or are used fictitiously, and any resemblance to actual persons, living or dead, events, or locales is entirely coincidental.

Editing by Jessica Peirce

Book Cover Design by Rebecca Ruger

When We Were Young

Copyright © 2022 Michele Brouder

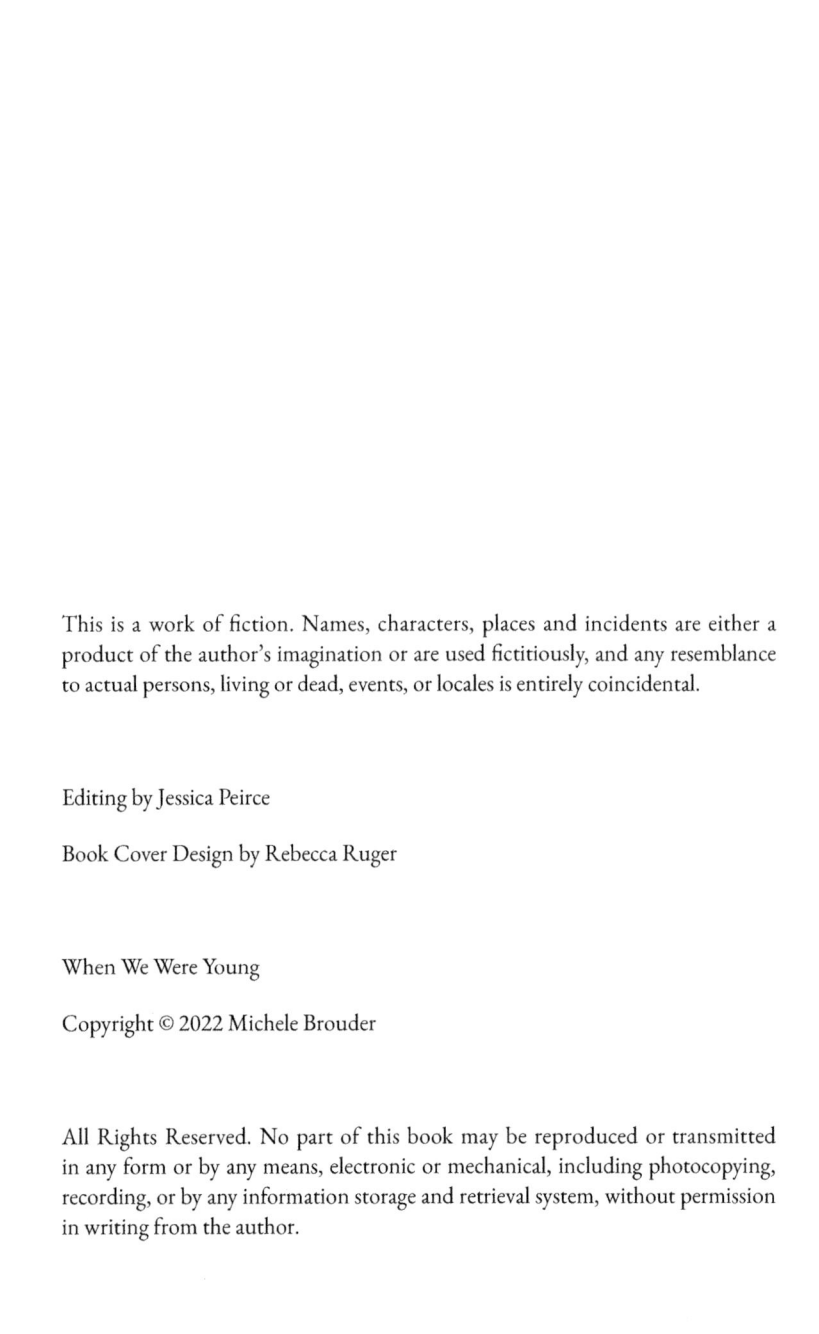

All Rights Reserved. No part of this book may be reproduced or transmitted in any form or by any means, electronic or mechanical, including photocopying, recording, or by any information storage and retrieval system, without permission in writing from the author.

Part 1

Present Day

CHAPTER ONE

Martha

MARTHA COTTER WAS STARTLED by a hooting and hollering behind her, nearly causing her to lose her grip on her walker. She'd just picked up her mail from the mailbox at the end of the driveway and was making her way back up to her grand old house on the corner of Star Shine Drive and Erie Street. With her jaw tight, she looked over her shoulder, deciding it required too much effort to pivot and investigate the ruckus. Immediately, she spied those Monroe sisters driving by in Isabelle Monroe's vintage cherry red convertible, singing at the top of their lungs to some song blasting out from the car radio. She hoped she wouldn't have to put up with that for the remainder of the summer.

She tut-tutted. "Who do those girls think they are?" Acting like they were in their twenties. Pretty soon, they'd be as old and frail as she. She continued up the asphalt driveway, taking her time because that's all she had, was time.

Her home was the largest house on Star Shine Drive. Until those new million-dollar builds up on the cliffs overlooking Lake Erie, it had been the largest home in Hideaway Bay. Her great-grandfather, Richard Newsome, had had it built in 1901, a fine Victorian with gingerbread trim and a large wraparound porch. It had remained in the family ever since, passed down through the matrilineal line. It was one of the few things that still made Martha smile.

The garden beds in front of the porch had been planted with low-maintenance shrubs. There wasn't a flower in sight. The grass had gone brown, showing evidence of the hot, dry summer.

Across from the house was an unobstructed view of Lake Erie and the beach, a long, wide swath of sand whose pale color always reminded her of cooked oatmeal. To the left of the house was Erie Street and directly across from the end of Erie Street was the weathered boardwalk that led to the beach.

Martha made her way toward the side entrance. She had a system. You couldn't do much in life without a system. The key to everything was organization. She shoved her mail into the deep pocket of her pink-checked tabard and opened the storm door. Gingerly, she stepped inside, leaving the walker next to the door inside the hallway. Three stairs stood between her and the main part of the house, where a second walker awaited her.

There's no future in getting old, she thought to herself.

She grabbed onto the handrails attached to the walls on either side of her and took the steps one at a time, arriving at the top with both relief and breathlessness. She no sooner laid her hands on her walker than the front doorbell rang. The sigh that escaped her could have shaken the house. *What now?*

Gripping the walker with a determined set to her jaw, she slowly headed toward the front door, cutting through the narrow hall that passed the dining room and through the front parlor.

The front door was a large carved oak affair with a glass window. As gorgeous as it was, it needed to be replaced. The wood swelled in the humidity in the summer, making it difficult to close, and the ancient brass letter slot the postal service had stopped using decades ago still encouraged too many businesses to drop their glossy colored postcards advertising everything from the new local Chinese restaurant to oil changes to dry cleaning. They ended up landing on the floor, and it required a lot of effort on Martha's part to pick them up. It all made her tired. As she approached the door, she noticed a small puddle of water from all the rain the previous night and made a *tsk* sound. Luckily, the new door was being delivered in the morning. The thought of it irritated her. It wasn't that she minded spending the money; what she minded was the inconvenience and upheaval it would cause to replace it. Thoughts of sweaty workers traipsing through her house and using crude language made her recoil.

Through the glass, she spied a teenaged girl standing on the front porch. The girl stood in profile, her nut-brown hair hanging down like a curtain. The girl swung her head around and rang the bell again, pressing longer on it.

"Just because you keep ringing the bell doesn't mean I'm going to move faster," Martha muttered.

Finally, she arrived at the front door, undid several deadbolts, and opened the door just enough to allow her form to fit through. To open it any wider would give the impression of blanket hospitality to every Tom, Dick, and Harry who arrived on the porch. That would not do.

Before the girl could speak, Martha rapped with a gnarled hand on the yellowed piece of paper taped to the door, which read "No Soliciting."

"Can't you read, young lady?" Martha demanded. She had no patience for impertinence or stupidity.

"Yeah, I can read, but I'm not soliciting," the girl said softly. She had brown eyes to match the color of her hair and a smattering of freckles across the bridge of her nose. Her young skin was dewy and soft-looking; she'd been spared the universal acne that seemed to plague teenagers.

"Then what is it you want?"

The girl broke into a grin and tapped her hands to her chest. "It's me, Gram—Mimi, or Martha the Eighth as I sometimes refer to myself." She was bright-eyed and chatting as if they'd spent all their lives together. But Martha had never laid eyes on her before.

Martha Cotter did something she never did: so caught by surprise, she let her mouth fall open.

"Mimi? Mimi Duchene?" she repeated. She moved her head half an inch and narrowed her eyes. She was delighted to see Mimi had inherited the wide-set eyes of all the women in Martha's family, coming down the French side of her mother's people. The nut-brown hair must come from Mimi's father, Edgar, a man Martha had never met. Nothing that could be done about that. Although it didn't look half bad on her.

"Can I come in?" Mimi asked. She had put her hands in the front pockets of her jeans, and her unflinching gaze never left Martha's face, as if she was considering her grandmother just as Martha had assessed her.

"What for?"

The girl swallowed visibly but she did not look away. "I thought I'd come find you. I wanted to meet you."

Martha frowned. Now why would a teenage girl want to meet her? Especially with her host of problems. She leaned her head to the right, peering around the girl to see if there was a strange car parked out front with her daughter, Martha the Fifth, sitting in it, afraid to come in, as well she should be.

"Where's your mother?" Martha demanded.

"Back home in Washington State," Mimi replied.

"How did you get here?"

"I took a bus," the girl said simply.

"Does your mother know you're here?"

Mimi shook her head.

"Did you run away from home?"

"Something like that."

"A fugitive, then," Martha remarked.

Mimi shrugged and smiled. Martha wondered if the child was always in such a good mood. That would get old fast.

With a put-upon sigh, Martha opened the door wider, allowing the girl inside. Over her shoulder, Martha said, "Wipe your feet on the mat. We'll call your mother and get you back home."

"I'm not going home," the young girl said firmly. "I want to stay with you."

Chapter Two

Mimi

She didn't spend all her Christmas and babysitting money on a bus ticket just to be turned around and sent back home. She didn't sit in a cramped, hot and sweaty bus for the last few days only to be told she couldn't stay.

Her grandmother stopped, and Mimi almost ran into her but managed to pull up short. It didn't look like it would take much to knock her over and break her hip. Martha clutched her walker, turning slowly to face her.

"What do you mean you're not going home?" she asked. She had an imperious air about her. Despite her frail appearance, her posture was straight and she gave off an impression of superiority, like she expected to be obeyed and never questioned.

"I can't stand here all day, young lady, waiting for you to respond," she said with a huff and turned around, shuffling slowly forward.

Left with no choice, Mimi followed her, her heart beating rapidly. For years she'd wondered what her grandmother was like. Her mother had spoken little about her over the years and the information was lacking. Her hope was to fill in some of the blanks while she was there. Or at least that had been her plan. She hadn't expected her grandmother to send her right back where she came from. *Sigh*. It wasn't going as she had hoped. She'd had in her head that it would be a tearful reunion, that her grandmother would throw open her arms and embrace her in a warm, vanilla-scented hug. Instead, her first reaction was to get rid of her.

Looking on the positive side, Mimi thought, at least she could put an end to all the speculation about her maternal grandmother, the fantasizing about her. Those daydreams were drying up faster than a shallow riverbed during a severe drought.

She didn't mind that the older woman walked slowly, as it gave her a chance to take a look at the house. It was huge, with high ceilings and lots of dark, heavy woodwork. Mimi didn't know where to look first. The showpiece of the front of the house was the wide staircase with its ornate handrail and banister. Parked at the bottom was an electric chair lift. She wondered if anyone ever slid down it as a child. But five minutes in her grandmother's presence and she was pretty sure it had never happened.

The wallpaper in the front parlor had a dark floral pattern, and there were pedestal stands with big, heavy green ferns on them placed around the room. A grand piano stood in the far corner, and she wondered if her grandmother played. Her mother certainly didn't, or at least not to her knowledge. The fireplace mantel was littered with black-and-white photographs and an old-fashioned clock. As much as she tried to picture her mother growing up in these rooms, she couldn't seem to make it all fit.

Mimi followed her grandmother through what must have been a butler's pantry—a small, narrow room with dusty shelves and cabinets on either side. From the pantry, they landed in the expansive kitchen, and Mimi's head continued to swivel in all directions. Here, too, the ceilings were high, but unlike what she'd seen so far, this room looked to have been updated sometime this century. The cream-colored cabinets had wood trim, and the countertop was made of artificial butcher block. The walls were painted a shade of scarlet. No sun shone in through the north- and east-facing windows as it was late in the day, heading toward evening. Other than a toaster, a can opener, and a small lazy Susan holding salt and pepper shakers and a dish of butter, the countertops were clear. The sink and the dish rack were empty.

"Sit down," Martha said, pulling out a chair for herself at the kitchen table. This must be the chair she always used, Mimi thought. It was the one closest to the sink and stove, and it had an extra cushion on it. An old cell phone sat within arm's reach on the table, along with an address book and a notepad and pen.

Mimi waited for her grandmother to sit before sitting down. She thought about sitting next to Martha but hesitated, thought better of it, and chose the seat directly across from her. She shrugged off her backpack and hung it on the back of the chair before sitting down.

Martha looked up at her and Mimi was able to get a better look at the elderly woman. Most of her impressions so far had been of her grandmother's backside. She had the same wide-set eyes as Mimi, and she wondered if they bothered her grandmother the way they bothered her. A kid at school said once that if her eyes were any farther apart, they'd be on the sides of her head. Her grandmother's hair was silver and worn short and neat. Her skin was translucent, highlighting a road map of blue and purple veins underneath. Her lips were pursed, and there was a sense of dissatisfaction about her. Mimi couldn't tell if it was because of her unexpected arrival or if that was her default state.

"Now, young lady—" Martha began.

"Mimi," Mimi reminded her, sitting up straighter in the chair.

"When did you stop using the name Martha?"

"The boy next door couldn't say my name when we were little, and he just started calling me Mimi," she explained, fingering the floral design on the linen tablecloth. The flowers were faded, and she thought the cloth might be as old as her grandmother. "He was only three at the time, two years older than me."

"Why it's up to a three-year-old to determine a lifelong nickname is beyond me," Martha said with annoyance.

Mimi didn't tell her what the next-door neighbor, now six foot one with blond hair and blue eyes, had only recently said to her, crushing her.

"Are you always so grumpy?" Mimi asked, pushing the boy next door from her mind.

Martha stared at her. "I'm not grumpy!"

Mimi laughed. "Yeah, you are."

"I am a lot of things, but grumpy isn't one of them."

"Okay, if you say so," Mimi said.

"Are you always so agreeable?" Martha asked.

Mimi shrugged her slim shoulders. "What's the point in arguing all the time?" There must be a gene in the family; her own mother always seemed to be looking for a fight. It was exhausting, always playing defense. More than once, she'd wondered how her father stood it.

"Tell me your mother's number," the older woman commanded.

With a sigh, Mimi dragged her backpack off the back of the chair and pulled out her cell phone. Resigned, she rattled off the numbers, interrupted by her grandmother only once to tell her to slow down. Martha studied the phone, a flip phone with enlarged numbers, squinting as she pressed the buttons.

"Why don't you put your glasses on," Mimi suggested.

Her grandmother's head snapped up and she said tightly, "I don't need glasses."

Mimi smiled slightly. "If you say so."

"I do say so."

Martha pressed the phone to her ear and announced, "It's ringing."

Why do people always tell you that? Mimi wondered.

Martha sat straighter, staring at something unseen over Mimi's left shoulder.

"Hello, Martine, this is your mother," she said, pausing. "I'm calling to inform you that Mimi turned up on my doorstep this afternoon, and you might want to get over here to pick her up."

Mimi sagged in her chair, resigning herself to the fact that she was going to be packed up and sent right back home. *So much for getting away from my warring parents and my unexciting life. This has to be the most short-lived adventure known to man.*

Chapter Three

Martha

It was the first time Martha had spoken to her daughter in almost eighteen years. Other than Christmas cards and the occasional letter to inform her of a new address or phone number, they had not communicated since that night years ago when words were spoken and things were said that couldn't be taken back. That was the problem with spoken words, especially when people didn't think before they uttered them. Spoken words were permanent and could sometimes be weapons of mass destruction.

Martine had changed her name when she was thirteen and going through a French phase, insisting that one Martha in the house was enough. The phone conversation hadn't lasted more than five minutes. And over the phone, Martha had heard a gamut of emotions in her daughter's voice. First, surprise to hear from her mother, and then shock to discover that Mimi was in Hideaway Bay. That had quickly morphed into relief that her daughter was safe and then anger that she had traveled cross-country on a bus. But by the end of the conversation, Martine had assured her mother that she would be on her way, although it would take a few days as she didn't fly. No pleasantries had been exchanged, no inquiries after each other's health or well-being. But then, what had Martha expected?

It had not gone unnoticed by Martha that her daughter had named her first child Martha as well. But maybe traditions died slower than feelings and connections. All the firstborn women in Martha's mother's family had been named Martha from the time of the American Revolution, in honor of Martha Washington. In the drawer of her bureau upstairs in her bedroom, she still had the birth announcements of Mimi and her younger brother, Micah. They were now yellow with age, the edges curled.

"Can I have something to drink?" Mimi asked.

So astounded to hear her daughter's voice after all these years, Martha'd forgotten Mimi was there, sitting right across the breakfast table from her, looking eerily similar to Martine many years ago, sitting in that same chair.

"Look in the refrigerator," Martha instructed. There wasn't much there, but then Martha wasn't used to serving refreshments to teenage girls.

Mimi opened the refrigerator door and stared inside, most likely hoping a better selection, other than milk and orange juice, would appear. Quietly, she closed it and sat back down.

"There's not a lot of choices, but I could make coffee," Martha offered.

"Don't worry about it," Mimi said. She stood. "I'll walk into town and get something."

Martha scowled. Who was to say the young girl wouldn't jump on a bus and head elsewhere now that she knew her mother was en route. She didn't know whether she could be trusted. She decided not to look too much into that thought, realizing it might be an indictment against herself. What grandmother didn't know everything about their grandchildren? Aside from their dates of birth, Martha knew absolutely nothing about Mimi and Micah.

"I'll be back in half an hour," Mimi said. "I want to check out the town and get something to eat."

"I've got things to eat here," Martha said.

"Like what?"

"I'm making liver and onions for dinner, there's more than enough for the two of us."

Mimi stuck out her tongue and said, "Ew, no thanks."

Martha's lips disappeared. This wasn't a hotel. "I've been eating liver and onions my whole life and I can tell you, it's delicious."

"Why don't you let me pick up some sushi or Chinese?" Mimi said.

"Raw fish? No thank you." Martha practically sniffed.

Mimi giggled. "You turn your nose up at raw fish yet you're okay to eat an organ from an animal."

"Loaded with iron," Martha said. The girl was pale; she'd benefit from a plate of liver and onions.

"What did my mother say? When will she be here?" Mimi asked. She stood behind her chair, her hands clasping the back of it.

"She can't get off work until the day after tomorrow, and she figures it's going to take three days to get here," Martha said. She remembered that Martine had a fear of flying.

"Oh, that soon?" Mimi asked, biting her lip.

Martha studied her for a moment, wondering what was going on either at home or at school that the young girl had run away in the first place. "Why don't you want to go home?"

The girl shrugged her thin shoulders. "I don't know. I wanted to meet you. Did you know that grandmothers and granddaughters have a special bond? Grandparents are natural allies with their grandchildren."

Martha wondered why the girl felt she needed an ally but instead asked, "Where did you come up with that?"

Mimi shrugged again. "I don't know. I read it somewhere."

"Don't believe everything you read."

"Mom always talks about her grandmother."

Another Martha. Martine had been close to Martha's mother since the day she was born. What was implied and understood in the girl's sentence was that Martine never spoke about her, Martha.

"Again, don't believe everything you read," Martha said sourly.

"Okay, Gram," the young girl said easily.

Uncomfortable with the topic lest the girl get any ideas about a bond forming, Martha said, "Is your mother still married to Edgar?"

"If you mean my father, then yes, she is still married to him," Mimi replied with a dimpled grin.

Martha scowled at Mimi to discourage her, but the child continued to grin. *My ability to intimidate must be slipping.*

"You better go to town now and get something," Martha said.

"Okay, I'll be back in half an hour."

"I'll trust you to return promptly."

"Do you need anything?"

"Like what?" Martha asked.

"From town. Something to eat? Groceries, maybe?" Mimi asked. "The newspaper?"

"No thank you, I have everything I need," Martha said curtly. She glanced at her wristwatch and said, "You might want to get going."

"Oh yeah, right," Mimi said, slipping her backpack over her shoulders.

Martha stood and reached for her walker, accompanying Mimi to the front door. "Watch that puddle there." She nodded toward the puddle on the floor.

"Do you want me to wipe that up for you? Do you have some paper towels?" Mimi asked.

"I'll get it," Martha said. She didn't want the girl to start becoming "useful."

As they stood at the front door, Martha said, "Now, do you know your way back?"

"Yeah, sure. Your house is the grandest house on Star Shine Drive," Mimi said with a smile. Her teeth were unnaturally straight. Martha thought people were too fixated on whitening and straightening their teeth. It was much more interesting when people let their teeth be. Her own front tooth slightly overlapped the one next to it.

Martha tugged at the door handle, but the door was sticking. She tried several times before it popped open. "The humidity makes the door swell, but soon it won't be a problem."

"Why?" Mimi asked.

"It's being replaced," Martha said.

"It's a beautiful door," Mimi said, studying it.

"It is, but there are a lot of problems."

Mimi waited, expectant, as if interested in hearing the list of issues with the door.

But Martha waved her on. "Come on, get going and I'll see you in half an hour."

"Okay, Gram."

"And no funny tricks, Mimi," Martha warned.

Mimi shook her head. "No, I'll be right back."

"Thirty minutes," Martha reminded her, and she closed the door behind her. She leaned forward on the walker and thought, *Now what am I going to do with a teenaged girl for the next four days?*

Chapter Four

Mimi

Mimi hopped off the porch, her backpack slung over her shoulders, walked to the end of the paved walkway, turned left on the sidewalk, and headed toward town, which was only a short walk away. She only had to cross Erie Street and she'd be on the main strip. She had known her grandmother's house was near Lake Erie, but she hadn't known it was *right on* Lake Erie. Her mother never said.

The beach was directly across the street, and the water shimmered in the afternoon sun. She'd love more than anything to kick her shoes off and trudge through the heavy sand and wade in the water. But she promised her grandmother she'd be back in thirty minutes, and she could not deviate. There were still a few days before her parents arrived and hopefully, she'd be able to go to the beach tomorrow or the day after. She hadn't thought to bring her bathing suit with her, but she'd figure that out later.

Ignoring the call of the beach, she lowered her head and stared at her feet as they took her into town. Tears stung her eyes. Her plan to meet her grandmother and stay for a bit had backfired tremendously. She didn't want to go home. And yet, she had nowhere else to go. She groaned at the thought of the inevitable confrontation with her mother. Everything was a fight with her. Mimi had already decided that when her parents got divorced, she would live with her father. She was almost eighteen, and her mother couldn't force her to stay with her.

She lifted her chin. Colorful striped awnings hung over each of the storefronts along Main Street, and her gaze swung from one to the next. She squinted her eyes to see better. There were all sorts of cute shops. It felt as if she were stepping back in time. She liked the look of this town.

Things must have been brutal between her mother and grandmother for her mother to leave and never return. Or keep in touch. Or even talk about it.

Though she'd only had a few glimpses of Hideaway Bay, she already preferred it to where she came from. Her family lived in a sedate suburb of Spokane—as far away from the beach as was possible. A beach was a big deal. Every time Mimi begged her parents to go to the beach, her mother shot her down with, "I had enough sand in my youth to last me a lifetime."

There wasn't much in the way of a grocery store and when Mimi asked someone, she was told it was out on the main highway. She hadn't a clue as to where that was, but it sounded as if she couldn't get to it on foot. There was a small pizzeria, and she went in and had a slice, leaning against the high counter that ran along the front window, then walked across the street to the Pink Parlor, thinking an ice cream might make her feel better.

Five minutes later, she walked out with two scoops of cotton candy ice cream on a cone. Glancing at her phone, she realized she had ten minutes to get home and began to head in that direction. In the distance, she could see the roofline of her grandmother's house. Ahead of her, a boy her age walked along the sidewalk, hitting the pavement with a stick. His hair was kind of longish, and he wore a black T-shirt and jeans. He must be dying in those clothes with the stifling heat, she thought.

"Do you get paid by the highway department or something?" she called out. She didn't know if she was intrigued or if she was simply bored and wanted to talk to someone her own age.

There was no answer, and the kid continued to beat the stick against the sidewalk.

"I said do they pay you to beat that stick against the sidewalk?" she asked, this time a little louder. Her ice cream dripped down one side of the cone and she licked it away.

The boy turned. "What's it to you?" he called back.

"It's nothing, actually, I was just curious, that's all," she said. She picked up her pace until she walked with him shoulder to shoulder.

He kept his eyes on the ground as they left Main Street, crossed over Erie Street, and landed on Star Shine Drive.

"I'm Mimi Duchene by the way," she said.

"Kyle. Kyle Koch."

"Do you live on Star Shine Drive?" she asked.

"No," he said, finally lifting his head. He had the clearest green eyes she'd ever seen on anyone. With a nod toward the last house on the street, he said, "I'm going to see Isabelle Monroe." He hit the ground with his stick a few more times before adding, "She's my dad's girlfriend."

He spoke about this person as if Mimi should know her. She didn't let on that she had no idea who he was talking about.

She flicked her wrist so that her ice cream leaned toward him. "Want some? It's cotton candy."

"No thanks," he said, returning his gaze to the ground.

She slowed her pace a bit, in no hurry to get back to her grandmother's but also aware of the time. Mimi would take it right to the last minute.

"You're not from around here, are you?" the boy asked.

Mimi shook her head, finishing her ice cream. Some had dripped on her hand, and she licked it off. "No, I'm from Washington. The state. I'm here visiting my grandmother." That sounded normal, she thought. Much better than saying she'd run away from home and landed at a place where there had been no real welcome.

Her other grandmother came to mind. She'd died when Mimi was eleven, and Mimi still missed her. The differences between her two grandmothers were like day and night. Grandma Duchene lived with them in the last years of her life. She used to let Mimi jump on her bed, and she'd laugh and clap as Mimi got up to no good. As grandmothers went, she was a pretty good one, and the teenager figured her other grandmother—her mother's mother—would be cast from a similar mold. But it had become apparent, eye-openingly so, that that wasn't the case.

Mimi pulled up short in front of her grandmother's house, studying the intricate gingerbread trim.

The boy walked a few steps but stopped and turned around, his hair swinging with him. "Why'd you stop?"

With a tilt of her head and a jerk of her thumb over her shoulder, she said, "This is me."

The boy's eyes widened. "*She's* your grandmother?"

"Yeah," Mimi said easily, trying to shrug off the insinuation.

"Is she nice to you?" he asked.

"Of course she is, I'm her granddaughter," Mimi said, realizing she walked a tentative line between reality and fiction. But fiction was always preferable. She looked up and down the street, realizing that her grandmother had the nicest house on the block. "Look, I've got to go in."

"Okay," he said, tapping the street with his stick as if for emphasis.

"I'll see you around," she said, and she dashed up the short walkway and took the steps two at a time to the front door.

Chapter Five

Martha

"At least you're on time," Martha said to Mimi as she slipped into the house. Martha hadn't expected a reply and pushed on. "Did you get something to eat?"

Mimi nodded. "I had a slice of pizza, and then I went to the Pink Parlor and had an ice cream cone."

"A slice of pizza? An ice cream cone? That's your dinner?" Martha pressed her lips together in disapproval until they all but disappeared. What was going on in Martine's house that her daughter thought fast food and an ice cream novelty passed for dinner?

"It was yummy," Mimi said.

"Dinner isn't supposed to be 'yummy,' it's supposed to be warm and nutritious," Martha said.

"I'm okay," Mimi said with a shrug.

Martha slapped her hands on her hips. "Let's review a few facts. First, you ran away from home. Second, you showed up here at the house of a person you've never met. And third, you ate an ice cream cone for dinner."

Mimi said nothing, waited.

"In my book, there is nothing okay with any of that," Martha said. She shouldn't care. Shouldn't invest emotion. The girl would be returning to the west coast in a few days.

"Maybe you're reading the wrong book," Mimi said with a grin and a twinkle in her eye.

"Don't be impertinent, Martha," her grandmother chastised.

The smile disappeared from Mimi's face, and she let out a long sigh.

"Now, follow me," Martha said. "I'll show you the bedroom upstairs you can use until your mother gets here."

As she'd done hundreds of times before, Martha lifted the side of the stair lift and pivoted it until it faced her. She sat in the seat and turned it a quarter turn, setting her feet on the platform. Once she buckled in, she set the armrests down and pushed the button on the remote, causing the chair to begin its slow ascent of the staircase along its metal track.

"That's a good idea," Mimi noted, following her grandmother up the staircase.

When the chair arrived at the top, Martha repeated the embarking process but in reverse. Once standing, she grabbed the walker parked next to the wall.

The upstairs hall was wide, and every door along it was closed. As below, the wallpaper was dark and the woodwork and trim heavy and ornate. The only light came from a window covered in heavy sheers at the end of the hall. Slowly Martha walked toward it.

"As you are a guest in my house, I would appreciate if you would not stick your nose in my things," she instructed.

"Okay," Mimi said behind her.

Over her shoulder, Martha asked, "Who was that boy I saw you talking to outside?"

"Oh, I don't know. I only met him when I left the Pink Parlor."

"Didn't your mother ever teach you not to talk to strangers?" Martha demanded.

Behind her, the young girl snorted, causing Martha to stop and turn around halfway. "Whatever is so funny?"

"Well, he's not really a stranger. He lives around here and he's my age," she said.

Martha went to say something, got as far as opening her mouth, but then muttered something inaudible and promptly turned away.

She stopped at the last door on the right, turning the knob with a gnarled hand and letting the door swing open.

"You can sleep in here, Mimi," she said.

Mimi stepped into the room and looked around. It looked like it hadn't been touched in decades, and it might be considered either outdated or retro, depending on who you asked. The walls were covered in wallpaper with yellow primroses on a white background. The trim had been painted yellow, and there was a yellow chenille bedspread.

"I keep the room as clean as I can," Martha said. "But feel free to dust if you want. There are sheets in the cupboard to make up the bed."

"Thanks."

"There is no maid service here so be sure to make your own bed."

"I can see the lake from my window," Mimi said excitedly.

Martha straightened up. "Of course, it's in the front of the house. This used to be my room when I was your age."

"How come you don't sleep in this room anymore?" Mimi asked.

"Because I don't want to," Martha said without elaborating further. Why did everyone these days feel entitled to know everyone else's affairs? This business of transparency was for the birds. Wasn't anything private anymore?

"All the rooms in this house are huge!"

"I suppose," Martha said, going over to the wardrobe against the far wall and pulling bedding from one of the shelves.

Where's your room?" Mimi asked, letting her backpack slide off her shoulders. It hit the floor with a thud. Martha looked at the offending item and scowled.

She answered Mimi's question with one of her own. "Is that where you're going to keep that?" She nodded toward the book bag in the middle of the floor.

The girl looked at it, taking a second to process the question. "Oh, no." Quickly she moved it to the side of the room, near the dresser.

"That's better. My room is across from yours. I'm at the back of the house," Martha said.

"Can I see your room?"

Martha scowled again. "Whatever for?"

The girl shrugged her slim shoulders. "Just curious."

"Curiosity never did anyone any good," Martha muttered, turning her walker to face the door. She moved forward and headed out of the room.

"Now what?" Mimi asked.

Martha frowned, lack of comprehension clouding her face. "Now what?" she repeated.

"What do you want to do now?" Mimi asked, her expression bright as if she'd just asked Martha if she wanted to hang out at the mall.

"I don't want to do anything," Martha said. She didn't want this girl to pin her down with expectations of companionship or a bond.

"Why don't we sit on the front porch? We could look at the beach and watch the people walking by."

"I don't sit on my front porch," Martha said evenly. She didn't add that sitting on the front porch would only encourage passersby to stop and make small talk, which she abhorred.

"That's a shame. There's a great view of the beach and the town," Mimi said.

It was said with such innocence and appreciation that it gave Martha pause, reminding her briefly what it was like to see things through the eyes of a seventeen-year-old. It was a long time since she'd been a teenager.

"Do you ever go to the beach, Gram?" Mimi asked.

"What is it with all the questions?" Martha snapped. She hadn't set foot on the beach since that incident all those years ago.

Mimi shrugged. "Just wondering."

Anxious for the questions to stop, Martha said, "Why don't you make up your bed and then come downstairs. I'll make you an egg and toast."

"I'm not hungry," Mimi protested.

"Be down in half an hour," Martha told her.

Chapter Six

Martine

"Well, I hope you're happy," Martine said to her husband, Edgar, as they pulled onto the thruway. She hadn't spoken to him in days. Not since Mimi had left. She blamed him for their daughter running away.

From his side of the car, Edgar stared at her, not in disbelief but in tired resignation. "Why is it whenever something goes wrong in our marriage, our home, our family, or in the world in general it is always, singularly, my fault?"

Martine ignored him, choosing instead to stare out the window. She leaned her chin on her hand. It had been raining all day. A light, steady stream whose rhythmic sound might have been relaxing if she weren't so tense.

"Come on, Martine, answer me," Edgar said.

"Because it *is* your fault," she said. "If you would just leave, we wouldn't be fighting all the time and Mimi wouldn't have run away."

"I'm sorry if I don't want to throw eighteen years of marriage out the window," Edgar said. He added bitterly, "Just because you might be going through a 'phase.'"

Martine tried to contain her fury at his dismissive tone. "It's not a phase, I assure you. The marriage isn't working. It hasn't worked in a long time, Edgar," she said wearily. "Surely, you must see that. You're an intelligent man."

"Every marriage has its ups and downs," he replied. "But you ride it out, fix it, do whatever you have to do. You don't just give up."

"After a while, you have to admit that it isn't working and move on."

She still did not look at him, although the scenery passing outside her window did not interest her either. It was an endless carousel of storefronts and gas stations. She dreaded the almost three-day drive to Hideaway Bay. Edgar thought if they drove fourteen or sixteen hours a day, they might be able to make it in two and a half. She was tense. She was upset about Mimi running away, about leaving Micah behind, about being stuck in a car with Edgar.

"Why would she go to your mother's house? She's never even met her," Edgar said.

"Good deflection," Martine murmured.

"Why?" he repeated.

"How do I know? She's got it in her head that we're supposed to be one big happy family." Martine had no idea why Mimi had run away to Hideaway Bay. It was one more thing that Martine was going to have to deal with. To endure. Her mother.

"I don't think that's an unreasonable expectation of a child," Edgar pushed.

Why is he still talking? Martine was perfectly content to drive all the way to Hideaway Bay in silence. She pressed her knuckles against her lips, her bracelets jangling on her arm.

They had no choice but to drive; she hated flying. For half a day they'd fought over Edgar going along. She'd wanted him to stay home, but he'd refused. She was perfectly capable of driving cross-country by herself to pick up their daughter.

They'd left Micah behind, dropping him off at Edgar's sister's house earlier that morning before they got on the road. She had two children close in age, and the cousins got on fine. As much as Martine hated to be away from Micah, it wouldn't have been fair to subject their nine-year-old son to incessant fighting in the car and then the ensuing drama when they finally did catch up with Mimi. Not to mention his meeting her mother for the first time. Even Martine wasn't that cruel.

With Mimi's disappearance, Martine had run the gamut of emotions from dread, terror, anxiety to livid anger when she discovered her daughter had taken a bus cross-country and landed on her mother's doorstep. She could imagine her mother, probably full of glee and *I told you so*s at Martine's epic fail as a parent and a wife.

"I don't know why you won't go to marriage counseling," Edgar said.

Martine sighed. What didn't he get? Why was he so obtuse? It was over. It had been over for a long time.

"We got married for the wrong reasons—"

"Not this again," Edgar said, his voice tight.

"Let's just be quiet for the next hundred miles, okay?" Martine asked. "Let's take a break."

"Whatever you say, you're the boss," Edgar said angrily.

Chapter Seven

Mimi

Mimi woke to the sound of a ringing doorbell. She blinked several times, looking around the unfamiliar room, wondering for a moment where she was. Sunshine splashed through the windows, making the yellow décor of the room appear bright and cheery. The window was open, and she could hear the sound of a man's voice down below on the front porch.

She flipped the sheet and the bedspread back and swung her legs over the side of the bed. Barefoot and wearing an old football jersey as a nightshirt, she stood, stretched, and glanced at the clock. It wasn't even nine.

There was the doorbell again.

Not bothering with her slippers, Mimi exited the room and tapped gently on her grandmother's bedroom door, not wanting to startle her.

"What is it?" Martha called.

Mimi opened the door just enough to insert her head in the opening. "Gram, there's someone at the front door."

"What time is it?" Martha asked groggily. She pushed her black satin eye mask up onto her forehead.

"It's nine," Mimi answered. "I can answer the door."

Martha propped herself up on her elbows and regarded Mimi with sleepy eyes. "Okay, but put on a robe and slippers."

Mimi didn't have a robe, but she hurried back to her room and slipped her feet into her slippers. She ran down the wide staircase as the doorbell rang a third time, sliding her fingers along the banister. Through the window of the large front door, she spied two men in beige overalls.

After unlocking the deadbolts, she peeked out and said, "Yes?"

"We have a delivery for Mrs. Martha Cotter," the older of the two guys said. An embroidered patch over the left side of his chest read "Chet."

"I'll take it," Mimi said.

The younger guy leaned back on his heels and rocked. "It's a replacement door. Where do you want us to put it?"

"Don't you have to install it?" she asked.

"Nah, we drop it off. The installers will be by tomorrow morning at eleven," Chet said.

"Elevenish," the younger guy added for clarification purposes.

"Hold on, let me ask," she said, and she closed the door and ran up the stairs to the end of the hall. She knocked once and popped her head into her grandmother's bedroom.

"Gram, it's a delivery," Mimi said. "A door?"

Martha had laid back down but now sat up again, albeit slowly. "Dang, in all the commotion of yesterday, I forgot about that."

Mimi took that to mean she was the commotion. The woman really didn't put out a welcome mat, that was for sure. Acutely aware that two sweaty men were waiting on the front porch, she added, "They want to know where to put it."

"They can put it in the garage," Martha said. In an exasperated voice, she added, "But it's locked."

"Where's the key? I'll unlock it," Mimi offered.

Martha grumbled something inaudible but finally said, "There's a key on the hook by the back door."

Mimi dashed out of the room with her grandmother calling after her, "And for the love of God, please put some pants on before you go outside."

Mimi stopped in her tracks, pivoted, and headed to her room to pull on a pair of shorts. She ran back down the stairs, instructed the men to bring the door around back to the garage, and then headed to the kitchen at the back of the house.

Keys hung on a rack on the wall near the back door. Out of the corner of her eye, she spotted the two men through the window, passing her and transporting a large wrapped object. The new front door was much bigger than either of them, but they made it look easy. One was even whistling as he carried his end.

Mimi found the key marked "garage," and went out the back door.

She let herself into the garage and turned on the light, illuminating the space. It smelled of fresh-cut lawn and gasoline. She eased past her grandmother's car, an older-model, pale-yellow Cadillac, and made her way toward the small black box above the light switch. She pressed the pad, and the garage door began its slide toward the ceiling.

The deliverymen brought the new door inside and leaned it against the side wall.

"Okay, you're all set," Chet said, wiping his hands on the sides of his coveralls as he and his partner retreated down the driveway toward their truck.

"Thank you," Mimi called after them.

She pressed the black finger pad, and the garage door clanked and rumbled as it came down. A squeal of tires indicated the deliverymen had left.

As she came back into the house, she heard the whir of the chair lift coming down the stairs. She dashed to the front hallway just as the lift delivered her grandmother to the bottom of the staircase.

"Good morning," Martha said. She was a confection in pink: a pink bathrobe and matching slippers. Her face was drawn, and she looked tired.

"Good morning, Gram," Mimi said. "Do you need any help?"

Martha stepped off the chair. "Mimi, I've been using this chair for the last few years, and I've been managing by myself just fine."

"Okay, but if you need help with anything, you can ask me," Mimi tried again.

"I'll tuck that away for future reference," Martha said, taking hold of the walker near the staircase and heading to the kitchen.

Mimi followed her. She was hungry.

"What do you normally eat for breakfast?" Martha asked.

"Whatever's there," Mimi answered truthfully. She didn't subscribe to the theory that just because it was breakfast one had to eat breakfast foods. Sometimes, she liked a slice of cold pizza in the morning. "Do you have any Pop Tarts?"

Her grandmother responded with a scowl. "I have cereal, oatmeal, or I can make you eggs," she said. She parked the walker near the counter and opened an upper cabinet, pulling down a bowl.

"Cereal's fine," Mimi muttered. She leaned against the other counter, crossing her arms over her chest.

Martha pulled down another cereal bowl and said, "You'll find juice glasses in the cupboard behind you." Mimi turned and pulled down two glasses and set them on the table.

"Grab some spoons from the drawer," Martha said, pointing in the direction of the cutlery drawer next to the sink.

Mimi laid two spoons on the table and added a teaspoon when Martha told her to. Martha filled the kettle with water, set it on the stove, and turned it on. Slowly, she made her way to the refrigerator and pulled out a carton of milk and a carton of orange juice, handing each one to Mimi, who set them on the kitchen table.

Mimi sat down, reached for the box of Corn Flakes Martha had set out, and poured some into her bowl until it was heaping.

Her grandmother slowly sat down, wearing a pinched expression. "Save some for me," she said, eyeing Mimi's overflowing cereal bowl.

Mimi nudged the cereal box in her grandmother's direction. "Okay."

There was minimal conversation as they ate their breakfast. Without making it obvious, Mimi looked around the kitchen, looking for any signs that her grandmother had a family, or interests, or even a life. The kitchen was clutter free; the only sign of the outside world was some coupons attached to the front of the refrigerator with a magnet. From where she sat, she could barely make them out. In her haste to run away, she'd left her contacts at home and who knew where her glasses were. Buried in a drawer somewhere in her bedroom.

"Do you wear glasses?" her grandmother asked.

"Contacts."

"Do you have them in now?"

Mimi shook her head, drinking the remaining milk from her cereal bowl.

"Next time, don't pour so much milk that you need to use your bowl like a glass," Martha said.

"Okay. And no, I don't have my contacts in now. I forgot them."

"What about your glasses?"

Sheepishly, she replied. "I forgot them too."

"You traveled across the country without your glasses?" her grandmother asked with a hint of incredulity in her voice. "I'll make you an appointment to get a pair."

"Not necessary. I mean, I'll be leaving in a couple of days."

"Wouldn't you like to be able to see while you're here?"

Mimi shrugged and stood. She picked up her empty bowl from the table and held out a hand for her grandmother's. Martha handed it over, and Mimi stacked it onto hers. She looked around the kitchen. "Do you have a dishwasher?"

"No, I live alone. No need for one."

Mimi carried the dishes over to the sink and rinsed them out. "Where's the dish soap?"

"Underneath the sink," Martha replied. "What are your plans today, young lady?"

"I was going to go to the beach," Mimi said. Bending over, she pulled out the bottle of dish soap from beneath the sink. "Do you have a towel I can borrow?" She put the drain stopper in place, squirted dishwashing soap into the sink and ran the water. "And is there a shop in town where I can pick up a bathing suit?" Quickly she washed and rinsed the dishes, stacking them in the drying rack.

"Try Brenner's, it's a discount store but since you'll only be here a few days, no sense in spending a lot of money on a bathing suit."

How cheery, Mimi thought.

"I'll get you a towel from the linen closet. Do you have sunscreen?"

"No."

"You must have left in a hurry," Martha said.

"Kind of."

"You can pick that up at Brenner's too." She paused and asked, "Do you have money?"

Mimi nodded. She'd spent the summer babysitting and had quite a pile of cash, which she'd hid in a sock in her backpack on her cross-country journey.

"Pass me a banana and hand me a knife," Martha instructed.

Mimi took a banana from the fruit bowl on the counter and pulled a butter knife out of the drawer and laid them on the table in front of her grandmother.

Martha peeled the banana and cut off a slice at a time, eating them as she went. "Do you want to tell me why you ran away from home?"

Mimi sank into the chair and appeared to hesitate. She wasn't sure how much she should tell this woman. In the short space of time she'd been there, she'd figured out that her grandmother was not the warm-and-fuzzy type. Not at all as her other grandmother had been. She supposed it was unfair to expect Martha to be like Grandma Duchene.

"I'm not looking for gossip, Mimi," Martha said. "I'm trying to understand why a minor would hop on a bus full of sweaty strangers and travel cross-country unannounced. Either things are rough at home, or you wanted to meet me. Which is it?"

"It's both."

"Could you possibly elaborate?" Martha asked, finishing her banana. She folded the empty peel neatly in half as if she were going to put it away in a drawer.

When Mimi said nothing, Martha narrowed her eyes at her granddaughter. "What's going on at home?"

"Mom wants a divorce," Mimi said.

Martha snorted. "No surprise there. I'm shocked the marriage lasted this long."

Tears sprung to Mimi's eyes. She hated that her vulnerability was exposed like this, afraid her grandmother might take it as a sign of weakness.

"You're upset," Martha said.

Mimi managed half a shrug. She bit her lip. She did not want to cry.

"Half of the marriages in the United States end up in divorce," Martha said. "It's almost like flipping a coin to see which one lasts."

"Dad doesn't want a divorce," Mimi said.

Martha sighed. "Marriage is difficult even under the best of circumstances."

Mimi wondered if her grandmother spoke from experience, but was too afraid to ask.

"Enough of that. Hand me the phone and my address book." She pointed to the phone on the counter.

Mimi brought the handset over as well as the floral fabric-covered address book. She waited as her grandmother leafed through the pages and pressed the buttons on the handset.

"Hello, Ray? It's Martha Cotter. My granddaughter is here and forgot her glasses. Can you squeeze her in today or first thing tomorrow morning?"

Mimi waved her hands in front of her grandmother, trying to tell her that it wasn't necessary, but her grandmother ignored her.

When Martha hung up the phone, she scowled at her granddaughter. "Why were you waving your arms in front of me like the house was on fire or something?"

"I was trying to get your attention. I'll be going home in a few days, and I don't need another pair of glasses."

"Don't be ridiculous. Of course you need to be able to see while you're here. What if you walk into a wall."

"I'm nearsighted, not blind."

Martha ignored her. "Anyway, the optician is on Main Street right across from the Pink Parlor. I'll drive you over myself. You probably saw it yesterday when you went for ice cream. Or maybe you didn't because you weren't wearing your glasses."

Mimi narrowed her eyes. "Was that a joke, Gram?"

Martha gave a slight shrug of her bony shoulders beneath her pink bathrobe. "Maybe it was. Maybe it wasn't."

Mimi smiled to herself. There was hope yet.

Chapter Eight

Martine

"Wʜᴀᴛ's ᴡʀᴏɴɢ ᴡɪᴛʜ ɪᴛ?" Martine asked as Edgar peered beneath the hood of their car.

Edgar put both hands on the hood, and Martine took a step back as he slammed it closed. His face glistened with sweat. A hot breeze that offered no serious relief blew past them.

"Well, if I knew that, we wouldn't be standing here on the side of the road."

Martine threw her hands in the air. "Just asking." She walked around to the passenger side of the car and leaned against the door. Irritated, she brushed her hair away from where it was sticking to the back of her neck.

Edgar walked back to the driver's side and got in. He pulled his cell phone from the well between the two front seats and began to scroll through his contacts.

"What do we do now?" she asked, trying to keep the panic out of her voice. Looking around did not assuage her nerves.

The landscape appeared unwelcoming. The simple asphalt road bisected gray and brown hills sparse with grassy scrub. Martine wasn't sure if they were hills or mountains. The lone stretch of road went as far as the eye could see. There was no one around, not a single dwelling. She swallowed hard and was glad she wasn't alone.

She crossed her arms over her chest. From inside the car came the sound of Edgar's voice on the phone. He sounded tense. She supposed they both were.

Edgar stepped out of the car and slammed the door.

"I just got off the phone with Triple A, they'll be here in about an hour," he informed her.

"An hour? We have to wait?" she asked.

"It seems that way."

"What are we going to do for an hour?" she asked.

He shrugged. "I don't know. Just hang out."

She made an expression of displeasure. "Then what?"

"We'll have to have the car towed to an auto shop to be repaired once they figure out what's wrong with it."

"That's going to set us back," she said.

"Yep," he said, joining her and leaning next to her against the car, mirroring her posture and crossing one ankle over the other.

"I better call my mother," she said with a sigh.

"Why don't you wait until we have the car looked at so we have a better idea of what's wrong, how long it's going to take to fix, and when we can expect to get back on the road."

Martine bristled. He always had a plan. Just once, she wanted to hear the words "I don't know" or "I'm not sure what to do."

"Call Mimi," he suggested.

She pulled her cell phone out of her pocket and dialed Mimi's number. After a few rings, it went to voicemail.

"She's ignoring my calls," Martine said, slipping the phone back into her pocket.

"You don't know that. She may be busy," Edgar said.

"You always take her side," Martine shot back.

"I'm not taking her side, only saying that there might be an explanation for why she isn't answering her phone," Edgar huffed.

Martine ground her teeth together, looked away, and sucked in a lungful of air. She didn't want to think too much about the hot air and how it made her feel. Did she feel breathless? Better not examine that too closely. They were miles from the last town they'd passed, in the middle of nowhere, and she'd bet a dollar the cell reception was spotty out here.

Anxious to get moving, she crossed her arms over her chest, looked at her husband and said, "What are we doing?" She didn't treasure standing out here in the brutal heat or suffocating inside the hot car.

Edgar turned to face her, his phone to his ear. "I'm going to start looking for a hotel in case we're stuck here."

It was funny how when everything around you was falling apart, including your marriage, everything about the offending spouse set your teeth on edge.

"Look, get on your phone," Edgar said, "and find another mechanic."

"Forget it," she grumbled, collapsing on the bed in the motel room. She could have sworn a cloud of dust puffed up with her exertions.

Two days. That's how long it was going to take to get the part to fix the car. They were stuck in this crappy motel in a small town she'd never heard of. She'd like to say the motel had seen better days, but she was doubtful. She had a feeling it had always been tacky and dated.

Edgar patted his back pocket for his wallet and whistled. Both those things aggravated her. She leaned up on her elbows, frowning.

"Are you going somewhere?" she asked.

"I was going to walk down to that corner store and get us something to eat and drink. Beer, preferably," he said. "There was a pizzeria down the road. We could walk over there if you'd prefer."

She didn't want to go anywhere. She was just going to put in her time and then leave as soon as possible, and hopefully it wouldn't be too long. "No, I don't want to go out."

"What did you want to eat then? I'll pick up something for you."

She shrugged, not wanting to list a litany of things she wanted. Too tired and annoyed to speak. Finally, she said, "The usual."

He nodded. At the door, he paused, his hand on the doorknob, and half turned to face her. "Did you want to come with me?"

She shook her head.

"I didn't think so, but I thought I'd ask."

Later on, he returned with groceries, including beer and some wine coolers for her. He went down to the common area where she'd spied a soda machine earlier and soon returned with a bucket of ice. He took out a package of fresh-cut ham, a loaf of bread, and a tub of butter spread and set to work making her an impromptu sandwich—butter on both sides of the bread—and another for himself. He whistled as he worked, and Martine realized she was gritting her teeth.

She hadn't known how hungry she was until the sandwich was set in front of her. They ate in silence, Martine sitting on the edge of the bed and Edgar at the small laminated table with the threadbare seats.

After fiddling with his phone, Edgar found a radio station and set the volume up higher. He uncapped a bottle of beer and made himself comfortable on the other bed, kicking his shoes off and placing one of the pillows behind his back. He took a hearty slug of the beer.

Martine opened up a wine cooler and settled in at the table, opening her phone and texting Micah to make sure he was all right. He didn't answer right away. She had her back to Edgar, trying to ignore his off-key singing and wondering if going to bed at eight was too early for an adult her age. As tempting as it was, she didn't want to wake up at three in the morning and be up for the rest of the night.

An old song came on the radio, a song that immediately brought back memories she chose to ignore but her husband did not.

From behind her, he said, "Do you remember this playing on the radio when we drove out to the Canyon?"

She did remember, though she preferred not to. Happy memories tended to be gold-plated, but she knew if she looked too close, they would appear tarnished.

"Don't do that," she said more sharply than she intended.

"Don't do what?" he asked. He sounded genuinely confused, but she wasn't sure. She wasn't sure of anything anymore.

"Bring up memories of when we first got together," she said.

"Why not?" he asked, his voice razor sharp. "They were happy times."

She snorted.

"They weren't? Or are you choosing to remember things differently?" he challenged. "At the time, you seemed pretty happy to me."

When she didn't bother to respond, he asked, "It wasn't all bad, was it, Martine?"

"No," she said truthfully.

She picked at the damp wrapper of the wine cooler, not looking at her husband, and listened to the loud hum of the air conditioning unit in the window, hoping it would drown out her thoughts.

Chapter Nine

Martha

"Now that's better, isn't it?" Martha asked Mimi the following morning after they left the optician's shop.

Looking both ways, Martha pulled her vintage yellow Cadillac out of the parking lot behind the optician's shop. Slowly, she drove home, hands in the ten-and-two position.

The glasses Mimi had picked out suited her face nicely.

"I look like a blockhead," Mimi muttered, hanging her head.

"My goodness, what does a blockhead look like?" Martha asked, aghast, or at least feigning it.

"This is an awesome car," Mimi said, running her hand along the leather seat, which had remained in pristine condition.

"Yes, it is," Martha said. Although she rarely left the house, when she did, she liked to travel around in the Caddy. It gave her a sense of security and well-being. She never walked anywhere even though everything was in walking distance from her house on the corner of Star Shine Drive.

She and Cal had purchased the car years before his death, and it was one of the few pleasures they'd shared together, that car. It was a big boat of a thing, a 1980 Cadillac Fleetwood Brougham. Over the years she could easily have upgraded to a newer model, but she was attached to this car. She was religious with its maintenance and upkeep. And now at her age, there was no point in getting a new one.

She reminded herself that just because she'd bought the girl a new pair of glasses didn't mean she was growing on her. Martha was eager to send her on her way home when Martine and Edgar arrived the following day. She braced herself for the meeting with her daughter. In the past, their meetings tended to be confrontational, and Martha doubted that time and distance would have tempered that.

It wasn't that she had anything against Mimi. The girl appeared, for the most part, well-mannered. But it was such a disruption. Martha had been rambling around in her old house for a long time by herself, and she was used to it. She didn't mind being alone. Admittedly, she was a slave to her routine, but she was okay. She might not describe herself as happy or even content, but it was probably best not to examine her own feelings too closely. She no longer ascribed much weight to emotions. They served no purpose but to get you all riled up.

At Martha's suggestion, Mimi went to the beach after returning from the optician's. That was fine with Martha; it meant she didn't need to make small talk and there was no worrying if Mimi was poking her nose into things. But even Martha had to admit that she worried about Mimi when she stepped out of the house. As idyllic as Hideaway Bay was, there were criminals everywhere. She had to keep her safe until the following day when her mother arrived. It was a shame that Martine had a fear of flying or she could already have been here, collected Mimi, and returned to her life in Washington State. And they all could have carried on with their separate, estranged lives at opposite ends of the country.

She watched from the front window as her granddaughter went off. She'd had the brand-new glasses on when she walked out the door but as soon as she crossed the street, Mimi paused, removed the glasses, slipped them into their case, and tucked them into her backpack. Martha sighed heavily.

The whir of an electric drill went off, and Martha bit her lip. Workers had arrived to install the new front door. She hated to part with the old one as it was original to the house but with it getting warped and water seeping in, it had to be done. Now with the damage to the hardwood, she'd have to have the whole floor refinished. Everything turned into a project. Nothing was simple anymore. But they'd promised her it would only take a few hours to install the door and collect their things and leave. Using her sternest voice, she'd made them promise they would clean up, leaving the area as they'd found it, minus the old front door, of course. She wasn't dragging her vacuum out to pick up sawdust and debris.

To better keep an eye on them, she didn't bother going to her usual spot in the back room but instead chose to sit in the front parlor to keep them in her line of sight. The front door was close to the staircase, and she didn't want them tempted to take a run up and have a peek. Sentinel, she sat on an old Victorian chaise, turned on the Tiffany lamp, and settled down to the newest issue of *Woman's Day*.

She put her back to the front window. Not that she'd be able to see anything due to the thickness of the sheers and the porch beyond that, but the sight of the beach unsettled her as it had for the longest time. It was why she tended to remain in the back of the house, whether upstairs or downstairs.

As the time passed, Martha became aware that the two workers removing the old door and installing the new one had either forgotten she was there or simply didn't care as their conversation became ribald with anecdotes and stories. If she had ever had a grown son who spoke like that, she would have washed his mouth out with soap; she wouldn't have cared how old he was.

It was getting to be mid-afternoon when one of the workers, a man in his thirties with the perpetual tan and muscle of those who do heavy lifting and work mainly outdoors, stood beneath the arch of the front parlor.

"We're all set, Mrs. Cotter, if you'd like to come and take a look at it."

"All right." More than the door itself, she wanted to make sure they'd cleaned up properly as they'd promised. The brand-new door looked stunning. It wasn't too much of a change from the old one—it, too, was oak, although not quite as wide as the original, because the original side window with the old mail slot had been replaced with a full-length pane of glass to allow more light in, or at least that's how the salesman had sold it to her.

Her appreciation of the new door came to an abrupt halt when she spotted a small pile of debris on the floor in the corner of the entryway. She frowned and pointed at it with a crooked finger.

"What's that?" she asked with a scowl.

The carpenter sighed and picked up the pile to show it to her. "This is all the mail we found in the wall. It must not have made it through the mail slot properly and somehow fallen down inside between the walls."

"You can toss that in the garbage," she said with a wave of her hand.

"You might want to look through it, Mrs. Cotter. There are a couple of letters here that look like they were dropped in decades ago. It might shed some light on the history of the house."

"Sir, my great-grandfather built this house. I was born here," she said with a lift of her chin. "I *know* the history of this house."

He said nothing, only pushed the pile toward her, indicating he would prefer for her to take it whether she knew the history or not.

Finally, she said with a nod toward the basket on the front of her walker, "All right, if it makes you happy, put it in there."

He did as she instructed. A quick glimpse at it showed her a few letters and flyers yellowed with age. Did she want to walk back into the past? She didn't think so. She'd leaf through it later.

"There are the keys, Mrs. Cotter," he said. He did a half turn and pointed to the set of keys on the console table against the wall at the base of the staircase. "Three sets, per your instructions."

"Thank you." Her eyes scanned the area, looking for any bit of sawdust, any mark on the floor or the walls, or any kind of disfigurement in the new door. She was almost dissatisfied that she found none.

"Let me show you how to operate the door," he said.

She shot him a withering look. "Young man, I've been using doors all my life. I'm sure I can figure it out."

He put his hands up. "All right. Anything else I can do for you?"

"No, thank you, that will be all," she said, edging toward the door to escort them out.

They'd set their toolboxes on the porch, and she waited until they cleared off, loading everything into the back of their van. She gave them a quick wave as they hopped into their vehicle.

First, she inspected the door again, thinking it was a fine door and her grandfather would have been pleased. She shut it, turned the lock, and tested the handle. *All's well*. It was remarkable how clear the new glass window was—she could see the beach perfectly. She would almost have preferred the old one.

Martha glanced at the mantel clock above the fireplace in the back room that overlooked the garden. Originally it had been a morning room where her great-grandmother had had her breakfast and attended to her personal correspondence. Over the ensuing years, it had morphed into more of a study or TV room, for lack of a better word. Martha hated describing the room that way. As if a television necessitated its own room. There was a TV there all right, but she only watched the news on it, her preference being crossword puzzles and magazines.

Mimi wouldn't be back for another hour and then they'd have dinner together. Martha settled in the wing chair. Although the fire hadn't been lit in decades, she still thought of this room as cozy. The windows faced east and south, allowing the sun to filter through the room in the mornings. As the day lengthened, so did the shadows. She'd carried a large brown paper bag in from the kitchen with the intent to sort through this pile of old mail and most likely, toss most of it into the garbage bag. She was pretty sure it was all junk but at the carpenter's insistence, she'd go through each piece one by one.

Once settled in her chair, she picked up the pile from her basket, gritty with the dust of many years. She set it down in her lap and picked up the first piece.

It was a colorful flyer and of a more recent vintage than what the carpenter had told her, though still quite outdated. As soon as she saw the word "pizza" she tossed it into the brown paper bag. The next one was a flyer on faded yellow paper from Reichman Jewelers, talking about layaway for the holidays. That was an old one. They went out of business more than two decades ago. There was an invitation on a postcard to Junie and Paul Reynolds's Bicentennial Party back in 1976. Martha had given the party a miss. Next, she picked up a small brown envelope with her old dentist's address in the upper left-hand corner. Using the letter opener she kept on the small table next to her, she slit it open along the top. She pulled out a small single sheet of paper and unfolded it. It was a bill. She looked at the date: July 27, 1988. She remembered this one. They'd sent her a past-due notice, and she'd been furious, insisting she always paid her bills on time. That red stamp that read "past due" had sent her into orbit. They'd insisted they'd sent the bill, and she'd denied ever receiving it. With a sigh, she realized they'd both been right. She'd left the dental practice shortly after that. *Oh well*. There were more flyers that she quickly tossed into the bag at her side. When she came to the small envelope with her name scrawled on it in that long-ago, once-familiar handwriting, her heart shuddered and nearly stopped.

She studied the envelope in detail. Her name, Martha, written across the front of it. It had not been delivered by the post office, but hand delivered. The small white envelope had yellowed with age. It had to have been in there for almost fifty years.

Filled with trepidation and with trembling hands, she used the letter opener and slit across the top of it carefully so as not to rip the paper.

Her heart thudded against the inside of her chest until it hurt. Her mouth went dry and she swallowed, trying to summon up some spit. Her head started to spin and with shaking hands, she pulled the single folded page out of the envelope. Without taking her eyes off the note, she reached blindly around on her side table for her reading glasses. Once found, she fumbled with them, putting them on.

Carefully, she opened the note.

Martha read the note again. And again and again, touching the faded ink and running her fingertips along the signature. The note, the instructions she'd waited for and spent more than five decades thinking had never come, had been lost to time and shoddy construction.

Her breathing picked up speed until she was gasping. The reality of her situation, how this lost letter had affected *everything* in her life was almost too much to bear. She leaned back in her wing chair, closed her eyes, and a guttural groan from deep within her escaped as if it were an echo of the heartache caused all those years ago. It had been a long time since she'd cried. She hadn't even cried when her husband died, having felt more relief for both of them. But now, she wanted to cry for the sheer helplessness of the situation.

Her life would have turned out differently if only she had received this note the day it was left for her. Nausea rose up within her. She retched and pulled a tissue from the box and put it to her mouth, but the wave of sickness passed. She burped, patted her chest, and leaned her forehead against the hand holding the letter, closing her eyes again. If she could only get upstairs to her bed. But she lacked the energy even for that. She didn't think she'd be able to get up out of the chair. Her shoulders started to shake as if she were crying, but no tears came.

"Oh God," she wailed. Her peripheral vision began to blacken, like walls closing in on her, until there was only darkness. Her hand fell to her side, the note sliding from her grasp and fluttering to the ground near her feet.

Chapter Ten

Mimi

MIMI SAT, KNEES BENT, arms wrapped around her legs, on an old bedspread Martha had given her to spread out on the sand. She had come down to the beach after their return from town at Martha's suggestion. Mimi sensed it was more to get her out of the way while the new front door was being installed. When she arrived at the beach, she'd run into Kyle, who gave her a wave and joined her. She was glad for the company; she'd have someone to talk to.

It hadn't taken Mimi long to fall in love with the beach at Hideaway Bay. Already, she dreaded leaving it, and her plan was to spend as much time as possible here until her parents arrived the day after tomorrow.

For a summer weekday, there was a decent crowd there of people of varying ages. She loved the smell of coconut that suffused the air and the way the lake looked in the bright sunshine, all shimmering and gleaming.

The sun was directly overhead, beating down on her, making her scalp hot. Her grandmother had advised on wearing a hat, and Mimi had scoffed at the idea, but now she wondered if she should have listened. Her feet were uncomfortably warm, and she kept burying them deep in the sand at the edge of the blanket, relishing the cool relief of it.

Kyle sat next to her, his long legs stretched out in front of him. They'd just come out of the lake, and beads of water slid down his back and chest. She envied him his tan; he was brown, whereas she was so pale she sometimes wondered when she looked in the mirror if she needed a transfusion.

Surreptitiously, she studied him with a few sideways glances. He would have benefited from a trim—his hair was too long and hid his most amazing feature: those glass-green eyes. Fine stubble ran along his chin up to his ears. He was lean and his belly flat. A thin strip of white skin was exposed directly above the waistband of his swimsuit. Realizing she was staring, Mimi immediately averted her eyes, feeling the blush in her own cheeks.

"I've got to get home soon, my grandmother will be wondering what happened to me," Mimi said.

"Five more minutes," Kyle said.

Her gaze moved to the lake. It amazed her how clear the water was at the shore. It was smooth and sandy on the bottom, no rocks, and so clear she could see her feet and the tiny minnows that tickled as they darted in and out around her ankles, making her laugh. The water was as warm as bathwater.

"That's Canada over there." Kyle pointed to the hazy, indistinct shape of the Canadian shoreline across the water.

She squinted and looked across the lake. Her brand-new glasses were tucked away in her bag. Playfully, she slapped him on the arm. "It is not. You're teasing me now."

Two splotches of red appeared on Kyle's cheeks. "I am not. Ask anyone." With a pause, he eyed her and said, "Don't you know your geography?"

She shook her head. "Nah, I like English and History."

"English? What's wrong with you?" he joked. "Jeez. Typical girl."

Realizing he was teasing her, she ignored his last comment and asked, "What do you like?"

"Science and Geography. I love natural disasters."

"What, like earthquakes and stuff?"

"Yep."

She knew she should start making moves to clear out and go back to the house, but she would have liked to stay here all day, swimming and sunning herself and talking to Kyle. She'd promised Gram she wouldn't be gone long, even though she sometimes got the impression her grandmother would have preferred her to be 'gone.'

Finally, she stood. "I really have to go."

"I can walk with you, I've got to pick something up on Main Street for my dad," Kyle said, hopping up.

"Do you like Isabelle?" Mimi wondered about this in relation to her own life. Her parents were getting divorced. Her father was a nice man and most likely would find another wife. As for her mother, no one would put up with her nonsense, not the way her father did.

She picked up her sunscreen and towel and shoved them into her bag.

Kyle shrugged. "She's all right. My dad likes her a lot," he said. "She's traveled to a lot of interesting places. She shows me pictures and slides. But the real reason I like to go to her house is her sister Alice is a great baker." He finished this sentence off with a laugh, unashamed.

"So, you're using Isabelle for a pan of brownies?" Mimi asked with a grin as she picked up the blanket and shook it out, the sand flying everywhere.

"Brownies? How about salted caramel brownies? Stuffed French toast. Cinnamon buns," Kyle enthused, helping her fold the bedspread.

Mimi had to admit that all sounded delicious. The food at her grandmother's house had been less than inspiring. She would have liked a brownie or some French toast. She tucked the blanket under her left arm and swung the bag her grandmother had given her to use for the beach over her right.

"Nice bag," Kyle said, grinning at the words printed on the side: "I'd rather be gardening."

Mimi laughed. She'd yet to see her grandmother step outside more than once. "There wasn't much of a choice. It was either this or one with a picture of Jesus on it."

Kyle winced and she giggled. "That's what I mean."

"Are you going to be around tomorrow?" he asked.

"Maybe. I'm not sure," she said, hopeful. "It depends on what kind of plans my grandmother has." It seemed Gram was more than happy for her to spend the day out of the house. She would have liked to get to know her better, but her grandmother didn't seem interested.

Right before they reached the street, Mimi bent and slipped a sandal on each foot, knowing that the asphalt would be hot—she'd learned that the hard way. She looked both ways before she and Kyle dashed across the street. From her vantage point, she could see that the new door had been installed.

Kyle walked with her as far as the end of the driveway.

"I'll text you later," she said as he walked away with a wave.

He looked back at her with those clear green eyes of his. "Okay."

Mimi didn't have a lot of friends back home, and she'd never had a boyfriend. Being here was like a new start, like being incognito. No one knew her, no one knew of her trouble at home. No one knew she sat alone in the lunchroom. No one knew she hated her high school and the people in it.

She bypassed the front door and the side door and went around to the back as instructed by her grandmother earlier. Somehow Mimi got the impression that there was no one beating a path to any door.

She shook out the blanket and the towel and hung them on the old rope clothesline as her grandmother had instructed, using wooden pegs from a basket in the garage. She hopped up onto the porch that ran the length of the house and went through the back door, where a second staircase led to the second and third floor where at one time, servants slept, according to her grandmother. She had asked if she could go up to the attic, but Gram had said no, that there was nothing to see up there. Mimi would have liked to be the judge of that; adults didn't necessarily know everything.

There was no sign of her grandmother. The kitchen was empty. There was no evidence of a dinner cooking: no pots on the stove, nothing in the oven. Her first evening, after she'd consumed her pizza and ice cream, she'd sat and chatted with her grandmother as she ate her plate of liver and onions. Martha had eaten everything on her plate with relish, washed up her dishes, and then sat down to watch the six o'clock news followed by the national news. Mimi had assumed this was part of her daily routine, but now she wasn't so sure.

She went through the kitchen and through the butler pantry, calling out quietly, "Gram?"

There was no response, and Mimi wondered if she had gone upstairs for a nap. She listened as she made her way through the house. It was quiet, nothing except for the continuous tick of the grandfather clock in the front room.

She walked to the back room where her grandmother liked to hang out, and poked her head in the doorway.

She frowned.

Her grandmother was slumped in her chair, her arm hanging over the side of it.

Advancing into the room, Mimi did not take her eyes off her grandmother.

Something was not right.

She reached out and shook her gently, and her grandmother mumbled something but didn't fully rouse.

"Gram," Mimi whispered, not wanting to startle the elderly woman. The only thing she could get out of her was an incoherent response.

Scared, Mimi ran out of the house and stood at the end of the driveway, looking left and then right. She put her hand on her forehead, pushing her hair up, trying to think. Should she call emergency services? She wished there was another adult around, someone else who could make the big decisions.

She spotted the house belonging to the Monroe sisters at the end of Star Shine Drive. Kyle had indicated that Isabelle and Alice were nice. Maybe they would help.

She broke into a run.

PART 2

1966

Chapter Eleven

Martha

The breeze blowing in off the lake whipped through Martha's long hair as she pedaled her bike from Star Shine Drive toward Main Street. She tilted her face up to the sun, letting the warmth bathe her.

It was good to be home.

Finished with her second year of college, she'd returned to Hideaway Bay for the summer. She was happy to be home with her parents and grandparents.

Martha had arrived on the train the day before, and the first thing she'd done was to pull out her old bright blue Schwinn bike and hose it down. She'd taken a bucket of suds to it and used a damp washcloth to wipe out the wicker basket that was attached to the handlebars. There were few things she loved more than riding around town on her bike. She liked how her hair flew behind her, and the way her heart rate increased the faster she pedaled. The breeze always felt like fingers running through her hair; she imagined it was what a lover's caress would feel like. She skipped Main Street and headed down Erie, crossing over one of the side streets. On one of the porches, she spied Mrs. McEllicott, who'd just celebrated her one hundredth birthday the previous weekend in the parish hall. Martha's parents had attended as had just about everyone in Hideaway Bay. She couldn't imagine being a hundred years old. She wondered if her hair would go white and her skin crepey like the town centenarian's. As she passed the porch, the old woman looked up and smiled, sporting a toothless grin. Some days the dentures went in and some days they didn't. Martha threw out her arm and gave a hearty wave.

"Hello, Mrs. McEllicott," she called with a generous smile.

"Welcome home, Martha!" the old woman called back.

Martha cycled around the back roads, waving to neighbors as she went. She came out at the other end of town, near the green where the war memorial stood. Her father's brother's name was etched on that shiny, smooth block of granite. She'd no memories of Uncle David; he'd been killed in action during the war. She herself wasn't born until after the war, when her father had returned from the Pacific theater.

Mrs. Walsh pulled her Buick into the driveway of her summer cottage. She and Dr. Walsh came down every summer. Their kids had grown up and left the area. The son, Mark, was a doctor in another state, and their daughter, Barb, was married now and living in California.

When Martha neared the green, she hopped off her bike, walked it across the grass, and leaned it against the gazebo. The space was well used during the big holidays: Memorial Day, 4th of July, and Labor Day. She trudged up the steps, admiring the fresh coat of paint on the lattice trim. Tired but invigorated, she sat on one of the benches that lined the inside of the pentagonal-shaped gazebo and kicked off her sandals. A slight breeze tickled her feet, and she flexed her toes.

She loved this view of Lake Erie. It was a little less populated down here, and the beach wasn't as crowded from this point as most people, residents and visitors alike, accessed it from the boardwalk on Star Shine Drive, not far from her home. Seagulls circled and swooped overhead, their shrieks piercing the solitude.

Martha crossed her arms over her chest and smiled. She didn't think she'd ever get tired of this view. Even from where she sat, she could hear the waves rolling in and the crash of the surf. It was so relaxing. She couldn't picture living anywhere but near a lake, especially this one. She wondered how other people tolerated living in landlocked states. She shuddered at the thought.

Her reverie was interrupted by the passing by of a young man. Martha frowned as she didn't recognize him, and she knew everyone in Hideaway Bay. That's what happened when you grew up in a small town, especially when you were from one of the original founding families of the community. No one was a stranger.

Her gaze followed him as he walked past, oblivious to her presence in the gazebo and going at a rapid clip. As if he was in a hurry. As if he had to be somewhere.

Martha leaned forward, suddenly curious. He was tall; he had to be six feet or more, and his blond hair was short and combed back neatly. She wished he would turn toward her so she could see his face, but he did not accommodate her. She watched his back as he disappeared onto Main Street.

She liked the look of him.

After a while, feeling rested, she hopped off the gazebo steps and rolled her bike away from the green space. She didn't hop on right away, not anxious to return home where her mother and grandmother would have a list of chores for her. She wanted to enjoy sinking back into the feel of her hometown, letting it envelop and embrace her. A block away, she hopped on her bike and began to slowly pedal, still in no hurry. She hadn't gone far when the familiar pink-and-white striped awning of the ice cream parlor beckoned her. She pulled her bike up on the curb and leaned it against the brick wall of the grocery store next to it, knowing that Mrs. Milchmann would come out soon enough to find out who the culprit was who dared leave their bicycle leaning up against her store.

The Pink Parlor—aptly named, Martha thought, with its interior walls the color of cotton candy, its sugar-white trim, and its white booths with dark pink vinyl seats—was crowded with townspeople.

A group of girls she had gone to high school with sat in the round corner booth in the front window and waved to her and called out as she walked by. She returned the greeting but headed toward the counter. She came to an abrupt halt when she spotted the mysterious man that had just passed her at the gazebo. Smiling to herself, she realized she now had the answer as to what he'd been hurrying to: he was an employee at the Pink Parlor. She'd be eating a ton of ice cream this summer. Weight be damned!

She watched the line ahead of her, trying to figure out which of the employees would end up waiting on her. A couple came in and stood behind her and she let them cut ahead, citing indecision over what flavor to choose. By her calculations, Mr. Mysterious would end up taking her order. As she stood in line, she shuffled her feet and chewed the inside of her cheek. The other employee, Cal Cotter, tried to catch her eye, and

Martha gave Cal a quick smile before returning her attention to his co-worker with the Scandinavian looks.

When her turn came, the new employee stepped up to the counter, their eyes locked, his mouth opened—it was a nice mouth, with full lips and somewhat straight teeth—and his previous customer cut ahead of Martha and asked, "Could I get some napkins?"

"Of course," he replied, turning around to get them, which left an opening for Cal to step up and take Martha's order.

"What can I get for you, Martha? The usual? Vanilla ice cream cone?" he asked. It was hard to be mad at Cal. Martha had known him her whole life. He'd been two years ahead of her in high school, and he was an all-around nice guy.

"No, I'll have the strawberry on a waffle cone," she said, sliding her eyes toward his co-worker.

"Huh, trying something different," Cal said, grabbing a cone from the pack and sliding back the cooler door. "Are you home for the summer?"

"Yes," she said without looking at him. She leaned over the counter and asked Cal with an almost imperceptible nod, "Who's that? Is he new?"

Cal turned his head and then looked back and smiled. "That's Ned Lindahl, he's working here for the summer."

"Ned Lindahl," she whispered to herself.

Her eyes were glued to Ned. He spoke softly and appeared sheepish as he took the order of the next person in line. He turned and his gaze met hers, and she was rewarded with a small smile that might just keep her going for the rest of the summer.

Cal handed her the ice cream cone. "I put an extra scoop on it for you." Without looking at her, he said, "Martha, would you like to go to the drive-in Friday night?"

Martha pulled coins from her change purse. This wasn't the first time Cal had asked her out on a date. And it wasn't that he wasn't good-looking, because he was, with thick wavy auburn-colored hair and kind hazel eyes. He had a high forehead, a strong chin, and an aquiline nose. But despite all these attractive features, the chemistry just wasn't there.

"Now, Cal, you know I think too highly of our friendship to ruin it with dating," she said lightly.

"I don't mind, Martha," he said quietly, taking the change she handed him and not even checking it.

She hated saying no to him, but it wouldn't be fair to lead him on. She thanked him, took her cone, and turned to leave. On her way out, she waved to the girls in the corner.

At the door, she paused, cone in hand, the strawberry ice cream beginning to soften and drip. Slowly, she turned to glance one more time at the fair-haired man. He stood there at the counter, watching her. She gave him a small smile, pushed through the door, and stepped out into the bright sunshine.

It was a beautiful day.

Chapter Twelve

"What's wrong, Mother?" Martha asked the following morning as she came down the stairs to find the front door wide open and her mother on the porch, bent over and peering through the brass mail slot in the paneled wood next to the wide oak front door. It had been there since the house was built back at the turn of the century.

"There's a piece of mail that's stuck and I can't seem to get at it," her mother said, sticking her fingers into the rectangular opening. "It's caught between the brass and the wood."

"Let me try," Martha said. She didn't like to point out that her mother's fingers were like sausages, a combination of the humidity and arthritis. She pushed the brass flap inwards and saw the corner of an envelope sticking out. If they tried too hard, the letter might be lost forever into the guts of the paneled wood. "Hold on, Mother, I have an idea."

She left her mother standing there with her hands on her hips and dashed up the stairs to her bedroom at the end of the hallway, grabbing a pair of tweezers from the top drawer of her vanity. She ran down the stairs, the tweezers in her right hand

and her left hand sliding along the satiny smooth finish of the intricate woodwork of the banister.

When her mother spotted the tweezers in Martha's hand, she smiled. "I didn't think of that." Merriment brightened her eyes and she quipped, "Your college education is definitely working out in our favor."

Martha laughed and knelt down, opening the flap and carefully pinching the edge of the letter with the tweezers. She pulled it out and handed it to her mother, who smiled. "It's a letter from my cousin Josie. I bet Helen has had her baby."

They were interrupted by the appearance of Martha's grandmother, also named Martha, as was her mother, a tradition coming down the matriarchal line of the family that started as an honor to Martha Washington. The female members of her mother's family were all members of DAR, Daughters of the American Revolution.

The look on her grandmother's face gave Martha pause. The lines in her forehead had morphed into a deep crease. One hand rested against her upper chest, fingers splayed, and the other hand was pressed against her abdomen.

"Mother, what is it?" Martha's mother asked, the letter from her cousin momentarily forgotten.

"Have you seen Grandpa?" she asked, looking toward the beach. Satisfied that he wasn't there, she looked up and down the street.

"When's the last time you saw him?"

"Breakfast?" she said.

"That was hours ago," Martha's mother fretted, her own forehead matching her mother's for anxiety and worry.

"I thought he was in the back room," Grandma Dorschel said, "but he's not there and the newspaper hasn't been read."

Grandpa Dorschel's morning routine was to enjoy a breakfast of one soft-boiled egg, one slice of toast with butter, and half a glass of orange juice, and then to retreat to the library at the back of the house with a cup of percolated coffee, black, no cream, no sugar, and go through the newspapers. But lately, he'd been forgetful and wandering off. It was happening with alarming frequency. It could be said that he was senile with periods of lucidity, for there were moments when he was sharp and as clear as a bell. But those moments were becoming few and far between.

"Go ask the neighbors if they've seen him," young Martha directed. "I'll get on my bike and ride around and see if I can find him."

She bounced down the porch steps and ran to the rear of the house, where her bike leaned against the back porch. The weather had been dry most of the summer so there'd been no need to park it in the garage and wrestle every day with lifting the heavy door, which warped in the heat. Her eyes scanned her immediate surroundings, looking for any sign of her elderly grandfather.

The fear with Grandpa was that he'd head to the beach and go into the water. The lifeguards did not come on duty until ten in the morning. And while nearly everyone in town knew him, many did not know that he'd been beset by confusion and could not be counted on to keep his own person safe.

Before she cycled down the side streets of Hideaway Bay, she went down the length of Star Shine Drive and back, surveying the beach to see if she could spot him in his white linen suit. She did not see him. Her grandmother was already knocking at the house next to theirs, and her mother had rounded the corner and was heading up Erie Street. The last time he'd disappeared, he ended up on Moonbeam Drive, but someone recognized him, saw that he was confused, and sat him down on their porch with a tall glass of lemonade before ringing the house.

Martha cycled past her mother, who gave her a wave. She pedaled down Main Street, coming out at the end of it at the town green space where she had sat just the day before, admiring the fine form of Ned Lindahl. As soon as she hit the green space, she spotted her grandfather in the distance, standing on the sidewalk and talking to none other than Ned.

From afar, her grandfather didn't seem to be upset or agitated. He could sometimes get like that. In fact, he slapped his knee and let out a hearty laugh. Ned stood with his hands on his hips and the sun shone on his golden hair, giving him an otherworldly look. He spoke to her grandfather, who pointed in the direction of Main Street. When Grandpa spotted her cycling toward them, he broke into a wide smile and gave a hearty wave.

Martha pulled her bike up to the curb.

"Grandpa, we've been looking all over for you," she said. She was a little breathless. In as ladylike a manner as possible, aware that Ned's eyes were on her, she got off her bike and lowered the kickstand.

"Why, I've been right here all along," Grandpa said benignly.

"He seems a little confused," Ned whispered to her.

Martha nodded. "Sometimes that happens."

"I was just going to walk around and see if anyone knows him," Ned said.

"Everyone here knows Grandpa. He was born and raised in Hideaway Bay."

"Except for me," laughed the fair-haired one. "My name's Ned Lindahl."

"Grandpa, meet Ned Lindahl," Martha said, laying a hand gently on her grandfather's arm. "Ned, this is my grandfather, George Dorschel."

"And you are?" Ned asked her.

"I'm Martha Hahn."

As much as she would have loved to stay there chatting with Ned underneath the shade of a chestnut tree, she knew she had to get her grandfather home. He'd lost interest in them and had walked a few feet away, standing on the sidewalk and staring up at a silver maple as if he'd never seen one before.

Martha looked at her bike and then at her grandfather, biting her lip as she tried to figure out how to get them both home. As in the past, her grandfather would probably need to be steered; he could be easily distracted when he was in this state.

"I'll walk your bike home if you want to mind your grandfather," Ned said.

Martha smiled. That was an acceptable solution. She approached her grandfather gently, laying her hand on his arm again. "Grandpa, let's go."

He mumbled something unintelligible but remained rooted to the spot. Carefully, Martha slipped her arm through his and said, "It's time for lunch." Lunch wasn't for another hour, but she supposed if she got him home, he could have his early.

This got his attention. "Is it liverwurst?" he asked. His eyes were clouded, as if there were a veil between the world he currently occupied in his head and the world in which they actually lived.

As it was liverwurst every day for him for as long as Martha could remember, she was able to say truthfully, "Yes, I do believe it is."

"Let's go, then."

Ned wheeled the bike behind them, and Martha kept her grandfather moving, talking softly to him to prevent him from becoming distracted by something else. Ned said nothing behind them, for which she was grateful. Her only goal was to get her grandfather home.

They made it as far as Erie Street, the house in view, when they were intercepted by Cal Cotter. Once he spotted the trio from across the street, he turned and trotted over to them.

"Hey, Martha, do you need help home?" Cal asked. He nodded acknowledgment to Ned.

Before Martha could answer, her grandfather asked Cal, "And who are you, young man?"

"Cal Cotter, sir."

A flash of recognition went off somewhere in Mr. Dorschel's mind. His expression became expansive, and he smiled and said, "Oh, from the hardware store. Spent many a time around the woodburning stove trading tales."

Martha and Cal exchanged a glance, both knowing that her grandfather referred to Cotter's Hardware, a place operated and owned by Cal's great-grandfather and no longer in existence.

"That's right, sir," Cal said easily, and he began to walk in the direction of the house on Star Shine Drive. "What tales have you to tell me today?"

Her grandfather said nothing, having returned to that interior place of his, but he walked placidly between Martha and Cal.

They rounded the corner onto Star Shine Drive just as Martha's mother and grandmother were returning to the house after their own search of the neighborhood. Ned walked down the driveway after setting Martha's bike against the side of the house. She caught his gaze and gave him a smile. She was grateful for his help.

Her grandmother and mother spoke at once, relieved and happy Grandpa was home safe.

"Oh, there you are!"

"We were worried about you!"

Grandpa Dorschel scowled, seeming not to understand.

"I told Grandpa it's time for lunch and he could have liverwurst," Martha said.

"Of course, we can have lunch now," Grandma Dorschel cried. She took her husband by the arm, and it always comforted Martha to see how his expression relaxed when his wife was around. She walked him up the driveway, her arm around his shoulder, her head bent toward him, speaking gently. "There's a nice chocolate cake in the icebox. You know how you love chocolate cake."

"I do, indeed, I do," he said.

Martha watched as her grandmother helped him in through the side door.

"Cal, thank you for helping Martha bring Grandpa home," Martha's mother said.

Ned neared them.

"No problem at all, Mrs. Hahn," Cal said.

"Mother, this is Ned Lindahl, he's here for the summer," Martha said, introducing Ned, trying to prolong his presence.

Ned extended his hand and shook Mrs. Hahn's.

Mrs. Hahn beamed at both Cal and Ned. "Boys, I can't thank you enough."

"No problem," Ned said.

"Would you boys like some lemonade and a nice slice of chocolate cake?"

Martha looked at Ned, hopeful, anxious for him to remain, but he said, "No thank you, Mrs. Hahn. I've got to get back and help my uncle."

But beside her, Cal said, "That'd be great, Mrs. Hahn. I'd love some."

Martha's mother headed toward the house with Cal in tow, but Martha remained on the sidewalk at the foot of the driveway with Ned.

"Are you sure you wouldn't like a piece of cake?" she asked. He had a quiet confidence about him that she found attractive. Actually, she found it irresistible.

"As tempting as it is," he said, his eyes never leaving hers, "I have to pass. Maybe another time, Martha."

He waved and walked away, heading down Erie Street, and Martha decided she liked the way her name sounded when it rolled off his tongue.

Chapter Thirteen

The breeze that blew in off the lake lifted Martha's cotton blouse away from her back. After her chores were done, she'd bolted out of the house. Her mother had been in the middle of making strawberry-rhubarb pies in the kitchen, and the house was stifling. Once she'd returned the canister vacuum and the feather duster to the broom closet, she told her mother she was going for a bike ride and went out the back door, running down the steps, anxious to get away.

The bike ride had been pleasant enough. The sun was high in a deep blue sky and although the temperature was hot, the humidity was low, making for a pleasant day. A monarch butterfly crossed her path, and Martha found delight in seeing it up close, even if it was momentary. It was when she was cycling around one of the side streets off of Erie that her pedals froze. Looking down, she made a face of annoyance. The chain had fallen off. She applied the brakes, slowing down enough that she could safely hop off the bike without getting hurt.

With both feet on the ground, she applied the kickstand and bent down to further inspect it.

"Drat," she said. She attempted several times to get the chain back on but was unsuccessful. For all her effort, all she was left with were black greasy smudges on her hands. She wiped her hands on the grass.

"Do you need some help?" asked a definitively masculine voice.

She didn't have to look up to know that it was Ned. She'd know that voice anywhere.

She was tongue-tied for a moment as she took in the sight of him. His white T-shirt clung to him, accentuating his broad shoulders and chiseled biceps. His face was red and damp with perspiration. His blond hair shone in the bright sunlight as if the gods had kissed him. She found everything about him attractive. An abandoned push mower stood on the lawn behind him.

Quickly she looked down at the sagging chain. "My chain fell off my bike and I can't seem to get it back on."

The blue-eyed boy nodded and walked around to her side. "Let me take a look at it."

Martha stood up so quickly that the top of her head bumped his chin.

"Ow," she cried, rubbing the top of her head.

He groaned and brushed his hand across his chin.

"I'm so sorry," Martha said. "Are you okay?"

With a laugh, he said, "I think I'll live."

"I'm usually not so clumsy," she muttered.

"Come on," he said. He took the bike by the handlebars and began wheeling it toward the garage at the back of the property.

The house was cottage style with a wide picture window next to the front door, looking out over a small porch. There was one lone window on the upper floor—a bedroom, Martha guessed—and she wondered if this was the room where he slept. Though small, the yard and house were tidy. There were flowers out front and as they walked toward the back, Martha spied a large vegetable garden.

"Do you live here?" Martha asked.

"I'm visiting. I live in Ohio, but my uncle had a stroke and lost the use of his left hand, so I came down to help him and my aunt out for the summer."

"That was nice of you," Martha said. "And you're working at the Pink Parlor."

Ned nodded. "I have a part-time job there for the summer."

The door of the garage had been pulled up to allow light in, as the other three walls were windowless. Though dark, Martha could see that the shelves and cabinets lining the other three sides were filled with various unidentifiable tools she found oddly mysterious. A strong smell of cut grass and gasoline permeated the space.

"Sit up there," Ned said, nodding toward a high wooden stool in front of a workbench.

Martha hopped up on the stool and crossed her legs, happy to watch him work.

Seeing the state of her hands, he picked up a clean rag off the work bench and handed it to her. "You can use this to wipe off your hands."

"Thanks," she said, giving both her hands a good rub, leaving black streaks on the rag.

Ned knelt down beside the bike and pushed a lever off the back cogset, resulting in the chain falling completely to the ground. He picked up the chain and threaded it back onto the teeth of the chain ring.

Martha stared, mesmerized, as the muscles along his back and shoulder worked together, rippling beneath his T-shirt. She'd be content to sit here all day with that view.

Ned stretched his arm out, the bicep pushing against the white sleeve of his T-shirt. If Martha were the swooning type, she might have asked someone to pass the smelling salts. He gave her pedals a spin and stood up.

He pulled a rag from his back pocket and wiped his hands on it. "There, all set."

"That was fast," Martha said, hopping off the stool. She had to admit to disappointment. It was a shame it was fixed as now she had no excuse to linger. "You must have done this before."

He smiled and when he did, his face lit up. "Once or twice. My kid brother has a bike whose chain always seems to be falling off."

"Lucky for me then that you know how to fix these things."

He held the bike out to her, standing on the other side of it. Martha placed her hands on it but did not look at it. She was held by his gaze. Up close, his eyes were fringed by almost-white blond eyelashes and in the shadows of the garage, his blue eyes appeared gray with gold flecks, reminding her of summer-morning sunrises.

Was it getting hot in this garage? Martha swallowed hard and said in a shaky voice, "I better get going . . ." Her voice drifted off as if all the words she possessed had fallen from her tongue and she had no more in the queue. Her mouth went dry, and she longed for something cool to drink.

She cleared her throat and gave a quick smile, broke eye contact, and took the bike from him. As she wheeled it out of the garage, he remained standing there, one arm up on the doorframe as if he were holding it up. She took one last look at him. "Thanks again, Ned."

With her back to him, she continued to wheel her bike down the driveway, not daring to turn around and look at him again, thinking it would be brazen to do so, though she wanted to.

"I'll see you around, Martha," he said behind her.

Her back stiffened and all the little hairs stood up on her arms and at the back of her neck at the sound of his voice saying her name.

Yes, she'd definitely be seeing him again.

As she cycled home, her thoughts circled around Ned—his beautiful face and the muscles that had stretched along his back beneath his T-shirt. She couldn't ever remember having a reaction to a man like that before. Of course, she'd had the silly schoolgirl crushes during high school where she'd doodle her name with the last name of her crush when she was supposed to be doing her homework, but this was different. She thought of the college boys she'd met over the last two years. There'd been some innocent flirting and lots of dancing but nothing where she'd been tempted to pursue it further. Not like this.

In the short space of time since she'd first encountered Ned Lindahl, her body had reacted in the most amazing ways. It was as if she possessed a heightened awareness and colors, textures, and sounds became more vibrant.

She saw the shiny red Buick pull out of a side street and she moved her bike over closer to the curb, but she was still startled when it blared its horn and she lost her balance and fell off her bike, landing on her right side on the curb. Wincing, she looked up and recognized the familiar profile of Mrs. Milchmann from the grocery store, disappearing down the street.

"Ow," she said, rubbing her hip. Looking down, she noticed a long brush burn running the length of her outer thigh.

Two elderly women who were walking along with their groceries set down their canvas bags to assist her. From her vantage point on the ground, Martha noticed how their stockings wrinkled around their ankles, reminding her of an elephant's legs. She started laughing, finding it funny.

Both women bent and peered down at her.

"Are you all right?"

When she continued to giggle, one of the women asked, "Did you hit your head on the pavement?"

"No, I'm fine," Martha said, forcing herself to stop laughing. The confluence of events in the past half hour had made her giddy. Once on her feet, she assessed the damage. The hem of her shorts had ripped along the side, and pinpricks of blood dotted the large swathe of the brush burn, which was starting to sting.

"You better hurry home and wash that off with some warm soapy water," said one of the elderly ladies.

"And then put some Bactine on it," said the other.

"Not mercurochrome?" asked the first.

"I don't use that anymore," said her companion with a moue of distaste, "too messy."

While the two women were in the midst of debating the merits of Bactine versus mercurochrome, Martha thanked them for their help, pulled her cycle up, and began to wheel it home.

As she neared her house, she spotted Cal Cotter seated comfortably on her front porch with a glass of lemonade in his hand. Next to him was her elderly grandfather.

"Oh, not Cal. Not again," she muttered to herself. He always seemed to be showing up. But she supposed that might be inevitable living in a small town. If she weren't bruised and sore, she'd turn around and cycle off in the opposite direction as neither of them had spotted her yet.

Her mother often sang Cal's praises, and her father thought he was a man with a "bright future." Martha wanted to get married someday but not to Cal Cotter. Since meeting Ned Lindahl, she'd realized there was something between a man and woman that was important: chemistry. And it was severely lacking with Cal. Not that that was his fault. They'd simply been friends for too long for her to see him that way.

By the time she wheeled her bike up the driveway and heard his laughter, she was clenching her teeth.

They both spotted her. Her grandfather gave a feeble wave and greeted her with a smile. He was a sweet old fella. Cal stood and walked down the porch steps.

"Hey, let me take your bike for you," he offered.

She shook her head. "No thanks, I'm just going to lean it against the house here, in case I want to go for a ride later."

"What happened to you?" he said, a frown forming on his face as he took in the large brush burn along the side of her thigh.

"It's nothing, I fell off my bike," she said.

"Are you all right? Does it hurt?"

"I'm fine, thanks, Cal."

"I was just having a nice conversation with your grandfather."

"Were you?

"I was telling him how I was hoping to take you for a drive around town this evening. I'm off and I've got my father's car," he said.

She faced him and said firmly, "Cal, please don't ask me out for any more dates. I'm not interested." He appeared to pale, and Martha added gently, "I am very flattered, but I think of you as a friend."

Cal took a step back and there was a scarlet blush to his cheeks.

Feeling suddenly awkward, she eyed the side door and said, "Look, I want to go in and wash this off."

"Sure. Sure. I'll see you around, Martha."

"Goodbye, Cal," she said. And before he could say anything else, she hurried around to the side door and slipped inside, acutely aware of the burning pain of the scrape along her thigh, but still dreaming of Ned Lindahl.

Chapter Fourteen

Later that evening, Martha sat on the glider swing on the porch. Her parents had gone to a charity dinner and dance, and she was left home with her grandparents with an admonition to keep an eye on her grandfather as he had wandered off earlier, before dinner. One of the neighbors had brought him home.

Her grandmother sat in one of the wicker chairs with its floral cushion, knitting a baby layette for the neighbor's daughter whose husband was away serving in Vietnam. It was yellow. It seemed almost all layettes were yellow. Wouldn't it be wonderful, Martha thought, if you knew if you were having a boy or a girl so you could buy pink or blue. It would certainly make things a lot easier. Instead, all newborns were dressed in yellow or green. She wondered about having children of her own someday, and an image of Ned Lindahl came to mind. Despite the darkness of the evening, she felt a blush stain her cheeks.

Her grandfather sat in the twin chair next to her grandmother, smoking a cigar. Since his return, he'd settled down.

No outbursts, no confusion. In fact, he'd been pleasant all through dinner, and Martha couldn't help but wonder if it was her mother's homemade strawberry-rhubarb pie that had done the trick. He had a terrible sweet tooth.

"You're going to wear that swing out by the way you're rocking on it," her grandfather said with a grin. This was the Grandpa she knew and loved.

"Yes, really, Martha, settle down," her grandmother said with a scowl. "You'll pull it right off its chain."

Martha caught her grandfather winking at her, and she had to stifle a laugh. But being the dutiful daughter and granddaughter, she slowed down and let her gaze drift to the beach. It was dark, and she could barely hear the surf for the cacophony of crickets.

"The crickets are loud tonight," her grandmother remarked, her clacking needles adding to the discordant sound.

"Crying for rain," Grandpa mused, staring off into the distance.

Martha turned sideways on the swing, lifting her leg up and placing it on the seat. She draped her left arm along the back of the swing. She debated whether to get up for a glass of lemonade but decided she was too comfortable to move yet.

Out of the corner of her eye, she spied a solitary figure walking along the sidewalk, coming their way. With an exasperated sigh, she hoped it wasn't Cal because then she'd be forced to retreat inside the house, and it was too hot and uncomfortable upstairs.

But as the figure got closer, she realized with unbridled relief that it wasn't Cal, but Ned Lindahl. Immediately, she sat up, setting her leg on the floor. She wondered what he was doing on Star Shine Drive as he lived on the other side of town.

She was torn between calling out to him or playing it cool but when he looked in their direction and waved, saying "Good evening," Martha opted for the former. She threw up her hand in a wave and said, "Hi, Ned."

"Martha," her grandmother admonished. "Must you be so common?"

If it got Ned's attention, then she must be, she concluded. And she was okay with that.

Ned stopped in his path and looked at her, his face illuminated by the streetlamp.

"Hi, Martha," he said. With his hands in his pockets, he walked up the front walkway, which was flanked by beds of roses on either side.

Martha bounded off the glider and rushed to the steps. Behind her, her grandmother gave a noise of disapproval, but her grandfather chuckled and said, "Ah, young love."

"Obviously, I was born in the wrong century," Grandmother said sourly.

"Any century would have been the wrong one for you," Grandpa quipped, slapping his thigh.

"Oh, you," she said.

Martha stepped off the porch and met Ned halfway up the walk.

"What brings you this way?" she asked, keeping her voice down because she knew her grandparents were listening.

"I just got out of work, thought I'd take a walk. I was thinking of taking a walk on the beach. The moonlight is just right," he said.

Martha glanced at the moon and decided he was right, but then it could have been covered in clouds and she would have thought that was perfect too.

With a nod toward the grand Victorian behind them, he said, "This is a mighty fine house."

Seeing the house through his eyes, the way he was unable to hide his admiration, she had to agree with him.

"My great-grandfather built it in 1901."

Ned's gaze swung from the house to Martha, circling her face. "Your family has lived in the same house all this time?"

She nodded. "That's right. I'm the fourth generation to live here." She tried to tamp down the pride in her voice. She didn't want to sound as if she were bragging.

"That's wonderful," he said. He hooked his thumb over his shoulder and half turned. "Would you like to come for a walk on the beach with me?"

"I would," she said easily. She didn't even have to think about it.

"Let me say hello to your grandparents first," he said.

Martha's eyes widened but before she could object—she couldn't be sure her grandfather would remember him—Ned was already making his way up the wide porch steps. She followed him and stood at his side, liking how the top of her head only reached his shoulder.

"Grandmother and Grandpa," she said, "this is Ned Lindahl. He works at the Pink Parlor." She turned her face up to Ned, and looking at him made her feel softer somehow. "And these are my grandparents, Mr. and Mrs. Dorschel."

Ned approached each of them and shook their hands. "Pleased to meet you."

"Lindahl is not a common name around here," Martha's grandmother remarked, her knitting needles still in her hands.

"No, ma'am, I'm from Ohio," he said. "I've come to give my aunt and uncle a hand as my uncle has had a stroke."

"That's terrible," Grandmother Dorschel said. "And who is your uncle?"

"Aaron Strassel," he answered.

"I know who you mean," she said, recognition lighting up her features.

At her side, Grandpa said, "Perhaps you'd care to enlighten me."

"Mr. Strassel's mother used to come here to the house years ago and do the laundry and the ironing."

"Why didn't you say so?" Grandpa asked.

"I just did, George," Grandma said with a trace of exasperation in her voice.

Martha interrupted them. "We're going for a walk." She did not tell them they were going walking on the beach, as her grandmother had an idea that no good things happened at the beach at night.

"You won't be long, will you?" her grandmother asked with a side glance at her husband. Martha did not miss the anxiety in her voice.

"I'll be back in half an hour," she promised.

A mosquito buzzed annoyingly around her face, and she slapped it away.

She was already off the porch when she heard Ned behind her, wishing her grandparents a good night.

Quickly, he reached her side. With a laugh, he said, "I didn't want to be rude."

She smiled at him in the moonlight. "You're not rude." She hadn't known him long but somehow, she doubted he was ever rude or even impolite. He seemed to have good manners written all over him.

As they crossed the street, Martha kept to the sidewalk and headed toward town.

"We can cut across the boardwalk," she explained. She didn't want her grandmother to see her walking onto the beach. The boardwalk was just enough out of the way that they'd be out of sight. She glanced toward Main Street. Most of the shops were darkened and the sidewalks were empty of shoppers and pedestrians.

She hoped he'd take her hand, as she felt compelled to touch him, but he shoved his hands in his pockets.

"This is a neat little town," he said.

She smiled at the use of the word "neat."

"Have you lived here all your life?" he asked.

"I have, but I go away to college," she said.

"Where's that?"

"Downstate," she said evasively.

"What's the name of your college?"

She hesitated before saying "Vassar." Just as people could be frowned on for being poor or of a lower socio-economic background, sometimes she felt she was at a disadvantage because her family had money. Lots of it. She was the only person from her high school to attend an Ivy League College.

Ned let out a low whistle. "Nice. Tell me, is it worth the money?"

Martha bristled, feeling she was being attacked.

Ned sensed this and said quickly, "Easy, don't get your dander up. It's just that I wonder if it's right to charge more for an education when you're reading the same books and studying the same subjects they're studying at the public universities."

She'd never thought of it that way. "Yes," she said without hesitation.

"And what do you plan on doing with your Vassar degree?"

She shrugged. She hadn't gotten that far. "I don't know yet." She'd gone to college to become educated, not necessarily to have a career, but something stopped her from saying so.

"It's an awful lot of money to spend to not know what you're going to do in the future," he pointed out.

She drew in a deep breath and crossed her arms over her chest. Why did she feel she was being ridiculed? Suddenly, he didn't seem as handsome as she'd previously thought.

"Oh, hey," he said, stopping in the middle of the boardwalk. "I didn't mean to insult you. Sometimes I think out loud about things when what I need is a filter for my mouth."

Martha's arms fell to her sides, and she laughed. When he put it like that, she couldn't stay mad at him.

When they reached the edge of the boardwalk, she kicked off her shoes and Ned followed her lead.

The sand was cool around her feet as they wandered toward the shore.

"What about you? Do you go to college?" she asked.

"I graduated with a two-year degree from the local community college. I'd love to go on to a public university, but that costs a lot," he said with a grimace.

"Right," she said. They walked along the shore, the water rushing in around their feet. The blinking lights of the ships and freighters making their way through the lake were visible on the black horizon. In the distance, Martha thought she heard voices.

"That's why I applied for a part-time job here in Hideaway Bay," Ned continued. "To earn an income while I help out with my uncle."

She hardly thought that working at an ice cream parlor would lend itself to the kind of money he would need to save to further his education, but she kept her mouth closed.

"I'm hoping to get a job up at Bethlehem Steel in Lackawanna in the fall," he said. "I figure if I work there for two years, I'll be able to save enough to allow me to return to Ohio and finish my education."

She couldn't picture him working there at the coke ovens or the blast furnace. Ned Lindahl was too fair, too nice for steel plant work. It didn't sound pleasant. In fact, it sounded dreadful. Somehow, she didn't think of the plant as a temporary place to work. Her father's sister lived up in Buffalo and had once said that young men left high school for lifetime jobs at the steel plant.

"What do you want to study?" she asked.

"Civil engineering," he said confidently. "What do you study at college?"

"Art history and English," she said, adding, "Dual major."

"I'm impressed," he said with a smile.

She looked at him quickly and decided he wasn't making fun of her.

"Why a dual major?" he asked.

"I love both subjects and couldn't decide, so I chose to pursue both," she replied. It sounded ambitious but the truth was, she didn't have to work and had the time to pursue a dual degree.

They walked on in silence for a moment and Martha brought the subject back around to him. "So, the steel plant temporarily and then back to Ohio." Every part of that plan took him out of Hideaway Bay and away from her.

"That's the plan, anyway," he said.

She sensed his mood changing, like a storm rolling in. Abruptly, she changed the subject. "How do you like Hideaway Bay?"

In the shadows of the night, she saw a smile form on his face, the cloud lifting. "I like it quite a bit. Everybody's so friendly, and they all seem to know everyone here." He looked at her, his stare intense as he said quietly, "The more I see, the more I like of it."

Embarrassed but in a good way, she turned her face away, afraid he'd be able to see the warm blush that had bloomed on her cheeks. Even though it was dark out, the moonlight was bright. She broke into a run, her feet kicking up water and splashing it about, the waves pouring in over her feet.

Ned had no choice but to chase after her. When he landed at her side, he reached out and let his fingers graze her arm before his hand fell away. Tiny pinpricks of light fired up inside of her at his touch.

"Have you ever been to the beach at night?" Martha asked.

He shook his head. "No, but I've always wanted to. Back home, we don't have a beach. We don't even have a local swimming pool."

Martha couldn't imagine that. She loved being near the water. Needed to be near it.

They stood together side by side, letting the surf roll over their feet. Ned had rolled his trousers up to his knees. His calves were thick and muscular, and Martha tried not to stare.

They didn't speak, but the silence was not uncomfortable. Martha tilted her face up toward Ned and smiled. Without hesitation, he smiled back at her, slipped his hand around hers, and pulled her away from the water.

"Come on, let's sit down for a few minutes before you have to go back," he said.

"Oh, I know what that's code for," she teased.

He looked at her and even in the moonlight, she did not miss his look of surprise.

"Never mind," she muttered. Her mistaken assumption made her cheeks go scarlet.

But Ned laughed. "You thought I wanted to sit down and do some necking?"

Now she felt humiliated and marched up the sand toward the street.

"Come on, Martha, I was only teasing," he said.

"I didn't realize you were such a boy scout," she huffed.

He ran up to her, reaching for her arm. "Stop. Actually, I was a boy scout up until my senior year."

She rolled her eyes and he laughed. He took both her hands in his. "It's getting late, and I don't want your family to worry about you. I just wanted to sit with you for a few minutes before I walked you home."

"Gee, thanks," she said sarcastically, still feeling a bit embarrassed. Why didn't he want to kiss her? She certainly wanted to kiss him.

His voice dropped to a whisper. "I want to kiss you, more than anything. But I won't rush it. And we don't have much time tonight." He rubbed her knuckles with his hands, and she could feel herself relaxing. "I know we just met but I really like you, Martha. Does that seem weird to you?"

"Not at all," she said truthfully. Something bloomed inside of her, hope maybe, that he felt the same way about her that she felt about him.

"On Christmas morning, I like to carefully open each gift and savor the moment," he explained.

Martha usually tore through the wrapping paper to get to her gifts, but she understood what he was telling her and she had to admit to being impressed.

Entranced by the way he'd wrapped his hands around hers, how her smooth hands felt vulnerable but safe in his bigger, calloused ones, she could only stare at him and nod. He lifted his hand and brushed a strand of hair away from her face.

"Martha, Martha," he said softly, "I like you way too much to rush my time with you."

The rest of the tension and embarrassment seeped out of her, and her body became as languid as jelly. He took hold of her hand and walked in the direction of the boardwalk.

"Come on, let's get you home," he said, pulling her behind him.

She didn't want to go home. She didn't think she'd ever want to leave him. She tried to slow her pace and memorize everything about this night. The small amount of cloud cover that began to cross the pale-yellow moon in the inky night sky. The blinking red lights punctuating the dark of the horizon. The warm breeze blowing across the beach and caressing her cheek, whisper soft. If only she could freeze this moment in time.

Chapter Fifteen

"You really like this boy, don't you?" Martha's mother asked, removing a blueberry pie from the oven. Steam rose through the slits in the top of the golden crust, blueberry juice bubbling underneath.

Martha nodded enthusiastically. "I do." For the past month, she'd seen Ned every day. Whether in the morning, afternoon, or evening, they had not missed a day. And every time she left him, she counted down the hours until she saw him again.

Her falling in love with him had not gone unnoticed by either her mother or her grandmother. It had been her mother's idea to invite him for dinner so they could all get to know him better. Martha was excited. She wanted her family to see Ned as she saw him: all that was noble and good. Everyone was enthused, but her father had added his own opinion. "Why doesn't Cal Cotter ever get invited to this house for dinner? He's a young man who's going places." They'd all ignored him and instead concentrated on the menu for the evening. Mrs. Hahn had decided on pork chops as it was still too hot to put the oven on for any length of time. Martha was fine with that;

her mother's pork chops were legendary—breaded and baked until golden brown, the meat tender and moist.

She carried the good crystal from the butler's pantry into the dining room, humming a tune. She laid the water goblets and wine glasses down on the table. She smiled at the heirloom tablecloth her mother had pulled out for use. Her great-grandmother had purchased it on her honeymoon in France, and it was only used on special occasions.

Grandmother Dorschel smiled at her. The eldest of the Marthas had the same wide-set eyes as her daughter and granddaughter. Her silver hair was pulled back into a bun at the nape of her neck. She moved from one large fern to another, on their pedestal stands, removing any dried brown fronds and watering the plants at the same time.

"We're looking forward to meeting your gentleman friend tonight," she said.

"Thanks, Gram," Martha said.

Her mother had referred to Ned as a "boy," making Martha think of their twelve-year-old newspaper delivery boy, Eddie, who threw the rolled-up newspaper onto their front porch every morning with a thud. But "gentleman friend" was no better. It made Ned sound elderly or as if he came from the last century, someone who used a cane and wore a monocle.

Ned Lindahl was a man. All man. He couldn't be anything but, not with that tall frame, those broad shoulders, and those muscular arms. He was neither boy nor gentleman caller. And he was hers. He'd said so, last night at the beach.

By six, everything was ready. Martha paced back and forth in the entryway, wringing her hands. She'd traded her usual capris for a sleeveless navy dress with a low-waisted skirt and a thin strand of red piping around the waist.

"Stop that pacing, you'll wear out that perfectly good rug," her grandfather called from the front parlor over the top of his paper.

"Martha, settle down," her mother said quietly at her side. "You told him to be here at six and it's only ten to. Give him a chance. If you say he's a fine young man, then he is."

Martha forced herself to stand still but took a step back as she didn't want to appear too eager, as if she had been waiting by the door, even though she had been. She couldn't remember if she'd told Ned that her grandparents would be there or not. He'd already met them briefly on the front porch that first night, but would he feel like he was facing the firing squad with four adults there? Her father would be imperious enough. Maybe she should have had Ned meet him first.

She was so lost in her swirl of agonizing thoughts that when the doorbell rang, she jumped. From the parlor, she heard her grandfather chuckle and mumble, "Someone has ants in their pants."

She smoothed down her hair with her hands one more time and drew in a deep breath. Her heart thumped so loudly she wondered if everyone else could hear it.

Slowly, she walked toward the front door, willing her heart to slow down and settle. Within her, everything tingled.

Through the glass, she spied Ned and her heart melted. She opened the door and gave him what she hoped was her best smile. He'd made an effort, swapping his T-shirt and jeans for a crisp, short-sleeved button-down shirt and a pair of pressed khaki pants with a crease running down the front of them.

"Hello, Ned," she said.

"Hello, Martha." He smiled. In one hand he held a bouquet of wildflowers and in the other, a box of chocolates. He held them up. "For your mother and grandmother."

"How thoughtful," she said. "Come in. You're right on time."

He stepped over the threshold and looked around. Martha realized he'd never been inside her house before. She wondered what it looked like through his eyes. From the other room, she heard the crumpling of the newspaper as her grandfather put the sections back together and set it aside.

Martha thought she'd start there. She took Ned by the hand and led him into the front parlor.

Grandpa wore his usual cream-colored linen suit. He had an uncanny resemblance to Mark Twain with his big mustache and wild white hair. He struggled to get up but once he was standing, he greeted Ned with a hearty handshake. He'd been having a good day; he was clear and bright. And Martha couldn't ask more than that.

"Grandpa, you remember Ned."

"I do, of course, good to see you again," her grandfather said.

"Mr. Dorschel, how are you?" Ned asked with a smile.

"Aside from a spot of rheumatism, I'm as fit as a twenty-five-year-old man," Grandpa boasted.

Martha suppressed a grin and, glancing side-eyed at Ned, saw that he was doing the same.

"You're not telling him about your spot of rheumatism and feeling like a twenty-year-old, are you?" Grandmother Dorschel said, entering the room. "It's good to see you again, Ned."

Martha's mother bustled through from the kitchen, wiping her hands on the apron that covered her housedress. "Oh good, you're here."

Ned turned to her, smiled, and held out his hand, which she took. "It's nice to see you again, Mrs. Hahn."

A faint pink blush spread across her cheeks and Martha lifted one eyebrow quizzically. Mrs. Hahn clapped her hands and said, "Dinner will be on the table in five minutes." She looked around the room and asked, "Where's your father?"

Martha shrugged. "I don't know."

"I'll start bringing the dinner out."

"Can I help you, Mrs. Hahn?" Ned asked.

Martha almost giggled at her grandfather's expression. Her grandfather and her father were both of the school where gender roles were clearly defined. She knew they had no idea what went on in the kitchen, and she often wondered if they thought the food just magically appeared on the table every day.

"That's very sweet of you, Ned, but I'll manage," Mrs. Hahn said, recovering from the offer. "Martha, why don't you show him around."

Mrs. Hahn retreated to the kitchen with Martha's grandmother following her to help out.

Martha didn't know what she should show Ned. It was a house, just like any other. She hesitated. Was she supposed to point out all the photos of her ancestors that lined the walls? Or the extensive collection of books in the library at the back of the house? Or the fireplace in the library that needed a new chimney?

Her grandfather took his place at the head of the table. She was just about to say something when her father appeared in the room. He marched forward with his arm extended. "So, you're the young man Martha's been telling us about."

"Mr. Hahn, it's nice to meet you. Ned Lindahl," he said, shaking her father's hand firmly.

"Is that a Norwegian surname?" her father asked. Mr. Hahn was six four, slightly taller than Ned. His back was ramrod straight, and he wore his salt-and-pepper hair cut short and sported a pair of black-framed glasses. He also had fixed, immutable ideas about things.

"It is, sir."

"Martha tells me you're from Ohio."

"That's right. I'm here to give my aunt and uncle a hand with the yard and other things."

"Good, hard manual labor is honorable work. This country was built on the backs of laborers," Martha's grandfather said from his seat at the dining room table.

"Well said, Grandpa," Mr. Hahn said.

"Martha tells me you graduated from a community college back home, Ned. Any plans to further your education?" Mr. Hahn asked.

"Yes, sir. I'm saving up some money so I can return to college and get another degree."

"Well done, young man."

Mrs. Hahn and Grandmother Dorschel pushed through the butler door from the kitchen, one carrying a platter of pork chops and the other carrying a big bowl of mashed potatoes. Both were set down on the table.

"Come on, everyone, sit down, let's eat while the food is hot."

Mr. Hahn extended his arm, indicating Martha and Ned should go first. Martha arrived at her seat at the table and tapped the back of the chair next to hers, letting Ned know he should sit there.

Ned held out her chair for her and once she sat, he settled into the chair next to her. Her mother and grandmother returned with bowls of green beans and mashed turnips. Her mother started to sit down but jumped back up and said, "Forgot the rolls."

She returned quickly and once she sat down to her husband's right, he picked up the plate of chops, took one, passed it along, and reached for the next serving dish.

Martha's nerves had settled, and she kept looking at Ned and thinking how handsome he was. He looked as if he'd always sat at the table with them. She could easily see it in the future. Her cheeks hurt from smiling so hard.

They spoke of generalities, and the conversation flowed. Ned was asked about his family back home and what they did for a living and how he liked Hideaway Bay. He told them he thought their home was impressive, and Grandpa Dorschel puffed up with pride.

"Have you received your draft notice yet, Ned?" Mr. Hahn asked, helping himself to a second pork chop.

Mrs. Hahn had stood to bring in a bowl of applesauce, which she passed around.

"No, sir, I haven't," Ned said.

"Will you join the Army or another branch?"

Ned shook his head. "No, sir, I won't be joining any branch. I'm a conscientious objector."

Forks and knives clattered to the table as every member of Martha's family stared at Ned, including Martha herself. The silence that quickly descended was as ominous as a funeral pall.

Ned straightened in his chair, but a red bloom spread across his cheeks. He rested a hand on the table, fingers clenched.

"What do you mean, a conscientious objector?" Mr. Hahn asked tightly. His second pork chop lay forgotten on his plate.

Martha's eyes widened and her mouth gaped. How had she not known this about Ned? She began to fear for him. He had no idea what sort of a bomb he'd just dropped on their dinner.

"Well, sir, I think it's wrong to take a life, no matter what the circumstance," Ned explained.

"Even in war?" Mr. Hahn asked, incredulous.

Grandmother Dorschel lowered her eyes and stared at her plate as if the food on it was the most fascinating thing she'd ever encountered. Grandpa chewed vigorously on a piece of meat, the muscle along his jaw ticking.

But it was Martha's father who worried her the most. The vein at his temple throbbed, bulbous and frightening.

"You won't defend your country during a time of war?" he demanded.

"I don't agree with this war, sir," Ned said bravely.

In her family, down both sides, during times of war, the men had taken up arms and gone to the front. No questions asked.

Martha sagged against the back of her chair, hopeless.

"You don't agree with this war," her father repeated, his voice rising.

"No, sir, I don't. I can't advocate the senseless killing of other men," Ned explained. "All in the name of the imperialistic policies of the American government."

Martha leaned forward, put her head in her hands, and let out a groan.

"What about the imminent threat of communism?" her father asked.

Ned shrugged. "With all due respect, sir, I have my own opinions and ideals."

"It must be nice to have the luxury of ideals," Mr. Hahn spat.

"Would anyone like more mashed potatoes?" Martha's mother asked nervously, lifting the bowl. No one answered her, and she set it back down on the table.

"All these young men dying senselessly," Ned pressed. "And for what? Because some politician in Washington says we must fight?"

Mr. Hahn jumped out of his chair and Martha looked up at him, afraid, realizing that the whole evening was ruined and there was nothing that could be done now to salvage it.

Ned looked at her and said, "I'm sorry, Martha, but this is who I am. This is what I believe."

Grandpa Dorschel spoke up. "Young man, our family has made a lot of sacrifices for this country."

"I don't doubt that, and I in no way mean to belittle their efforts. My own family made their share of sacrifices in the name of war going back to the Civil War."

"My brother died in the battle of Guadalcanal," Mr. Hahn stormed, his hand in the air. "His body came home in pieces!"

Martha wanted to cry.

"I'm sorry for your loss, sir, but going off to war does not honor your dead brother. The only way we can honor him is by not going to war again," Ned explained quietly.

Mr. Hahn went the color of puce. "What kind of poppycock is that?" he demanded.

"Martin, sit down," Martha's mother pleaded. She half stood, then thought better of it and sat back down. She put her hand to her hair nervously and then touched her throat. "You'll have a heart attack."

"I don't care what I have. I won't listen to this kind of drivel in my own home."

Grandpa Dorschel cleared his throat as if to remind his son-in-law whose house it actually was.

"Sir, I beg to differ—" Ned started.

"You can beg all you want, young man, but it won't change my opinion of you," Mr. Hahn said. "There's a word for men like you: coward."

"Dad!" Martha hissed.

"I think it's time to put war and politics aside," Grandmother Dorschel said. "Let's finish our dinner. It's getting cold."

"I've got indigestion," Mr. Hahn said. He remained standing.

The rest of them bowed their heads and picked up their forks. Martha, with her head lowered, wanted to look at Ned but was too afraid to. Her hand shook as she picked up her fork. She stared at Ned's hand, but he hadn't picked up his utensils. His hands remained on the table, on either side of his plate, steady.

"Will you please sit down," Mrs. Hahn asked her husband.

"I cannot, not with a traitor at my table."

Ned threw his napkin down on the table and stood, pushing his chair back. His eyes were steely.

Martha's eyes widened and instinctively, she reached out for Ned, but he was just beyond her grasp.

"Just because I disagree with you doesn't mean I love my country any less." With his voice shaking, Ned said, "I am not a traitor, sir."

"I'll ask you to leave this house and never come back," Mr. Hahn said.

Ned turned to the table and his gaze bounced from Martha to her mother and then to each of her grandparents. "I apologize for ruining your dinner. Thank you for your hospitality."

He did not look back at Martha as he strode past her father and out of the dining room. The silence was punctuated by the closing of the front door behind him.

"Ned!" Martha jumped up, but her mother restrained her with a firm hand.

"Let him go, Martha," she said softly.

Her father turned to her. "I forbid you to see that man again." He stood and, without another word, he stomped out of the room.

Martha hung her head in her hands and sobbed.

"There's no use crying, Martha, over something that can't happen. He seems like a well-mannered boy, but his politics are too different from ours," her grandmother said gently.

"Your grandmother's right, nothing to be done. Move on," Grandpa Dorschel said and then, looking at his daughter, he said, "Might as well bring that blueberry pie out. Someone is going to have to eat it."

Chapter Sixteen

Martha didn't wait for the pie to be served. Instead she threw her napkin down on the table, pushed back her chair, and ran up to her room. She couldn't stop crying or shaking. How would she get past this? Her father would never allow her to see Ned again.

It had started off so well, too. She flopped on her bed, burying her face in her pillow, and sobbed. She'd finally met someone she liked. Someone she thought of as "the one." But now it was all destroyed by a difference of opinions, and she appeared to have no say in the matter. Decisions about her choice of a boyfriend, partner, husband were going to be made by someone other than herself. It made her feel helpless. Powerless.

It wasn't long before she fell asleep, exhausted from crying. Hours later, a noise woke her, and she tried to place it but was unsuccessful. She lifted her head from her pillow, still damp with her tears, and squinted in the darkness to read the bedside clock. It was after midnight. There was that sound again:

Tck. Tck. Tck.

It sounded liked something was hitting the window.

She slid out of the bed and adjusted her dress as the waistband had twisted while she slept. She crept over to the window and peered through it, spotting Ned standing on the sidewalk, tossing pebbles at her window. She feared he might wake her parents, and that was something she'd rather miss. She slid the window open, the old frame grunting in protest. She opened it just enough to stick her head and shoulders out.

When Ned spotted her, he said in a loud whisper, "Come outside."

Martha hesitated. Her father would kill her if she did.

"Please," he said.

Not wanting to wake her father, she said nothing in response, only nodded.

She left the window open so as not to make any more noise. Quietly, she slipped out of her bedroom, closing the door softly behind her. She carried her shoes in her hand and tiptoed down the long hall, past her parents' and her grandparents' bedrooms.

Quickly, she made her way down the grand staircase, avoiding those familiar creaky spots. She bypassed the front door as the heat and humidity warped it and made it stick, and she did not want to call attention to her nighttime activity. She tiptoed through the house to the kitchen and went out through the back door. Gently she closed the door behind her, slipped on her shoes, and hopped off the back porch.

Ned stood at the end of the driveway, his hands on his hips. He broke into a wide smile when he spotted her running down the driveway.

When she reached him, he pulled her into his embrace, hugged her, and kissed her. But Martha pulled away, still afraid her father might spot them. She stared at the darkened house, everything covered in shadows. Even though the lights were out in her parents' bedroom, she didn't want to stick around. She tugged at Ned's hand and said, "Come on, let's go to the beach."

The warm breeze blowing in from the lake was as gentle as a caress against her skin. There was no one out at this time of night. She kept looking over her shoulder to make sure she hadn't been found out, only relaxing slightly when the house was out of sight.

Together they ran through the sand; the beach was deserted. The lake was inky black, like the night sky, and it was hard to make out the horizon.

She didn't stop running until she was winded, and then she collapsed onto her knees, sinking into the cool sand and dragging in a ragged lungful of air. Beside her, Ned hardly seemed out of breath. He put his hand on the small of her back and a thrilling sensation coursed through her, making her forget about the earlier unpleasantness at dinner. A fine sheen of perspiration lined her hairline. She rolled over onto her back, her hands over her abdomen, and looked up at the dark night sky. There was too much cloud cover to make out the stars or the moon. It was pitch black, and it all felt heavy and ominous to Martha.

Ned joined her on the sand, turning over onto his back. He lined up against her until they were shoulder to shoulder. He reached over and took hold of her hand and gave it a gentle squeeze, pulling it to himself.

"Well, that went well," Martha quipped, and they both burst out laughing. What else was there to do about it?

When the laughter subsided and they were left to stare quietly at the sky, it was Ned who spoke first. Martha was relieved as she didn't even know where to start.

"I'm sorry, Martha, I should have told you about my feelings about the war in Vietnam," he said quietly.

"I suppose we would have gotten to it eventually. I didn't know it would be brought up tonight at dinner," she said sadly.

Her father had been adamant that she was not to see Ned again and once her father made up his mind about a subject, he remained unmovable. Although she'd always thought of herself as a dutiful daughter, she couldn't imagine not seeing Ned anymore. She had never disobeyed her parents in her life. But she supposed there was a first time for everything. She thought too much of him not to see him again.

"I won't kill another human being, and I won't go and fight in a war I don't believe in," he said.

Martha had many questions. Was that a blanket statement? What if he were attacked in a dark alley; would he kill if he had to defend himself? What if it was her being threatened? Would he defend her, or would he stand idly by, leaning on his principles? She posed these thoughts to him.

"That's a little different. There's a difference between going to war and defending yourself—or someone you love." He turned his head to face her. "I hope it never comes to that, but I'd do what I had to, to protect myself and those I care about."

Martha was confused. If it were anyone else, she'd say his principles had more holes in them than a colander. But in the short time she'd known Ned, she'd learned that he was sincere and genuine, if a little idealistic. Maybe his ideals and principles were sound for him. Her idea of men going off to war was rooted in her own family's history of sacrifice. Her thoughts were automatic, but Ned's principles forced her to look at her own opinions. Wasn't that one of the reasons she was going to college, to learn not only to think for herself but to think critically as well? Maybe she needed to examine this issue more closely.

She sat up, her hands tracing patterns in the sand on either side of her.

Ned rolled over onto his side and propped himself up on his elbow, facing her.

"My father has forbidden me to see you," she said softly.

"I realize it's a big ask to hope you'll continue to see me," he said.

"I hate the thought of sneaking around behind my parents' back," she said. She hadn't been raised like that: to employ deception to get what she wanted.

"All I ask is for you to think about what I've said. You know where I stand, but where do you stand? Could you be with me if your ideals clash with mine?" he asked.

There it was. Could she be with him? Up until tonight, her answer would have been a resounding yes. There would have been no hesitation. No thought whatsoever.

"May I be honest, Ned?"

"I would want you to be nothing else, Martha," he said.

"I'm confused right now about the war, about you being a conscientious objector and how I feel about that. How it would be to be with you. I mean, let's be honest, in the general scheme of things, your position is bound to make you unpopular."

Ned chuckled. "I got that impression tonight." He added hastily, "But not in all circles."

With her finger, she drew a series of circles in the sand. "I want some time to think about this," she said.

"Take all the time you need. I'm here for another six weeks, and then I go back to Ohio."

She nodded.

"How will I know?" he asked. "I don't want to get you in trouble."

Martha thought for a moment, wiping the sand from her hands. "I'll come into the Pink Parlor some night when you're working. And I will let you know either way."

"In the Pink Parlor in front of everyone?"

She sensed his hesitation over a public meeting, especially if she were to tell him it could go no further.

"How about we devise a code that only the two of us know," she said. She liked the intimacy of that. Something just for the two of them. A shared secret.

"Okay, like what?" he asked.

She could practically hear the smile in his voice. "Let's keep it simple so it's not confusing," she said. "Or we'll be all over the place."

"Right."

She thought for a moment. "If I order a vanilla ice cream cone, then you know it's a go. But if I order anything other than vanilla, then it's off."

"Okay, Martha," he said solemnly. "Do you know when you'll know?"

"No, I don't. I want to look into your side of things and decide for myself."

"I'm glad, because I want an equal as a partner and a wife."

The mention of the word "wife" sent a tingle down her spine. Before things got out of hand, she jumped up, brushing sand off her backside. She had to get back home before someone noticed her missing.

Ned scrambled to his feet.

"I've got to get home," she said. "It's getting late."

Ned took both her hands in his. "Can I kiss you goodnight?"

"Yes."

He slid his arms around her waist and pulled her close to him. Martha liked how she felt in his arms. She wrapped her arms around his neck, brushing her fingertips against the nape of his neck. On her tiptoes, she leaned up to him. His lips pressed against hers, gently at first, then he deepened his kiss, and Martha felt sensations she'd never experienced before. She pulled away, panting, before it led to other things, things she wasn't ready to give. His eyes were dark and heavy lidded.

"I have to go home," she said. She knew if he continued to kiss her like that, she wouldn't have to investigate anything about the pros and cons of the Vietnam War, that her answer to him would always be yes, a thousand times yes.

She ran toward home, leaving him standing there near the shore with the sound of the water hitting the beach.

When she was far away enough from him to feel safe, she turned and waved. He returned the wave, and she continued on her journey home.

Chapter Seventeen

"I was thinking of going up to Buffalo for a couple of nights. To visit Aunt Helen and maybe do some shopping before I head back to school," Martha announced one morning at breakfast. Buried deep within the newspaper last night was a mention of an anti-war information meeting at one of the colleges up in Buffalo. It was an opportunity that had dropped into her lap.

Across the breakfast table, her father lowered his newspaper so that only his eyes were visible across the top of the paper. It had been a week since Ned had been at the house for dinner. His name hadn't been mentioned again. But Martha was determined to educate herself. She'd gone to the Hideaway Bay library two days in a row but found nothing. When she had asked the librarian for information on protests on the war, the librarian, Miss Peckinpah, gave her a funny look and responded with, "Now, why would you want information about that?"

Thinking quickly, she said, "I'm doing some research for a class I'm taking at college in the fall."

"That's the problem with those liberal-slanted colleges," the librarian huffed. "All I have are newspaper articles."

Martha had started there, but it only led to more questions. She could find her answers at college, but she wasn't returning there until the end of August, and Ned would have gone home by then.

She needed her answers now.

"I'm sure Helen would be delighted to see you," her father answered slowly. "She hasn't seen us since Christmas."

"That's what I was thinking," Martha said. "It might be nice to go up to the city for a couple of days."

"When were you thinking of going?" he asked, lowering his paper even further.

"I thought I might take the train up on Wednesday morning and return Friday evening," Martha said.

Her father nodded. "I'll call Helen later and let her know what train you're going to be on."

"That's great," Martha said.

Her father picked up his paper and resumed reading it, saying nothing more.

The train ride up to Buffalo was less than an hour, and Aunt Helen was waiting at the station when Martha's train pulled in, right on time. It had been raining all day, and the humidity was high. Aunt Helen, tall and solid like Martha's father, stood on the platform beneath a wide black umbrella. Her hair remained dark, and her red lipstick contrasted sharply with her thickly penciled eyebrows.

"Martha, it's wonderful to see you," she said. She wrapped her niece in a stiff embrace and then pulled back and looked at her. "You look well. Pretty as ever."

"Thanks, Aunt Helen," Martha replied. She picked up her small suitcase and walked beneath the umbrella beside her aunt.

"My car is parked right out front; it isn't far," Aunt Helen said.

Martha's aunt was a schoolteacher and had never married. She lived in a big, rambling house on Lexington Avenue with her best friend, Lillian, who was an artist.

As they walked toward the car, the rain continued to come down from the dark sky, and cars whooshed by, sending up spray from the puddles. Aunt Helen dodged the splatter expertly, but a splash hit the back of Martha's legs.

Aunt Helen's green Buick was parked across the street. Martha had always thought the car seemed a little flamboyant for her aunt, as her aunt always seemed staid to her, but then who was she to judge.

"Lillian and I were delighted when your father called and said you'd like to come for a few days," Aunt Helen said.

"Yes, I need to do some shopping for school, and I might meet a friend or two," Martha said evasively. She kept it general, but she wanted her aunt to know that there might be some time when she'd go out alone.

Martha was quite fond of Aunt Helen, although at times she thought her father treated his younger sister with dismissiveness. But then Martha was beginning to figure out that was how her father treated most women.

"We'll have to go to lunch then," Aunt Helen said with a definitive tone. She opened her car door, and Martha skipped around to the passenger side and threw her small suitcase onto the floor of the back seat.

"How's Lillian?" Martha asked.

"She's fine. Busy painting," Helen said.

"Good."

Lillian was an interesting person. A bit bohemian, she tended to favor colorful kimonos and was known to smoke a cigar on occasion. But she was a lot of fun. And Martha was glad she lived with Aunt Helen. They were two single women who had never married or had children, and Martha thought it was practical of them to combine their resources as far as housing and bills went.

The rain continued all the way to Aunt Helen's house on Lexington Avenue. On the ride over, Aunt Helen inquired after Martha's parents and grandparents. Martha did not mention Ned's name, not even when asked if she was going steady with anyone.

Aunt Helen pulled her Buick into the driveway of the three-story house on Lexington, parking behind Lillian's bright blue Falcon station wagon. The house was Victorian in features like the one Martha lived in down in Hideaway Bay, and it was just as grand. The three stories were painted the color of coffee, and the trim was all done up in cream. The front door stood in the center with large windows on either side of it. On the second floor were two bay windows, which made the house look impressive. Martha pulled her small suitcase out of the back seat and followed Aunt Helen up onto the porch.

Lillian waited for them in the front living room. She was dressed casually in a vibrant purple-and-orange kimono, with her long gray hair swept up in a loose bun. She removed her reading glasses and jumped up from the settee and set aside her sketchbook as they entered.

"There she is!" Lillian said. She wrapped Martha in a warm hug. She smelled of lemongrass and cedarwood. "We're so happy that you decided to come up to see us."

"Just for a few days," Martha said, feeling guilty that her real reason for coming to Buffalo wasn't to visit them but to find out more about the protests against the Vietnam War.

The three of them sat in the living room, catching up, until Aunt Helen told Martha to bring her things up to the spare bedroom on the second floor. When Martha returned downstairs, she found her aunt in the kitchen making cube steaks for dinner. The air smelled of frying onions, and the meat sizzled when her aunt added it to the pan.

"Lillian's gone out to the studio to paint. Go on and see what she's working on, because dinner will be half an hour," Aunt Helen said.

"Do you need any help?" Martha asked.

Aunt Helen shook her head. "No, I could do this with my eyes closed."

"I can set the table if you want," Martha offered.

"It can wait."

"All right, I'll go see what Lillian is working on," Martha said, and she slipped out the back door and dashed along the paved brick walkway, her head bent against the raindrops. She tapped on the door of Lillian's studio and entered when she heard Lillian say "Come on in."

The studio had once been a garage, but Lillian had had it renovated into a studio. It had high ceilings, and lots of windows had been added to throw natural light against the plain white walls.

Lillian had changed into a paint-splattered pair of overalls and a loose-fitting light blue blouse. Along the far wall, running nearly the entire length and height of it, stood the huge canvas she was working on. Lillian painted abstract art, and Martha always thought her work was breathtaking.

"Wow, Lillian, that's beautiful," Martha said truthfully, studying the colorful canvas.

"It's a work in progress," Lillian said, picking up a small can of bright turquoise paint which at first she splattered across the canvas, then adjusted with a different brush.

Martha hopped up onto a wooden stool near Lillian's desk. The rolltop desk was littered with all sorts of paraphernalia, from Scotch tape to chewed pencils and an envelope with "Albright-Knox Art Gallery" in the return address corner. There were little dots of paint over some of the desk. A half-chomped cigar sat in a gray glass ashtray, and there was a calligraphy set that looked as if it was well used.

As Lillian worked, they spoke of generalities: How were things down in Hideaway Bay? How were things up in Buffalo? Lillian asked if Martha was looking forward to returning to college, to which Martha had said yes, even if she didn't know how things would turn out for her and Ned.

As they talked, something else on the desk caught Martha's eye—some pamphlets protesting the war.

Seeing an opening she had not expected but desperately needed, Martha asked, "What do you think of this war in Vietnam, Lillian?"

"Do you want me to give you the company line, or will I tell you what I really think?" Lillian said, pausing with her paintbrush in her hand. The tips of her fingertips were smudged with paint.

"I'd appreciate your honesty," Martha said. She knew Lillian to be a straight shooter.

"I'm against it," Lillian said.

"Why?" Martha asked, somewhat surprised.

When Lillian didn't respond right away, Martha explained, "I'm trying to educate myself about it, and I need facts."

Lillian nodded, set her paintbrush down, and picked up a rag and wiped at her hand, barely removing any of the paint stains. "Mostly, it's immoral. The draft mainly draws from lower- and middle-class men and minorities. Are we really trying to stop communism or does the US government have another agenda? Why can't we let the Vietnamese determine for themselves the future of their country?" Lillian ticked these points off on her fingers.

Martha chewed on this.

"What brought this on?" Lillian asked, her steely-eyed gaze planted firmly on Martha.

Martha decided she wouldn't insult the older woman by lying and poured out her story about Ned and the confrontation with her father.

Lillian nodded. "Your father is more conservative in his thinking . . ." And her voice trailed off.

"I'll say."

"Do you like this Ned Lindahl?" Lillian asked.

Martha didn't hesitate. "Very much."

"So, you didn't come up here to visit with us," Lillian said with a grin.

"I always want to see you and Aunt Helen, you know I'm fond of you both," Martha was quick to say. "But I was hoping to attend a protest meeting I saw mentioned in the paper."

Lillian laughed. "I know, I'm just teasing you. But if you're talking about the meeting at the college tomorrow night, I can take you."

"You will?" Martha asked, unable to mask her surprise. She couldn't believe it.

"Sure. They're non-violent protests," Lillian said with a shrug. "If it's information you want, you should go."

"What about Aunt Helen?"

"What about her?" Lillian asked.

"Will she tell my father what I'm doing here in the city?" Martha asked. She didn't want to offend her aunt, and she didn't want to get in any more trouble with her father either.

Lillian smiled. "Helen?" She shook her head and picked up her paintbrush. "She's the one who got me to join the anti-war movement in the first place."

Martha's mouth was still hanging open when her aunt poked her head inside the door and said, "Come on, you two, dinner's ready."

Martha exchanged a smile with Lillian, and they followed Helen back to the house.

Chapter Eighteen

Martha wrung her hands as she left the house, trotted down the front steps, and headed along the sidewalk toward town and more specifically, the Pink Parlor. She'd told her parents she was taking a walk around the block. If they'd heard one mention of the ice cream shop, they would have vetoed that.

It had rained all day but had cleared up by the time dinnertime rolled around. There were still puddles on the sidewalks, but Martha sidestepped them. The air smelled like wet earth. The occasional breeze ruffled the leaves of the trees, sending leftover raindrops falling to the ground.

She hoped Ned was working tonight. And she knew what she had to order. She hadn't seen him around since that night on the beach after the disastrous family dinner. She'd looked for him from her front porch and her bedroom window but he'd kept his distance, respecting her need for time to think, and she thought she loved him more because of it.

The Pink Parlor was full. It was as if everyone had been eager to get out of their houses once the rain stopped. All the small white bistro tables on the sidewalk had been wiped off and were filled with customers, and all the tables and booths inside were occupied as well. She got into the line behind three people and waited her turn, hoping it was Ned who waited on her. Cal was working as well and when he spotted her, he gave her a quick smile.

Ned was in the process of making a banana split and when he spotted her, he paused for a fraction of a second, locked eyes with her, and then resumed his task, putting a finishing cherry onto one of the three mounds of ice cream in the long, narrow bowl.

The line moved slow. There was someone up ahead who kept changing their mind. First, they wanted lemon sherbet, then chocolate, then strawberry, before finally deciding on orange sherbet. Martha rolled her eyes in frustration.

It was almost her turn. Ned was just putting a scoop of strawberry ice cream on a regular cone. She couldn't help it that a smile spread across her face. Every sensation was heightened, from the way the goosebumps rose on her arms from the too-cold air conditioning, to the sound of the music playing over the loudspeaker ("Along Comes Mary" by the Association), to the smell of the woman's perfume ahead of her—*Emeraude,* she guessed. For the rest of her life, she would associate those three things with this moment.

Martha didn't realize she was holding her breath until Ned handed his customer his order and then turned his full attention to Martha. She became unaware of anything else inside the Pink Parlor. She felt like she could barely breathe.

"Can I help you?" he asked. She could tell from his expression that he feared the worst.

She smiled to reassure him.

"I'd like a vanilla ice cream on a waffle cone, please."

His smile grew large and generous, lighting up his eyes, and his posture relaxed. "One vanilla ice cream on a waffle cone coming right up!"

As Ned made up her order, she never took her eyes off of him, thinking—no, knowing she'd made the right decision. She walked out of the Pink Parlor with her cone in her hand, feeling as if she were walking on a cloud. It was probably the best ice cream cone she'd ever eaten.

They started to meet secretly in the middle of the night, both of them sneaking out of their houses to meet at the far end of the beach. They didn't dare meet during broad daylight, too risky, too chancy that someone might spot them and report back to Martha's parents or grandparents.

Two weeks later, after having met every night, Martha knew as she neared Ned that something was wrong. She saw it in his demeanor. The sagging shoulders, the head down, and the hands stuffed in his pockets.

Immediately, she reached out for him. The lake was wild tonight, with the water crashing to the shore. She had to raise her voice to be heard. The pale orb of the moon, high in the sky, ducked in and out of the nighttime clouds rolling over it.

Ned threw an arm around her shoulders, pulled her close, and kissed the top of her head.

Martha steadied her hand against his abdomen as they walked along the beach. The wind whipped around them, pushing her hair back. She looked up to Ned, concern flooding her. Even in the shadows, he looked pale. "Tell me what's wrong," she said.

"I had a call from my mother today. My draft notice came in the mail, and I have thirty days to report," he explained.

"What are we going to do?" she cried.

"I've given this a lot of thought all day," Ned said.

She supposed he'd been thinking of it long before today, of the inevitable arrival of his draft notice. What would happen to them? Ned stopped walking and turned to face her.

"Martha, I'm going to be blunt here," he said.

She nodded. "Please."

"I'm in love with you, and I can't imagine spending the rest of my life with anyone else," he said.

"I feel the same way. I love you too," she said.

Overwhelmed, he pulled her into his embrace, hugging her tight. "It's wonderful to hear you say that."

"What will we do?"

"I have a plan," he said. "I'm going to Canada soon."

Her heart sank. "To Canada?" she repeated.

"Yes, and I want you to come with me," he said. "As soon as we cross the border, we can get married since we're both over eighteen."

Martha blinked several times. "You want to marry me?"

He laughed. "Yes, of course." He went quiet. "Don't you want to marry me?"

She envied him his surefootedness until she realized she was in possession of that same certainty about him. About them. He was the only one for her as well.

Quick to put his mind at ease, she said, "Yes, I want to marry you too."

A grin spread across his unblemished face. "Whew. You had me scared for a moment. I was beginning to think I had gotten it all wrong."

She hooked her finger in his belt loop. "No, you haven't gotten it wrong."

"Let's start making plans to leave," Ned said. "I'll look into train schedules. We can take a train to Buffalo and then go to Canada from there."

"We'll need a car to get to Canada," she said. Aunt Helen and Lillian came to mind, and she smiled. "I think I might know someone who can help us."

"Good." he nodded.

Suddenly, the sky opened up, and a deluge of rain began to fall.

"Come on, let's get out of here," Martha said, grabbing his hand and running.

"Where can we go?" he shouted after her.

"I know a place," she said.

She ran along the beach until she reached Star Shine Drive, but she didn't head in the direction of home. At the other end of the street was an abandoned house that had stood empty for years. All the neighborhood kids ended up there at one point or another.

It was totally shrouded in darkness. The "for sale" sign on the front lawn—if you could call it that—flapped in the rainy breeze. Martha couldn't remember anyone ever living in this house, not in recent memory. Her mother had said the family had left a long time ago and had never returned and even when Martha pressed her, she could not recall many details about the people who used to live there.

It was a two-story house with an attic, the color of the paint on the exterior unknown given that the clapboards were perpetually covered in dust and dirt. The shutters hung haphazardly around broken windows.

Once they were on the front porch, Martha pressed her forefinger to her lips and whispered, "Shh." She'd noticed a light on in the house next door, in one of the upstairs windows. She didn't need rumors to start maligning her reputation.

The front door was locked, but she reached carefully through the broken pane of glass in the door to unlatch it. They stepped inside and closed the door quietly behind them.

They were alone. It was dark, and that was just as well. Any kind of light or movement seen from outside would surely be investigated. Besides, the electricity was most likely turned off.

The two of them stood there and looked around. Even though Martha had long been aware of the derelict house, she'd never been inside. At first glance, it looked as if the former occupants had gotten up and left with the intent to return. As if they'd gone out to dinner or run up to Milchmann's grocery store to get a bottle of milk. Martha rubbed her bare arms as goosebumps erupted.

Furniture and belongings were still present in the front room. A couch had been moved away from the broken front windows and now stood in front of the fireplace. The drag marks on the hardwood floor were still evident. Old books crammed the bookshelves that flanked the fireplace. Paintings—all of horses—now water-damaged and faded, lined the walls. Bare patches of wallpaper were brown with dirt and mold.

"How long has this house been like this?" Ned asked in a quiet voice beside her.

"For as long as I can remember," Martha answered.

"I'd love to look through the rest of it," he said, his gaze sweeping over the room.

She shook her head, slid her arm around his waist, and said, "Not tonight. We don't have time. I've got to get back before someone notices I'm gone."

"Right, we'll investigate another time," he said, putting his arms around her. She leaned into him, the side of her face pressed up against his chest. She closed her eyes, thinking she could stay like this forever.

Martha reminded herself to take a deep breath. Things were starting to happen. It felt like a current, where you would get caught up in it and just be going along for the ride, not sure where it would spit you out.

She knew she loved him. She liked his ideals and his manner. He was perfect for her. She also liked the fact that he was going to take her away from this town. Although she'd miss her parents and grandparents, she knew her place was with Ned. With him, she could be the kind of person she wanted to be: an independent thinker.

He kissed the top of her head and pulled away. "Come on, I'll walk you as close to home as I can."

Reluctantly, she stepped back, releasing him from her hold and already missing him.

He brushed a lock of hair away from her forehead, gazing at her face.

"Soon, we'll always be together, and no one and nothing will come between us," he said.

She liked the sound of that; it comforted her.

"Meet me here tomorrow night at the same time," he said. He looked around again. "This is the perfect place for us for the time being."

"I will," she said. Impulsively, she threw her arms around his neck and pulled his face down to hers to kiss him. He responded in kind, his hands roaming up and down her back.

She lingered in his kiss for a few minutes, but he pulled away. "As much as I want to keep kissing you, we have to go. You need to get home."

Although she could have kept on kissing him for hours, she agreed with him. Once they were out of Hideaway Bay, they'd have plenty of time for that.

"Until tomorrow night."

Chapter Nineteen

The following night, Martha thought her father would never go up to bed. He usually went upstairs at ten but that night, he was still downstairs at eleven. And for Martha to sneak out of the house, her father needed to be in his bed and sound asleep. For a few anxious moments, she wondered if he knew about her sneaking out of the house. But he would have said something, she was sure of that.

Her mother and grandparents had gone up earlier. Grandpa hadn't had a good day. He seemed restless, pacing from one end of the house to the other, insisting he had business to take care of in town. He went from the front door to the back door and became frustrated when he found them all locked, the keys safe in a hiding place. Upset to see him so agitated, Martha tried to distract him by pulling out old photo albums and looking through sepia-colored photos from when he was younger. But he was either disinterested or showed no recognition—which, she could not tell.

Martha sat on the sofa with her legs tucked up beneath her, going through the same magazine for the third time.

"What are you still doing up?" her father asked, coming from the back of the house.

"Just wanted to finish reading this before I head up," she said, holding up the magazine, even though by now she had it memorized.

"Well, don't stay up too late," he said. He stopped at the grandfather clock in the front hall, pulled his pocket watch out of his vest pocket, compared the times, and adjusted the grandfather clock accordingly, twisting the key in the lock, opening the glass door, and repositioning the hands on the clockface.

"Are you coming up?" he asked, shutting the door.

"In a little bit," Martha said, making a point of not looking up from her magazine.

"All right," he said. "Be sure to turn off all the lights before you come upstairs."

"Yes, Father," she said.

Without another word, he trudged up the stairs, the steps creaking under the bulk of him, the noises both familiar and accusing.

When he reached the top of the stairs, the light in the upstairs hall went off.

Martha let out a long sigh. She glanced at the grandfather clock. It was eleven thirty. She had only thirty minutes to sneak out of the house to meet Ned. Hopefully, because it was late, her father would skip his habit of reading before bed and go right to sleep.

At five minutes to midnight, she turned off all the lights downstairs and tiptoed to the back of the house, exiting out the back door as she'd done before.

When she reached the front of the house, she saw the light on in her parents' bedroom.

"Damn," she muttered. It was too risky to continue that way. She spotted Ned at the boardwalk. They made eye contact and she pointed to the upstairs window. He looked, and nodded.

She pointed to the backyard and then down the street toward the abandoned house at the end. She'd have to cut through the yards to get to it. He nodded in understanding.

Martha trotted carefully along the driveway to the backyard, cutting across the dark lawns behind her neighbors' houses, only once tripping over a croquet hoop and landing on all fours. Hurriedly, she jumped up and looked around, but there were no lights on in the upper windows and no shouts from those windows. She brushed off her knees and continued on her way. Thankfully, none of her neighbors had fences; she wasn't too sure of her climbing abilities.

Ned was waiting on the porch of the derelict house. A smile spread across her face as soon as she spotted him, and she picked up her pace, breaking into a run. She leapt into his arms. He swung her around before setting her down and leaning in to kiss her.

This was when she was happiest: when they were together. There weren't enough hours in the day for how much she wanted to be with him.

"I've got some news," he said. "First, there are several trains that leave Hideaway Bay in the middle of the night, so it's just deciding which one."

Martha thought a minute. "Any train after midnight, but preferably not too close to dawn as I don't want my father coming after us," she said. This was her biggest worry. "I want to be in Canada by the time he wakes up."

"What about your contact in Buffalo?" Ned asked.

Martha smiled. "That would be my Aunt Helen and her friend, Lillian." She had yet to call Aunt Helen and Lillian and ask them for their help. She was afraid they would try to talk her out of running away with Ned. She'd wait until the very last minute to contact them.

Ned hesitated. "Can you trust them?"

"Yes, I think we can. They're involved in the anti-war movement up in Buffalo."

He frowned. "You're sure she won't call your father?"

Martha shook her head and spoke with conviction. History had shown her that Aunt Helen wasn't easily bullied by her father. "No. We can count on them to help us."

"Can they get us to Canada?"

Martha smiled, thinking of Helen and Lillian. "They'll probably drive us themselves."

He nodded, rubbing his hands up and down her arms. "Everything's going to be all right, Martha," he said. "Do you believe me?"

She nodded quickly. But not for the first time, she couldn't help but feel as if she were caught up in a fast-moving stream.

He threw his arms around her and pulled her into his embrace, kissing her.

Chapter Twenty

On the eighth night of meeting at the abandoned house at the end of Star Shine Drive, Martha and Ned arrived at the property to see a "Sold" banner across the sign on the front yard. All the broken windows had been boarded up and the front door replaced, with a lock. At dinner earlier, Martha's father had mentioned something about the property being purchased by a young couple with a daughter from Buffalo, but she hadn't paid much attention. She was too excited after her phone call with Aunt Helen and Lillian.

"Come on," she said to Ned, looking around the deserted street.

There was no one around, but you never knew who might be peering out their windows from behind the curtains. And seeing a couple out walking this late at night would surely get tongues wagging all the way back to Martha's house.

She took Ned by the hand and pulled him along. Avoiding the street, they crossed over to the beach and walked the length of it to the boardwalk, coming up around the old Big Red Top, a building that had been abandoned for years but had recently been purchased by someone Martha didn't know, someone by the name of Stanley Schumacher.

"Come on, we can cut across to the gazebo and sit for a few minutes. No one will see us there for the trees," Ned said.

Martha wouldn't be able to relax until they were out of sight. They were just about to cross Main Street to the town green, where the gazebo and the war memorial were shrouded in darkness, when they ran straight into Mrs. Milchmann walking a small white French poodle with a rhinestone collar.

Oh no, Martha thought to herself.

"My goodness, what are you doing out on the streets this late at night, Martha Hahn?" Mrs. Milchmann said. "I couldn't sleep, I thought a walk might do both Sadie and me a bit of good."

Even in the dim light cast by the streetlamp, Martha could make out the gleam in the other woman's eye and the smirk on her lips. She lived for drama, especially if it would land someone in hot water.

"Just out for a walk ourselves, Mrs. Milchmann," Ned answered coolly.

With glittering eyes, Mrs. Milchmann looked from Martha to Ned and then back to Martha.

"Does your father know you're out here prowling the streets with Mr. Lindahl?"

That was the problem with small towns. There was no privacy, and everyone knew everyone's business. To Mrs. Milchmann, gossip was currency, and she'd just hit the motherlode.

When Martha didn't answer her right away, Mrs. Milchmann raised an eyebrow and said, "I thought as much. No good will come from this kind of consorting, Martha." She cast an eye of disapproval at Ned. "Go home, before you make a mistake you might regret."

"Yes, Mrs. Milchmann," Martha said, her cheeks turning scarlet. She had to get home. It was a foregone conclusion that by morning, her parents would know she'd been sneaking around at night with Ned. Not that she had anything to feel guilty about other than disobeying her parents, but it was the optics of it as viewed through the lens of a small town. She and Ned would literally be the talk of the town.

"She has nothing to regret," Ned said. The muscle ticked along his jaw. "And Martha has done nothing to be ashamed of."

Mrs. Milchmann turned a steely eye on Ned and said in a sharp voice, "You're new to Hideaway Bay, Ned. You don't know how we operate here. And taking a young lady—most likely without her parents' permission—out in the middle of the night to get up to all sorts of trouble is just not a thing that is done around here. And that *is* something to be ashamed of."

"With all due respect, Mrs. Milchmann, I find your assumptions insulting and offensive."

"I don't care how you find them, young man," Mrs. Milchmann snapped.

Martha groaned.

"You'll take Martha straight home from here," she ordered.

They didn't say anything. Martha turned toward home, but Ned remained rooted to the spot. She tugged his hand and whispered, "Please, Ned." This wasn't the time to stand his ground and take on Mrs. Milchmann. They had bigger problems looming on the horizon; namely, her father discovering her deceit and treachery within hours. Her stomach tied itself in knots.

Ned finally relented, and they walked side by side down Main Street in the direction of Star Shine Drive. No sense in hiding now. By daybreak, Mrs. Milchmann would report the encounter all over town.

"I won't be able to meet you anymore at night," Martha said glumly. She was afraid. Afraid of her father's reaction when he found out. Afraid of never seeing Ned again. Afraid that someone or something might come between them.

"She won't tell anyone," Ned said, but his voice lacked conviction.

"She'll be on the phone first thing in the morning. You don't know her like I do," Martha said.

"Give me a minute to think about this," he said.

They walked in silence down Main Street. Martha was anxious to get home and get to her room. Not that she'd sleep tonight. It was going to be a long night.

At the intersection of Main Street and Erie, Ned stopped. "I've got an idea."

"What is it?" she asked, feeling as if she might throw up.

He stopped in front of the now-darkened Pink Parlor and turned Martha to face him. He took her hands in his. "I'll come by tomorrow morning and ask your father for your hand in marriage. No more hiding, Martha."

Martha's eyes widened but her heart broke. His idealism was one of the many things she loved about him.

Tears filled her eyes, and she reached up and caressed the side of his cheek. "I love you, Ned Lindahl," she whispered. "I want you to know that one thing."

He turned his head until his lips landed on her palm. He kissed it. "Martha—"

"As much as your idea has merit, it won't work. In fact, it will only infuriate my father more," she said sadly. She loved the fact that he was willing to stand up to her father and take the blowback. She couldn't have loved him more than she did in that moment.

They walked along in silence. "I've got another idea," he said.

Despite her nerves, she had to laugh. "You're full of ideas tonight!"

He smiled down at her. "I've got to report to the draft office soon. I think we should leave right away."

"When?" she asked.

"Give me a day or two to sort out arrangements and train tickets," he said.

"But how will you get in touch with me?"

"Could you come into the Pink Parlor?"

"I won't be able to leave the house for the foreseeable future," she said.

He appeared thoughtful for a moment. "I'll have to call you on the phone."

Martha shook her head. "My grandmother answers the phone. All day long."

"What if I say I'm someone else?"

"Like whom?"

They looked at each other and said at the same time, "Cal."

"Yes, just say you're Cal Cotter," Martha said. But then she shook her head. "No, Granny knows Cal's voice. And she'll start asking you questions you don't have the answers to."

"What if I slip a note through your mail slot?" he suggested.

"Anyone could pick up the mail off the floor during the day."

"What about in the middle of the night?" he asked.

"I can't keep going up and down the stairs to check for a note. My father will know something is up for sure."

"All right, then, let's do this. Come down once a night, between two and three a.m., but be ready to leave if the note's there. I'll try to give you a day's notice." He paused and added, "If your father questions you as to why you're going downstairs in the middle of the night, tell him you're getting a drink of water."

It wasn't the best plan, but it was all they could come up with in the short space of time.

"It's going to be fine," he said. "Look for the note sometime in the next week. Have a bag with a few things ready to go at a moment's notice. Take only what you need. I've been saving my paychecks all summer. That'll get us started."

She didn't expect him to bear the financial burden alone. "I won't be able to take any money out of the bank, it would be too risky, but I have some cash in my dresser drawer."

Ned shook his head. "Don't worry too much about that. Just bring what you can."

Martha was making mental notes and going through her room in her mind, thinking of what she'd take along with her. She couldn't take a big suitcase, but she had an overnight bag that would do. She thought about what she'd say in her goodbye note to her parents and grandparents.

Suddenly talk of running away to Canada was becoming real. They were going to do this. Start a new life together in another country with Aunt Helen's help. Aunt Helen's parting words on the phone had been "Just get to Buffalo, we'll take care of the rest."

"I'm afraid," Martha said.

"You don't ever have to be afraid of anything when you're with me, Martha."

Right before she crossed over to Star Shine Drive, she threw her arms around Ned's neck and kissed him hard on the lips. She never felt more alive than when she was with him.

He laughed against her lips and hugged her tight. "I love you, Martha Hahn."

Chapter Twenty-One

Ned

Two nights later, Ned waited for Martha at the Hideaway Bay train station. He sat on a bench parked against the tan clapboard siding of the depot. The stain finish on the wooden seat was sticky in the humidity. Off in the distance, thunder boomed, and bolts of lightning lit up the night sky, bright flashes of white light. If he were a superstitious sort of person, he would have thought the weather was a portent.

He knew that what he was asking of Martha was a long shot. That she'd have to give up everything she loved and held dear. But it wasn't anything he wasn't willing to do himself. Canada had been the last option. The only option. What choice did he have? He wasn't proud of what he was about to do, but he had to stand by his principles.

He waited all night. At three in the morning, when the thunder and lightning rolled in closer to Hideaway Bay and the rain came down in buckets, he stood in the small breezeway between the offices and waiting area, watching the water sluice off the edge of the roof, thinking the weather was apropos. She still hadn't shown up.

An urge built inside of him, telling him to run through the pouring rain to her house and pound on the door and demand an answer for why she'd chickened out in the end. To declare his love for her. To face her father and tell him he couldn't stand in their way. But that was something that only happened in movies and, always concerned for her, he didn't want to cause a scene at her home or get her into any trouble, especially if she'd changed her mind. He couldn't bear that—the look on her face that would tell him she wasn't going with him.

When the rain let up in the early hours of the morning, it left behind an oppressive mugginess. Ned's shirt stuck to his back, and his eyes felt scratchy. Weary, he collapsed on the bench and dozed off, waking only when the five fifteen came rumbling down the tracks, its brakes screeching. Fisting his hands, he swiped at his eyes, trying to wake up. In the distance, toward the east, the sun was coming up over the horizon, all gold and pale, creating a thin stripe of yellow light beneath the blanket of the night.

Slowly, he stood, stretched, looked around, and saw no one. Still no sign of Martha. Irritated at the cheerful song of some bird, some kind of overachiever in the avian world, he strode back into the depot and marched up to the ticket window.

"Still here, son?" the ticket master said.

"I am," Ned said, trying to keep the annoyance out of his voice. If he was standing there, wasn't it obvious that he was still there?

The ticket master had been there all night. Sometimes, Ned caught him staring out the small window and watching him, probably wondering about him, especially since he'd purchased two tickets and had been alone all night.

Ned slid the two train tickets across the counter. "Can I exchange these for a single ticket?"

"I'm sorry but that train has come and gone. You should have exchanged them before it left the station," the ticket master advised him.

The muscle along Ned's jaw ticked, and he ground his teeth together. Sighing, he pulled his wallet out of his back pocket and unfolded it. "I need a one-way ticket on the next train to Buffalo."

"All right, son," the ticket master said. He told him the price, and Ned slid the correct amount across the counter and accepted the ticket.

"That train is leaving in forty-five minutes from Platform B," the ticket master advised him.

Ned nodded. He would go on without her. He had no choice. She'd made her decision, and now he'd made his.

As soon as he was able to board the train, he slumped in his seat by the window, his cheeks ruddy from disappointment. It wasn't relief that filled him when the train pulled out of the station, it was anger and sadness. He watched the town and the lake pass by out the window, and he promised himself he would never set foot in Hideaway Bay again.

CHAPTER TWENTY-TWO

Martha

BY THE FOURTH DAY, it was impossible not to panic. Martha had had no word from Ned. She was grounded and was unable to leave her house for a month. Her father had gone through the roof when he'd found she was sneaking around at night, just as she thought he would. She had to stay in the company of her mother or grandmother, not even her grandfather would do.

During that week, as Martha waited for a message from Ned, her father did not speak to her. If she asked him a question, he ignored her. Her mother and grandmother cast her sympathetic glances and her grandfather, when he was lucid, would scowl in disapproval at her father, but Martha was more worried about the lack of communication from Ned than her father's cold shoulder.

By the fourth night, she paced all evening until her mother warned her she was going to wear out the carpet. Her father, misunderstanding her anxiety, said, "Maybe next time, you'll learn to obey your parents."

When she went to bed, she couldn't sleep. Shouldn't she have heard from him by now? There was no way to get in touch with him. She couldn't go to his aunt and uncle's house, she couldn't go to the Pink Parlor, she couldn't even use the phone without being overheard. Cal had stopped by once, but he was turned away by her father, who told him to come back in a month when Martha had learned her lesson. For once she would have liked to see Cal; she could have gotten information from him, like whether Ned was still working at the Pink Parlor.

Not for one minute did she think Ned had left without her. He must be delayed, or maybe something had happened to his uncle. She began to entertain the latter as a possibility in earnest.

After a week, panic set in. He was supposed to have reported to the draft board the day before. Surely, he wasn't still in town, or was he? And if so, what was he waiting for? Her overnight bag had been packed and stowed underneath her bed since they first made the plan. Every night she made several trips downstairs, anticipating finding the letter on the doormat, but there was nothing. She wondered if her father had somehow intercepted it, but he wouldn't have remained silent about the discovery of their plan; there would have been shouting and posturing and more punishment.

Aunt Helen called one evening.

Martha took the call in the front hall, close to where her parents and grandparents sat in the front parlor.

"Can you talk?" Aunt Helen asked.

"No," Martha replied.

"All right, I'll ask yes-and-no questions. Are you and Ned still coming to Buffalo?" she asked. Martha did not miss the anxiety in her voice.

"I don't know," she replied.

"Have you heard from Ned? Is he still in Hideaway Bay?"

"No, and I don't know."

"All right. There must be a good reason for the delay," her aunt said. "Call me if you hear anything."

"I will."

"Good night, and try not to worry, Martha, as hard as it is."

"Okay," Martha said, but she didn't know how she could avoid worrying. It was all she'd been doing: worrying and waiting, wondering where Ned was and when he was coming for her.

When her month was up, Martha hurriedly dashed out of the house as soon as her chores were done and grabbed her bike, which had not seen any use in the previous four weeks. She hopped on and pedaled like mad down the driveway and headed toward the Pink Parlor.

The bike hadn't come to a complete stop before she was hopping off of it. She leaned it against the wall out front and pulled the door open. She saw neither Ned nor Cal.

Didi, the owner, manned the counter. "Hello, Martha, what can I get you?" she asked. Her red curls framed her face beneath her pink cap. She was in her late forties and had never been married. She'd never left Hideaway Bay, and Martha often wondered if people like her were dissatisfied with their lives.

"I don't want any ice cream, thanks, Didi," Martha replied.

Didi laughed. "I thought it was a bit early in the day for ice cream."

As casually as she could, Martha asked, "Is Ned working today?"

Didi frowned. "Ned Lindahl?" She shook her head. "Ned gave his notice a month ago."

"He did?" Martha asked, her heart sinking. She leaned against the counter for support. She thanked Didi and headed out, grabbing her bicycle again, hopping on and making her way to the house of Ned's aunt and uncle. She cycled as fast as she could, not believing that he was gone. There was no way he would have left Hideaway Bay without her. Never in a million years. As her heart pounded in disbelief and fear, tears stung her eyes.

The front door was open at Ned's uncle's house. His aunt sat in a chair on the porch, snapping green beans and throwing them into a large pot. She set the beans aside when Martha landed in her driveway, hopped off her bike, and let it crash to the ground. Martha ran to the front porch but remained standing on the footpath.

Ned's aunt stood at the top of the porch steps, appearing hesitant. Martha couldn't blame her; she'd arrived like a whirling dervish with her hair flying out behind her.

"Can I help you?" the aunt asked, her expression wary. Martha could see Ned's Nordic genes in his aunt's features.

"Is Ned here?"

"Who are you?"

"Martha. Martha Hahn."

The expression on the older woman's face changed dramatically. She went from tentative to fearful in a matter of seconds.

"Look, we don't want any trouble," she said, taking a step back.

"There won't be any trouble," Martha said.

Ned's aunt shook her head. "Your father was here a few weeks back and threatened us with all kinds of trouble."

Inside, Martha seethed at her father. "Where is Ned?"

"Ned left," his aunt said. "And now you should go too." She turned her back on Martha and opened the front door.

"Where did he go? Where can I find him?" Martha cried out behind her.

But the woman remained silent and went inside, closing the door behind her.

Martha fisted her hands and wailed, kicking at some loose gravel. She put her arms over her head and stomped her foot. How did you let out a primal scream? How did you get that out in a small town with people everywhere, all around you, listening?

He'd gone without her. How could he? He'd said he loved her. He promised! But he left anyway.

The rage, fury, and sorrow mixed within her and rose up from an unimaginable depth. She needed to scream. With her heart pounding, she cycled her bike to the beach, pumping the pedals as fast as she could until she felt the stinging burn in her calves, her blood rushing through her. She dumped the bike on the sidewalk and ran toward the water, fit to burst with a seething rage and agony inside of her, wanting to growl, wanting to scream with fury and pain. Without any regard for her clothes or her shoes, she pushed forward through the water, not caring that people pointed at her, ignoring the stares and whispers.

From behind her, she heard, "Martha Hahn, what do you think you're doing?" But she pushed on. As soon as she was waist deep, she pointed her arms in front of her, her hands almost in a prayer position, and dove into the water, her clothes now soaked and clinging to her, wet and heavy.

Beneath the water, she screamed until her lungs burned, bubbles bursting forth from her mouth. But then a sob escaped, and she took in a mouthful of water. She popped out of the lake, coughing and choking, then took a deep gulp of air and went back under the water, letting out another scream and watching the slew of bubbles stream out of her mouth into the murky water. She kept doing this, not caring if she drowned, until she heard splashing behind her and the displacement of the water around her. When she surfaced for the fifth time, she heard someone calling her name. It sounded like Cal Cotter, but she couldn't be sure. And she didn't care.

She ignored his frantic pleas, choosing instead to continue to submerge and scream. She spied him within arm's reach of her, but she dove out of reach and swam to keep a distance from him. Beneath the water again, she screamed and sobbed. When she burst forth from the lake she coughed and sputtered, and finally Cal reached her, his shirt and pants soaked, the material dark right up to his chest. He took hold of her arm, putting his other arm around her shoulder. When he had a good grip on her, Martha collapsed against him and let out an agonizing sob.

"He left without me," she wailed, her heart shattering. "He promised to take me with him!"

"It's all right, Martha, come on," Cal whispered. "Everything's going to be all right."

"It'll never be all right again!" she screamed. She leaned against his shoulder and let out another sob.

Cal held her close and helped her out of the lake, shielding Martha from the gape-mouthed stares of the beachgoers. She glimpsed townspeople standing there, frozen, silent, their incredulous stares glued to the two of them. But she didn't care.

By the time they reached the front door of her house, she was shivering, and Martha didn't have the energy to get up the stairs. She stared up at Cal, her friend, his face full of kindness. "I can't do it," she whimpered.

"Yes, you can," he said, coaxing her up the stairs.

"I can't," Martha said, shaking her head.

"Come on, Martha, we've had enough excitement for one day."

The front door flew open, and Martha's mother appeared, throwing her hands to her cheeks and exclaiming, "What's going on?"

And that led Martha to lean into Cal and sob again.

Her mother ran down the stairs, her face contorted in fear and worry. Grandmother Dorschel appeared in the doorway, holding a dish towel she soon dropped when she spotted Martha and the state she was in. "What is it? What's happened?"

The three of them managed to propel Martha up the steps. Her grandmother guided her through the front door, her arm tightly circled around Martha's waist. "Let's get you out of these wet clothes before you catch a chill. Come on, I'll take you upstairs and run a hot bath for you," she said soothingly.

Mrs. Hahn hung back, and Cal quickly recounted for her in whispers what had happened at the beach.

"Oh no," she muttered. She thanked Cal for his help, stepped into the house, and closed the door behind her.

Martha's father appeared from the back of the house. He saw the state of the three women and bellowed, "What the hell is going on?"

Martha's eyes widened, and she pulled away from her grandmother's grasp. "You! You! He left because of you!" And she launched herself at her father, landing on him, pushing him against the wall. Blind from tears and fury, she lashed out at him, pounding on his chest with her fists.

Her father took a quick step back, out of Martha's reach. He blinked his eyes rapidly. "Martha...." His voice was shaky.

"Martha, come on," her mother said firmly. She threw her arm around her daughter's shoulders and led her away.

The tears came now, heavy, loud, and ugly. Snot ran from Martha's nose. She could not imagine feeling any other way than she did at that moment. Or ever feeling happy again.

Part 3

Present Day

CHAPTER TWENTY-THREE

Mimi

MIMI RANG THE DOORBELL at the last house on Star Shine Drive. Her body trembled and her heart thudded against her chest in fear, and she was breathless from the quick run down the street. When there wasn't an immediate answer, she banged on the screen door. Peering through the screen, she spotted the woman named Isabelle walking toward the front door.

Engulfed with panic, she yelled, "My grandmother needs help!"

Isabelle threw the dish towel she was holding, and it landed on the back of a chair. She pushed through the screen door, placing a hand on Mimi's shoulder.

"Who's your grandmother and where is she?"

"Martha Cotter—"

Before Mimi could say anymore, Isabelle dashed off the porch and ran toward the big old Victorian at the corner. Mimi caught up to her, and when they arrived on Martha's porch, she dashed straight inside, having left the big door wide open in her hurry to get aid. She guessed if her grandmother was conscious and knew what she'd done, she'd have a fit.

"What happened?" Isabelle asked as she followed Mimi into the house.

"I was out, and I came home and found her slumped in the chair. I tried to wake her but she's not answering."

"Okay. I'm Isabelle Monroe, by the way," the woman said.

"I'm Martha's granddaughter. Mimi." She led Isabelle to the back room, where her grandmother remained in her chair but was now sitting upright, leaning on the arm with her head in her hand.

"Mrs. Cotter? Are you all right?" Isabelle asked with a frown.

Martha could barely lift her head and although she opened her eyes, she didn't seem to notice them. Her complexion was waxy, and Mimi was alarmed at the whiteness of her lips.

Isabelle stood, pulled out her phone, and dialed 9-1-1 and requested an ambulance.

"Mimi, do you know where the Hideaway Bay Medical Center is in town? On Main Street? There's a sign hanging outside of the building."

Mimi didn't know the place, but she nodded anyway. Main Street wasn't that long, and she was sure she'd be able to find it.

"Run down there and see if Dr. Morrison is available. Tell them your grandmother is ill and we've called an ambulance."

Mimi nodded, flooded with relief that someone else was in charge. That there was an adult present. She was only seventeen; what did she know? Absolutely nothing.

"I'll stay here with your grandmother. Leave the front door open for the ambulance. Okay? Go on now," Isabelle said. She pulled the little embroidered footstool closer to Martha's chair and sat on it, and took Martha's hand and began to speak softly to her.

Mimi ran out of the house and hopped off the porch. She ran all the way down Main Street, circumventing a mother pulling her toddlers along in a red wagon, feeling that running on grass slowed her down.

Just as she arrived at the entrance to the medical center, she heard the blare of sirens in the distance. There was only one person in line at the reception desk, and Mimi hopped impatiently from one foot to the other as the elderly woman ahead of her rattled off a litany of complaints to the beleaguered-looking receptionist. Another woman appeared behind the receptionist and said to Mimi, "Can I help you?"

The words poured out of Mimi. "My grandmother is sick. I came home and found her slumped in the chair and she doesn't seem to be with it—"

"Who's your grandmother?" the woman asked.

"Martha Cotter."

The woman's tone was calm but no-nonsense. "Did you call an ambulance? Is she home alone?"

"There's a neighbor with her right now—she's the one who called the ambulance. The neighbor told me to come down here."

The woman nodded. "I'll let the doctor know. Go home and wait there."

Mimi nodded, feeling like things were getting done. She ran all the way back home to her grandmother's house, her heart rate picking up again when she spotted the ambulance backed into the driveway.

She ran through the house to the back room, where the paramedics were attending to Gram. Isabelle stood off to the side with her arms folded across her chest.

Martha looked awfully pale in her chair. Her face was contorted in a grimace. When the EMT tried to place the blood pressure cuff around her arm, she slapped his hand away.

"Mrs. Cotter, we just want to grab a set of vitals," he explained patiently.

Without opening her eyes, Martha thrust her arm out.

Relief filled Mimi to see her grandmother was returning to her old, feisty self.

Isabelle leaned over to Mimi and whispered, "She seems to be coming around. She asked where you were, and I told her you went to alert the doctor."

They watched as the paramedics assessed the elderly woman. One stood with a clipboard, asking Martha questions. Slowly, she rattled off her list of medications.

"Blood pressure is a bit high," the paramedic said, removing the black cuff from around her arm. "160 over 100."

Martha waved him away. "I'm fine." Despite what she said, her voice was shaky.

Mimi was startled to hear a voice behind her. Isabelle turned and said, "Oh, Dr. Morrison. Thank you for coming."

"I happened to be in between patients," he said. He made his way through the small crowd of people and knelt down in front of Martha.

"Are you misbehaving, Martha?" he asked with a smile.

Mimi liked him right away; she thought he seemed nice.

"As usual, Dr. Morrison," her grandmother answered.

"What happened?" he asked.

"I didn't think doctors made house calls anymore," Mimi whispered to Isabelle.

"They don't, but Dr. Morrison will come out for an emergency."

"That's good to know."

"I just had a little bit of a fright, that's all," Martha said, lifting her chin.

"What are her vitals?" the doctor asked the paramedics.

The EMT rattled off her blood pressure, heart rate, and respiratory rate. They'd hooked her up to a monitor. Dr. Morrison glanced at it.

"Were you unconscious?" he asked.

"I don't know. Maybe I was just sleeping," she said. She didn't look at him. Her gaze traveled around the room, noting the occupants.

Mimi piped up. "When I came home, I found her like this in the chair except she wouldn't wake." Her grandmother leveled her with a withering glare, but Mimi didn't back down. "It's true, Gram, I really tried."

The doctor turned toward Mimi with a questioning look on his face.

Isabelle placed her hands on Mimi's shoulders and said, "This is Mimi, Mrs. Cotter's granddaughter."

He nodded and turned his attention back to Martha. He asked her name, the date and if she knew where she was, all of which she answered correctly. He removed a pen light and asked her to look straight ahead and shone it in her eyes. Satisfied, he asked her to grab both his hands and squeeze. She did so.

"Martha, although everything seems fine, I think as a precaution a trip to the hospital is in order, to run some tests," he said. "And these fine gentlemen will give you a ride."

"Nope, no way," she said, shaking her head vigorously.

"We really need to run some tests," Dr. Morrison said again. "It's not natural to lose consciousness for any period of time."

"I was probably in a deep sleep."

"You might have had a little stroke," he said. "We should check things out, at least to rule out that possibility. It's important to get treatment quickly for strokes."

But Martha shook her head. "No, I'm not setting foot in a hospital. I haven't stepped into one since my mother died. And I have no plans to either. It's a one-way street. You go in but you don't come out."

"That's not necessarily true," Dr. Morrison said.

Martha put up both her hands in protest and said sharply, "Look, I'm fine. I had a little bit of a shock, and it may have knocked me on my keester, but that's all. I'm fine." She said the last word with emphasis.

"We can't force you to go, although it is in your best interest to do so. It's your right to refuse, although I don't agree with it and I will document it as such," the doctor said.

"Dr. Morrison, you write down whatever you need to, but I'm staying put." Martha leaned back in the chair, tucked her head in the corner of it, and folded her hands in her lap.

Mimi took a step forward. "I'll be here. I can look after her."

The doctor looked at her, obviously unconvinced, but Martha spoke up immediately. "Yes, my granddaughter is here. I won't be alone." Her features softened a bit, but only briefly.

She looked around at the doctor, the paramedics, and Isabelle, and spoke pointedly. "Now, I appreciate your good intentions, but I really must ask you all to clear out of my house. I'm tired and I want to go to bed."

The doctor exchanged a look with the paramedics as if to say *what can you do?*

Dr. Morrison wrote out a prescription and left it on the table. As he did, he frowned, bending down to pick up a small piece of notepaper which Martha immediately snatched from his hand.

"Thank you very much, Dr. Morrison, I was looking for that," she said and without looking at it, tucked it into the pocket of her pink-checked tabard.

The room gradually cleared until only Mimi, Isabelle, and Martha remained.

"I want to go to bed," Martha said wearily.

Mimi thought she suddenly looked pale and wondered if they should call the doctor back, but Martha spoke again.

"Come on, between the two of you, you should be able to get me to the staircase."

Mimi hung back, waiting to follow Isabelle's lead, anxious about her grandmother standing up and walking all the way from this room to the staircase at the front of the house. There was a narrow stairway in the back hall off the kitchen, but there was no chair lift on it.

"Gram, do you have a wheelchair?" Mimi asked.

"I don't need a wheelchair," Martha barked.

Mimi took a step back, her face reddening.

Martha pursed her lips and put her hands on the edge of the armchair, trying to boost herself up. "I'm sorry, Mimi, I didn't mean to snap at you. I'm just tired."

"It's okay, Gram, I know you've had a rough afternoon," Mimi allowed.

"You don't know the half of it," Martha quipped.

"Are you able to stand by yourself, or do you need help?" Isabelle asked. She stood on one side of the armchair, and Mimi positioned herself on the other. Martha's walker was placed directly in front of her.

After three tries and waving off any offers of assistance, Martha was finally able to pull herself up to a stand. She closed her eyes and stood for a moment to catch her breath, gripping the edges of the walker with a white-knuckle grip. With Isabelle beside her and Mimi behind her, Martha slowly made it through to the front of the house.

"I see you got a new door, it looks nice, Mrs. Cotter," Isabelle said.

"I should have replaced that door fifty years ago," Martha said, leaning over her walker. "It would have spared me a lot of grief."

Isabelle and Mimi exchanged a glance but had nothing to add to that statement.

When they arrived at the base of the grand staircase, Martha directed that Mimi should go to the top to help her get off the chair. Mimi dashed up the stairs and waited for her grandmother to make her way up on the mechanical stair lift. Isabelle remained at the foot of the staircase, watching Martha ascend. Mimi was glad she was there.

Once the chair landed at the top, Mimi helped turn it. Isabelle came up to give them a hand. Relief filled Mimi when her grandmother seemed to be able to stand without difficulty and made her way with her walker down the hall toward her room.

As they entered the bedroom, Mimi looked around. She had never been in there before. It was a spacious room with a large window that overlooked the backyard. Although the view wasn't as nice as the one from Mimi's bedroom window, it was such a beautiful room that you could forgive it for the lack of a view.

The backyard wasn't much. It was mainly grass, and the garage needed a fresh coat of paint. Along the wall of the garage was a row of flat trellises that had perhaps once been used for climbing roses, but there were no flowers there now. In the middle of the backyard stood a stone birdbath whose base had a crack, making it look like it was listing. There was no water in it, just a small pile of dirt and debris that had landed in it over the years.

"I need to use the bathroom first, and then I want to put on my nightgown and get into bed," Martha said.

"Would you like one of us to assist you in the bathroom?" Isabelle asked.

Mimi blanched. She wouldn't know where to begin in the bathroom with an elderly woman.

"I would not," Martha said sharply. Then, her voice softening, she added, "But thank you anyway." She turned to Mimi and said, "My nightgown is hanging on the inside of the wardrobe." She nodded toward the large wardrobe on the other side of the room, a pretty piece of furniture with magnolias painted on a yellow background. Carefully, she stepped into the bathroom and closed the door behind her.

Mimi opened the wardrobe door, which creaked in protest, and removed a thin, short-sleeved yellow cotton nightgown with a daisy print and laid it over the back of the armchair next to the four-poster bed.

"Kyle has mentioned you, Mimi, I understand you're a friend of his," Isabelle said with a smile.

Mimi blushed.

"Look, why don't I give you my number," Isabelle continued, pulling her phone out of her back pocket. "You can call me any time, day or night, if you need some help." Mimi rattled off her cell phone number, and Isabelle inputted it into her phone and sent her a corresponding text.

From the bathroom came the sound of the toilet flushing and then water running in the sink.

When Martha finally emerged from the bathroom—albeit slowly—she looked surprised to see them there. "You're still here."

"We only want to make sure you get into bed all right," Isabelle told her.

This was met with Martha scrunching up her nose and making a face of displeasure.

"I've given Mimi my phone number, you can call me anytime if you need anything," Isabelle said.

Martha said nothing but did nod in acknowledgment. Slowly, she made her way to the bed.

"Take your time, Gram," Mimi advised.

Martha stopped in place and looked at her granddaughter. "It's all I've got, is time."

Slowly, she shuffled around to the far side of the bed. She backed up until her legs hit the side of the bed, and she sank down onto the edge of the mattress, sighing. "Almost there," she said quietly, closing her eyes for a moment.

"Mrs. Cotter, can we help you get into your nightgown?" Isabelle asked.

Mimi looked back and forth between her grandmother and the neighbor. She wasn't in any hurry for Isabelle to go home.

"If I need help, I'll let you know," Martha said tartly.

First, she removed her pink tabard, folded it in half, and laid it next to her on the bed. Then she reached over and pulled the piece of notepaper Dr. Morrison had found out of the tabard pocket and clutched it in her hand before setting it down on the nightstand beside the bed. "Where's my nightgown?" she asked, looking around.

"Right here, Gram," Mimi said, pulling the nightgown off the back of the chair and handing it to her grandmother.

Martha took it from her and laid it across her lap. With stiff fingers, she undid the buttons on the front of her floral blouse, shrugged it off her shoulders, folded it in half lengthwise, and laid it on top of the tabard.

Mimi glanced around the room, looking for something to do, not really wanting to stand there and watch her grandmother—the one she'd only met days ago for the first time—get undressed.

Isabelle stepped toward Martha. "Can I unhook your bra for you?"

"Please. It hurts my shoulder to reach behind me," Martha said. She leaned forward slightly to give Isabelle greater access.

The straps of her bra slackened, and Martha held the cups against her chest. "Please put my nightgown over my head."

Isabelle gathered it up and slipped it over Martha's head. Feeling as useless as a screen door on a submarine, Mimi picked up the clothes off the bed and asked, "Where should I put these, Gram?"

Martha removed her bra beneath the cover of her nightgown and laid it on top of the pile in Mimi's arms. "Lay them on the chair. Those clothes are clean, I can wear them again tomorrow."

Mimi did as her grandmother requested.

"Now, Mimi, I'm going to stand up and pull down my slacks," Martha said.

Mimi didn't know why her grandmother was notifying her.

Martha stood, hooked her fingers into the sides of her slacks, pulled them down to her thighs, and sat back down on the bed with another sigh. Guessing what she had in mind, Isabelle removed the walker and Mimi knelt down in front of her grandmother, untied her shoes, removed them, along with the socks, and lastly, slipped the slacks off.

"The socks should go in the hamper. In case your mother never told you, you should change your socks and underwear every single day," Martha said. "I'll need that walker, Isabelle, to stand back up. Mimi, pull the bedcovers down so I can get in."

Mimi did as instructed, and they helped Martha into bed. As soon as her head hit the pillow, she closed her eyes and whispered, "Oh God, that feels wonderful."

"Gram, do you want a cup of tea or something?" Mimi asked, worried as it was only five in the afternoon. Surely she couldn't be going to bed for the night? She had no idea about the habits and routines of the elderly.

"Thank you for your help, Mimi, but I don't need anything right now." She stared at the ceiling for a moment and then closed her eyes. "All I want is to go to sleep."

"Is it okay if I check in on you?" Mimi asked, frightened not only to leave her grandmother alone but also to be on her own in the big house.

Martha appeared to consider this for a moment. "All right, if you must, but if I'm asleep please don't wake me."

Isabelle said goodbye and Martha thanked her for her help, and Mimi was the last one out of the bedroom, closing the door quietly behind her.

Mimi chewed the inside of her cheek as she followed Isabelle down the hall and down the staircase. Once Isabelle left, she'd be the only one left in the house with an old woman who probably should be in the hospital.

Isabelle paused at the front door. "Are you sure you're all right?"

Mimi nodded with a confidence she didn't feel. Suddenly coming here seemed like it wasn't the brightest idea she'd ever had. It might have been easier staying home and being miserable and talking smack to her mother.

"You have my number, you know where I live," Isabelle said. "And my sisters, Lily and Alice, live there as well. If you can't get a hold of me, you can run down to the house."

Mimi nodded, hoping she wouldn't have to call her and wishing at the same time she didn't have to leave.

"Have you called your mother?" Isabelle asked.

Mimi shook her head. "Not yet. But she's on her way here anyway."

"You might want to give her a quick call to tell her what's going on. I'm sure she would want to know."

Isabelle slipped out the front door. "Call me if you need anything, Mimi, even if it's just because you're not comfortable staying alone."

"I will, I promise," Mimi said, hoping that whatever came up, she'd be able to handle it on her own.

She pulled her phone from her back pocket, glancing at all the missed calls from her mother. She supposed she should call her and fill her in.

Chapter Twenty-Four

Martha

Once the door clicked quietly closed behind her granddaughter, Martha opened her eyes and stared at the ceiling. She was glad to be alone. Everyone had left, and she needed the peace and quiet so she could think. She'd had a great shock.

Oh, Ned.

To her surprise, tears pooled in her eyes and slid out from the sides, falling to her hairline. The surprise was the amount. She'd suffered from dry eyes for as long as she could remember. Couldn't recall the last time she'd cried. Even Cal used to say that she had no tears because she had no feelings. She used to think that might be true, but now she wasn't sure anymore.

Fumbling around for a pair of reading glasses, she managed to open the case and put them on. She took the notepaper from the nightstand, unfolded it, and read it again. One lost piece of paper, with only a few words written on it, had changed the course of her life forever. And not necessarily for the better. So many lives had been affected: not just hers and Ned's, but Cal's and Martine's as well.

Tears flowed like small rivers, and memories of the past floated on them like boats adrift.

Chapter Twenty-Five

Martine

When she saw her daughter's name flash across the screen, Martine was filled with a sense of relief that quickly turned to anger. Who did Mimi think she was to ignore her mother's calls for more than two days.

"Nice of you to call," Martine said with a flash of irritation when she answered her phone. Before her daughter could respond, she added, "You could have at least called your father and let him know you were all right."

"Hey, Mom," Mimi said casually as if she hadn't just run away from home and traveled clear across the country.

Martine pressed her lips together, warning herself to count to ten and not go off on a rant.

"I guess you guys will be here soon, right," Mimi said, her voice rising.

"Well, sweetie," Martine started sarcastically, "if you had answered your phone, you'd know that we had car trouble and have been delayed for three days."

"Three days!" Mimi repeated. "What's wrong with the car?"

"Something with the carburetor, I don't know. Anyway, it's not the shop, it's the part, it's back-ordered and, fingers crossed, it'll be here in two more days."

"Jeez," Mimi whined.

Immediately, Martine sensed something wasn't right with Mimi and her mother. Her mother wasn't everyone's cup of tea; maybe Mimi was finding that out for herself. "Why? What's going on?"

"It's Gram, she's sick."

Martine's brow furrowed. "What do you mean, she's sick?"

Beside her, Edgar looked up from his phone.

"I don't know. She had kind of a spell earlier today. The doctor and an ambulance came out, but she refused to go to the hospital. They were wondering if she'd had a stroke," Mimi's voice was now high-pitched.

"A stroke? And she still wouldn't go to the hospital? That's Mom. She hates hospitals. Avoids them at all costs since my grandmother's death," Martine explained. "How is she now?"

"I don't know. She went to bed. I think she's crying in there."

Martine snorted in disbelief. "My mother does not cry."

"She's going through an awful lot of tissues," Mimi said.

"Tissues?" Martine repeated, unsure. "Does she have a cold? Or sinuses?" She tried to think back. Did her mother have issues like that? She couldn't remember, but then how would she know—she hadn't seen her mother in almost eighteen years. A little stab of guilt hit her; her mother certainly wasn't getting any younger.

"I don't know what to do," Mimi said.

Martine could hear the anxiety in her daughter's voice and immediately chose to remedy it. "Is she in any pain or discomfort?"

"She says no, but like I said, she can't stop crying," Mimi said.

The frown deepened into a ridge along Martine's forehead. She wasn't so cold that she wasn't a bit concerned about her mother. "What is she crying about?"

"I don't know," Mimi said. "And she won't get out of bed."

"Is she eating?" Martine asked.

"Yes, but not much. I've been bringing things upstairs. She had some chicken noodle soup and crackers. And she drank some tea."

"That's better than nothing," Martine said, trying to reassure her daughter. It was hard to imagine her mother lying in bed and crying. She'd never been the warm, fuzzy type. At one time, Martine had accused her mother of being cold and devoid of feelings. She couldn't imagine what would cause her to take to her bed in that kind of a state. Now she was worried, though she was loathe to admit it.

Martine thought for a moment. "Look, I know how she is," she started. "But try and see if she'll tell you why she's upset."

"I'll try, but she's not exactly open and besides, she doesn't really know me," Mimi griped.

Martine decided to ignore the possibility that that remark was an attack on her and said instead, "Just do your best, and I'll get there as soon as I can."

"Where are you?"

"Somewhere in North Dakota. We'll get on the road as soon as we can," Martine reassured her.

"Couldn't you fly?" Mimi asked.

Martine hesitated before saying simply, "No, that's not an option."

"What about Dad? Can he fly out?" Mimi said.

"No, he cannot," Martine snapped. "Maybe you didn't think this through, running away to a grandmother you've never met and learning it's not as ideal as you thought."

She was hot and sweaty, and she wasn't going to be berated by her teenage daughter for a bad decision she'd made. She'd had that the whole time she was growing up; she wasn't going to let her kids be critical of her as well. Maybe the whole experience of arriving at her grandmother's house only to have to look after the ornery woman would be one of those character-building exercises for Mimi people were always talking about.

Mimi huffed on the other end of the phone.

Before the conversation deteriorated any further, Martine said, "All right, let's hang up. You better go check on your grandmother. Call me if there's any more problems or if you need to talk. And please, answer your phone when I call."

"Okay, Mom," Mimi said quietly.

"Would you like to say hello to your father?" Martine asked, turning to face Edgar, who sat next to her on the bed with his back against the headboard and his legs stretched out before him. He looked up at her.

"Yeah," Mimi said easily.

Martine handed over her phone. "Mimi wants to talk to you."

Edgar took the phone from Martine and spoke into it. "Hey, pumpkin," he said with a broad smile on his face.

Martine rolled her eyes. She hated that he had nicknames for their children. He'd called Mimi "pumpkin" ever since she was a little girl. Hearing it was like nails on a chalkboard. And the big smile—she could never remember him smiling like that when he spoke to her. She half listened to his conversation with Mimi, her thoughts drifting back to concern over her mother. This behavior did not sound like Martha Cotter at all, or at least not the woman she knew and who'd raised her. Her mother was what, seventy-seven? Seventy-eight? Maybe it was a medical issue. A mild stroke, like the doctor had suggested, or the beginnings of dementia, possibly? She remembered her mother saying that her own grandfather had had dementia, with a tendency to wander off around Hideaway Bay.

Edgar ended his conversation with Mimi and handed the phone back to Martine.

"She doesn't sound too bad considering everything she's been through," he said.

Martine rounded on him. "For everything she's been through? She made the choice to run away. And now she's stuck with the consequences: looking after my mother."

When he didn't reply, Martine plowed on. "You didn't even scold her for taking off. You're too easygoing, which is why she walks all over us."

"She's seventeen, she's just a kid," Edgar said. "She's had a rough few years."

"And here we are stuck in the middle of North Dakota because of her poor choices," she pointed out. "And you're acting like what she's done is okay. You practically condoned it over the phone."

"There's no sense in both of us criticizing her," he ground out.

"You always take the easy job," she huffed. "I'd like to be the popular parent for a change."

"It's not a popularity contest, Martine," he said, impatience tinging his voice.

"Easy for you to say."

Edgar stood and grabbed the empty ice bucket. The muscle along his jaw ticked, the tell-tale sign that he was angry. She waited. Now he'd leave so they wouldn't have a huge blowout. Sometimes, she'd like to have a blowout, thinking it might relieve some of the tension in their marriage.

"I'll get more ice," he announced.

"Whatever."

He stopped at the door and looked at her. "When we first got together, you complained about how critical your mother was, and you vowed you wouldn't be that kind of parent. That you'd raise your children with love and affection instead of constant criticism." He paused, stared at her, and threw out a parting shot: "How's that working out for you, Martine?"

He slipped out the door and closed it behind him.

Martine sat on the bed and crossed her arms tightly across her chest as if trying to suppress her emotions. But in the end, they always found a way out, either through words or tears. In this case, her eyes filled up and she pressed her lips together to try to hold it all in.

Chapter Twenty-Six

Mimi

It would be at least another few days until Mimi's parents arrived. What was she supposed to do until then? What if her grandmother kept refusing to get out of bed? Or worse, what if she died? Then what would happen? What would Mimi do? She wasn't a nurse; she wasn't even out of high school yet. She carried the kettle over to the big one-basin sink and filled it with water, then returned it to the stove and turned the burner on beneath it. She'd found a tray in the butler's pantry, had wiped it off with a damp cloth, and was using that to carry food and drink up and down to her grandmother. She was glad for the distraction of making tea or heating a small pot of soup. The tasks kept her mind off of the unknown and scary.

The sun shone brightly through the kitchen curtains. Kyle had texted her and asked if she wanted to go to the beach. She texted him back and told him she couldn't. Then she quickly sent him another text explaining that her grandmother was sick, and she couldn't leave the house. It was a beautiful hot summer's day, and although she hated to be stuck inside, she knew she had to stay put and look after Gram.

The doorbell rang and Mimi glanced at the clock. It was almost one. She was in the middle of emptying a can of beef barley soup into a small saucepan to heat up for lunch. She turned the burners off on both the soup and the kettle and ran to the front door.

Through the glass, she spied Dr. Morrison. Thank goodness. Even if it was just for a few minutes, someone other than herself was going to be in charge of the ornery almost-eighty-year-old woman who was refusing to get out of bed. She was beginning to wonder who the surly teenager was in this situation.

She unlocked the front door, sliding back the three deadbolts her grandmother had had installed. Who was she trying to keep out, anyway? She hurried, afraid the doctor might change his mind and leave.

He wasn't that tall, but he had a nice shock of brown hair, cut close. And there was something about his eyes. They were a deep brown, warm and kind. Just looking at them made her relax.

"I'm on my lunch break and I thought I'd pop over and see how your grandmother is doing," he said, carrying a small black leather bag at his side.

"She's okay. Seems better, but she's refusing to get out of bed," Mimi said, closing the door behind him.

The doctor looked up the staircase. "Let's see what she has to say for herself."

Mimi glanced toward the kitchen, deciding the lunch could wait. "Come on, let's go up." She went upstairs with the doctor following her.

"How long are you here for, Mimi?"

"My parents should be here in a few days," she told him.

"How do you like Hideaway Bay?"

"I love it. The beach is amazing," she said. Not that she'd be seeing much of it in the next day or two, but she was still hopeful. She couldn't believe she was staying in a house that was right across the street from the beach.

When she arrived at her grandmother's bedroom door, she knocked softly, opened the door, and poked her head in. "Gram, Dr. Morrison is here to see you."

In the darkened room, a thin hand raised from beneath the bedcovers and waved them in.

Mimi opened the door wider and stepped into the room, her eyes adjusting to the shadowy darkness. The doctor followed her in and went around to the other side of the bed.

"Good afternoon, Martha," he said.

Mimi opened the drapes at the far window, letting in floods of light. The blanket and towel she'd hung on the clothesline were still there, unmoving in the still heat.

"Mimi tells me you're not getting out of bed," Dr. Morrison said, standing there with his hands on his hips.

Martha glanced over at Mimi and her lips thinned. "Mimi talks too much."

Dr. Morrison chuckled. "Your granddaughter is concerned about you."

"Mmm."

Mimi stood as unobtrusively as possible at the far end of the room.

Dr. Morrison set his bag on the chair beside the bed and looked out the window. "It's a beautiful day outside."

Martha looked toward the window with a slight frown as if she was just noticing the day for the first time. "I suppose it is."

"Would it be all right if I examined you? Took your blood pressure?"

"Is it necessary?"

"I want to make sure you're okay. Any more spells?"

"No, I'm fine," she said.

"If you won't get out of bed, then maybe you're not as fine as you think," he countered.

"You have an answer for everything, don't you, Dr. Morrison?" she said.

Mimi watched her grandmother, wondering if she was going to get snappish, but she thought there was a glimmer of a grin on her grandmother's face.

"Are you married?" Martha asked the doctor.

He laughed and shook his head. "No."

"I doubt you'll be single for long," Martha mused.

"Are you feeling depressed, Martha?" he asked.

"Good deflection," she said earnestly.

"Are you?" he asked, pausing, holding his stethoscope in his hands.

She slowly sat up. "Maybe. But it's not what you're thinking. I found out some news that has upset me, and I'm just waiting for it to pass."

"Anything you'd like to share?" he asked, assisting her in sitting up.

"No, thank you," she said. "Some things are better left private."

He nodded and instructed her to dangle her feet over the side of the bed for a minute. "Do you feel dizzy now? How about when you sat up?"

"No," she said.

Mimi took a couple of steps closer. Her grandmother looked thin and frail in the cotton nightgown. When she was dressed, she appeared sturdier. She waited quietly while the doctor listened to her grandmother's heart and then wrapped the blood pressure cuff around her upper left arm and pumped it up with the stethoscope placed in the crease of the elbow.

When he was finished, he removed the cuff and tucked it and the stethoscope away in his bag. "Your blood pressure's good."

"That's good news," Martha said.

"Now, what about this depression?"

Martha placed her hands on the edge of the bed next to her hips and leaned forward slightly. "It's something I'll deal with in my own way."

"Maybe I can help," he offered.

"I'm sure you can, but I prefer to deal with it myself."

"There's no harm in asking for help when you need it," he countered. When she responded with half a shrug, he asked, "Do you ever sit out on your porch?"

She looked wistful for a moment. "I haven't sat out on the front porch in years. When I was growing up, we always sat out there, my parents and grandparents."

It was the first time Mimi had heard any mention of parents or grandparents. She had a hard time picturing Gram with either. Since she'd met her, she'd only imagined her as living by herself, certainly not with a houseful of people.

"Maybe it's time to get back out there. You could watch the world go by," he said.

"I've already seen things pass me by," she said softly.

The doctor looked toward Mimi. "Maybe you could sit with your grandmother on the porch for a bit."

"Sure," Mimi responded eagerly. At least it was outside of the house and getting closer to the beach. The heat had been sweltering, and there was no air conditioning in the house. All the windows were open but that helped minimally. The house was dependent on any breeze coming in off the lake, of which there had been none since she arrived.

"There's no furniture for the porch," Martha protested. "Well, there is, but it's in the garage and I don't know how clean it is."

Anxious to get out of the house, Mimi said, "I'll bring it out, Gram, and clean it off."

Martha shot her a look that indicated Mimi wasn't being helpful. Or maybe she was being too helpful.

"Let's see if we can get you downstairs today and sitting out on the porch for a little while," Dr. Morrison said. "Then next week, I'd like to see you in the office."

"So soon?" Martha asked, unable to mask her displeasure.

Dr. Morrison laughed. "Yes, so soon."

Mimi nodded behind him, determined to get her grandmother to the doctor. But she abruptly stopped nodding as it dawned on her that she wouldn't be here. Next week at this time, she'd be back in Washington State. Her grandmother wasn't the only one who was depressed.

Chapter Twenty-Seven

Martha

She'd let that handsome doctor with the warm brown eyes convince her to come downstairs, and now she regretted it. By the time she'd reached the bottom of the staircase using the lift, she was exhausted and ready for another nap. Just getting dressed had sapped her of what little energy she had. She hadn't wanted to get dressed, but she couldn't sit out on the front porch in her nightgown and robe. What would the neighbors think? Not that she cared, but still.

Mimi held the front door open. "Take your time, Gram."

She was aware of how anxious the teenage girl had been the last couple of days. She could hear her running up and down the stairs as if she were running to put out a fire. Could hear the worry in her voice with every question asked. Probably not what she thought she was signing up for when she ran away from home and ended up here, becoming the primary caregiver for an old woman. Poor kid.

Martha lifted her walker over the threshold and set it on the porch. Mimi had carried two chairs from the garage and wiped them off with a damp cloth. Martha eyed the furniture, still functional though dated. But it would do for now. Besides, she had no idea how long she'd be sitting out here. It might only be a one-day affair.

"I wiped them down," Mimi said with a glance toward the chairs.

Martha nodded. She reminded herself not to be critical. The girl was doing the best she could under the circumstances. She'd probably be glad to get back home to Washington State.

"Which chair did you want to sit in, Gram?" Mimi asked, hovering.

Anxious to get off her feet, Martha grabbed hold of the arm of the chair nearest to her and sank down into it. Her mouth went dry, and she put her head in her hand for a moment, feeling slightly nauseous. The unrelenting heat didn't help.

"Are you all right?" Mimi asked.

Martha did not miss the concern in her voice.

"I'm okay. I'm just thirsty." She lifted her head and looked at the lake across the street. She'd spent a lifetime avoiding looking at it. Maybe it was time to look at those things she'd ignored for so long and start considering them.

"I can make you a cup of tea," Mimi said. "Or how about some beef barley soup?"

Martha shook her head. The thought of either made her slightly queasy. "It's too warm a day for anything hot."

"I bought some iced tea, if you'd like that instead."

Martha thought that sounded more refreshing. "Iced tea. Can you add some ice cubes to it?"

"Sure," Mimi said, and she ran into the house.

Martha looked around. It felt strange to be sitting out here when she hadn't done it in such a long time. Decades. When she was younger, the porch was always full with either her grandparents or parents or cousins or friends. There used to be a swing along the side of the porch, and she'd sit there for hours in the evenings, gently rocking. Those were some of the most peaceful hours of her entire life. But those days were long gone. The swing had rotted, and she had it taken down and put it into the garbage and hadn't bothered replacing it. Sometimes she felt like she was the only one left from those days. And she supposed she was.

Thelma Schumacher walked by on the sidewalk in front of the house. She gave a hearty wave as she passed by.

"Hello, Martha, good to see you out!"

Martha nodded and put her hand up in greeting. To her dismay, Thelma made her way up the walkway toward her and joined her on the porch. Although Thelma was only a few years older than Martha, she was in better health and appeared to be spry. Martha used to spot the other woman zipping around town on foot while Martha drove everywhere in her old Cadillac.

"Hello, Thelma, how are you?" she asked politely.

"I'm fine, but I heard that you were under the weather," Thelma said with a frown.

Martha gave a dismissive wave with her hand. "It was nothing. Just a little spell. I'm fine now," she said, although she wasn't sure she'd ever be fine again.

"I was wondering if you wanted to join our card club down at the parish hall. We meet weekly," Thelma prattled on. "It's for widows and widowers."

This wasn't the first time over the years that Thelma had invited Martha. But Martha always refused.

"I appreciate that, but for now I'll say no."

Thelma nodded and rambled on. "Della from the Hideaway Bay Olive Oil Shop is starting up a new social club. Probably geared for people closer to her own age."

Martha knew of Della, the owner of the olive oil shop. She'd gone in there a few times. She couldn't tell if Thelma was offended or not by Della's forming of a new club. Either way, it wasn't her concern.

Mimi reappeared, holding two tall glasses full of ice cubes and iced tea. Martha reached out for hers, impatient to take a sip of something cold and sweet. She felt parched.

"Hi," Mimi said to Thelma.

"You must be Mimi," Thelma said. "I'm Thelma Schumacher. I'm a neighbor of your grandmother's. It's a good thing you're here."

Mimi nodded. "Would you like a glass of iced tea?"

Thelma shook her head, her iron gray curls shaking. "No thanks, just stopped by to say hello to Martha." She turned her attention back to Martha and said, "Would you think about it? Joining the club, that is. We'd love to have you."

"I will," Martha promised.

She would give it thought, but she couldn't see herself leaving the house to play cards. She wasn't one to join things. She had been once, back in high school and college, but then things had changed.

Thelma waved goodbye and headed off toward the home of the Monroe sisters. She and the girls' grandmother, Junie Reynolds, had been inseparable when Junie was alive.

Martha took another sip of the iced tea and sighed. It was sweet and refreshing. She took a couple more sips and steadied her glass on the arm of her chair. Mimi plopped down in the other chair. Martha remembered what it was like to be young.

How you could fall down and bounce right back up. But as you got older, you were slower to get up. If you got back up at all. Slower to recover.

"Gram, I know we really don't know each other, but can you tell me what's bothering you?"

Martha regarded her. Her granddaughter had been a godsend, going up and down the stairs several times a day with bowls of chicken noodle soup, toast, tea, and whatever else she could make in her limited capacity, playing nursemaid for a grandmother she hardly knew. It was a nice change to have someone waiting on you when you were so used to doing things by yourself for so long.

Martha had never imagined talking about Ned again after he'd left. Not that she hadn't thought about him, because she had. In the beginning, it had been a curse to think about him all day and all night long. But as the years went on, it became less and less so. She'd be reminded of him at the most unexpected times. It could be a simple turn of phrase, a song that had played on his tinny transistor radio, or a smell, like gasoline and freshly mowed lawn or even vanilla ice cream. Sometimes the memories would slam into her, but sometimes they would return whisper soft, almost like a caress, to remind her that there had been a great love in her life.

If she spoke his name out loud, would it change anything? Lessen her purgatorial pain?

She eyed her granddaughter, deciding she liked her open, honest expression.

"I suppose we should start at the beginning," she said, sighing. She set the glass on the arm of her chair, looked at it to make sure it wouldn't fall, and reached into the pocket of her cardigan and pulled out the lost note.

She opened it, still not quite believing it after all this time. That it had been there all along. Just waiting for her.

> *My darling,*
>
> *Meet me at the train station Thursday night at three a.m. From that moment, we will start our lives together. The thought that you will be at my side for the rest of our lives is the only thing that gets me through the days.*
>
> *All my love,*
>
> *Ned*

She reread it again, although by now she had it memorized; it was burned into her soul. She gave Mimi a tentative smile as she handed the lost note over to her to read.

Chapter Twenty-Eight

Mimi

MIMI HELD THE YELLOWED note in her hand, looking back and forth between her grandmother and the lost missive. She'd read it three times, not comprehending.

Martha stared out at the lake but did not see it. Her eyes were wet with tears.

"Who was Ned?" Mimi finally asked, her voice sounding loud in the silence.

Her grandmother turned her head toward her as if she'd forgotten she was there. "Ned was the love of my life," she answered quietly.

Mimi realized she was staring at Gram with her mouth hanging open, and quickly closed it.

"We were supposed to run away together and get married," Martha said. "But that note got lost in the mail slot. It was only found the other day by the door installers."

Mimi's shoulders sagged. "Oh no," she whispered. "That's awful." She appeared to digest this news. "You didn't get the note until the other day?"

"No, I did not."

"What did you think happened? At the time, I mean," Mimi asked. What had been the consequences of that lost note? Was the estrangement between her mother and grandmother one of them?

"I thought he left without me, that he'd changed his mind," Martha said with a small smile. A lone tear fell, and she swiped at it, annoyed.

"Oh, Gram," Mimi cried. "That's terrible."

"Yes, it was terrible," Martha said, looking down at her folded hands in her lap. "At the time, I thought I'd never survive it."

Sensing gloominess and not sure what to do, Mimi said brightly, "But you did, you're here."

"Barely," Martha whispered.

Mimi had lots of questions she wanted to ask. "Where were you going? And why did you have to run away?"

Martha told Mimi all about Ned's objections to the war and about the disastrous dinner where her father had accused him of being a coward.

"Ouch. That's harsh," Mimi said.

With a slight nod, Martha said, "It was more than that. Father had lost a brother in World War II and well, it colored his perspective, understandably. He forbade me to see him."

"What did you do?" Mimi asked, inching closer to the edge of her seat and staring at Martha.

"We were madly in love. We used to meet in the middle of the night at Isabelle's house." Martha smiled at the memory of it.

"They let you?"

"The house was abandoned then. We met in secret. But we were found out, and I got into a lot of trouble. I was on house arrest," Martha remembered bitterly. "So, we made plans to run away. He was going to drop a note through the mail slot in the middle of the night. We were going to take the train to Buffalo, where my aunt was going to help us cross the border to Canada. That's where the draft dodgers were going in those days. But as you can see, I never got the note."

"Whatever happened to Ned?"

Martha shrugged. "I don't know. I never saw him again after he left Hideaway Bay."

"That's the saddest thing I've ever heard," Mimi said.

"Yes, it's very sad," Martha agreed.

They sat quietly for a bit before Mimi felt compelled to ask, "What about my grandfather?"

"Cal? What about him?"

"Did you love him? Did he know about Ned?"

It was a while before Martha answered Mimi's question, as if she was carefully and thoughtfully choosing her words. "I'd known Cal since I was a little girl; he was a good friend of mine. Before he went away to serve in Vietnam, he was one of the kindest people you could ever meet. I loved him as one loves a friend, but I didn't love him the way I loved Ned."

"Oh," Mimi said, looking at her with that frankness that young people have when they're trying to get answers to their questions. "Do you regret marrying Granddad?"

"No," Martha said without hesitation.

As Mimi sat next to her grandmother, digesting all this news, all sorts of questions raced through her mind. In a short period of time, she'd certainly learned a lot about the grandmother she'd only met recently.

"Didn't you want to find Ned and see him?" she asked. This genuinely perplexed her. But on further thought, maybe she could understand why her grandmother hadn't searched for him.

"I figured he'd made the choice to leave without me, so there was no point in chasing him," Martha replied.

Mimi could understand that. She used to harbor a terrible crush on her next-door neighbor, and he'd stomped on her dreams in one afternoon. After that, Mimi had avoided him at all costs, not wanting any reminders of her humiliation.

"But now that you know the truth—that he didn't leave without you, that he waited for you—don't you want to find out what happened to him?" Mimi asked. If it were her, she'd want to know. Her curiosity would be insatiable.

Martha shook her head. "No, it's too late. I don't even know if he's still alive. Or where he even is. Still in Canada somewhere? Who knows. And perhaps it's best to leave the past in the past."

Mimi didn't necessarily agree. The other half of the equation was Ned, who'd left Hideaway Bay thinking Martha had never shown up. How sad was that? Her mind whirred with possibilities, and she was about to present several suggestions to her grandmother when she spotted Isabelle's younger sister Alice making her way toward them, carrying a covered dish in her hands.

When Alice turned onto the short footpath, Martha sighed. "This is why it isn't a good idea to sit out on your front porch. Everyone feels compelled to stop by."

Mimi gave her grandmother a warning look. "Gram, be nice."

"I'll try," Martha said. "But I make no promises."

Mimi chuckled.

Alice bounced up the steps, and the sunlight caught the diamond solitaire on the ring finger of her left hand.

"Hello, Mrs. Cotter, how are you feeling?" Alice said. She held up a square ceramic dish that was covered with a dish towel. "I've made you some apple crumble."

"Yummy," Mimi said.

The cuisine here at her grandmother's house tended to favor mid-twentieth century American: reliance on canned vegetables and meat fried in a pan on the stove. Admittedly, Mimi missed the more adventurous menu from back home, but she couldn't admit that just yet. One evening when she'd suggested they order Thai, her grandmother had frowned and said, "Why? We've got baked potatoes and pork chops tonight."

Martha glanced at Alice and said, "That was thoughtful of you."

"Just a little something," Alice said.

She handed the dish to Mimi, who took it into the house and set it on the kitchen table. It was still warm. Mimi lifted up the dish towel and smiled at the sight of the golden crumb crust. She leaned back to make sure her grandmother wasn't in sight through the front door, then grabbed a spoon from the drawer and took a small taste. She closed her eyes in delight as the flavors of apple, butter, and cinnamon hit her tongue.

When she returned, Alice had taken Mimi's seat. Mimi hopped up on the wide railing and sat sideways on it.

"Isabelle, Lily, and I are right down the street if you need anything," Alice offered.

"I appreciate that," Martha said.

Mimi had to smile at her grandmother. She probably wasn't used to all this polite conversation and hospitality in one day and might need a nap afterward.

"You're an attorney, isn't that right?" Martha asked.

"Yes, I went into partnership with Ben Enright, out on the highway," Alice replied.

"How do you like being back in Hideaway Bay?" Martha asked. Years ago, she'd heard from the girl's grandmother that Alice was living in Chicago. Small-town life must be a big change.

"I love it," Alice said enthusiastically.

With a nod to the diamond solitaire on her finger, Martha mused, "It seems like you might love someone, too."

Alice looked down at the ring and smiled. "Yes. I'm engaged to Jack Stirling."

Mimi had no idea who that was, but the way Martha nodded indicated she at least knew of Alice's fiancé. Mimi would ask her about it later.

"I love weddings," Mimi said.

"Me too," Alice gushed.

Mimi knew her own parents had had a low-key affair, married by the justice of the peace with a small reception at her other grandparents' house. She knew Martha had not been there. And although her parents never mentioned it, she was able to do some quick math and conclude that her mother was already pregnant with her when she wed her father. Mimi didn't mind. She wondered if her grandmother and Cal had had a big wedding. Although there were loads of framed photos adorning just about every available inch of wall space downstairs, she hadn't seen any of her grandparents or of their wedding. The photos were mostly of dead ancestors, most of whom had lived in the house at one time or another.

"When's the date?" Martha asked.

"Next year," Alice said. "We'll be getting married right here in Hideaway Bay."

Mimi thought Alice would make a pretty bride with her clear complexion and that abundance of curly red hair.

"Where will you live?" Martha asked.

"We're not sure yet," Alice said. "To be determined." Quickly she added, as if sensing there might be grist for the mill, "Either Jack's house or we might start over in a new home of our own."

"I'd advise you on the latter," Martha said.

After a few more minutes, Alice stood, saying she wouldn't keep them any longer and they could return the dish any time. Mimi could see that her grandmother was relieved as she was beginning to wilt with all the small talk.

"She's a nice girl," Martha said when Alice was halfway to her home and out of earshot. "And it was thoughtful of her to drop off an apple crumble. I haven't had that in years."

Mimi nodded.

Martha looked at Mimi and with a wry grin, she asked, "How did it taste?"

Slightly mortified, Mimi stopped swinging her leg and asked, "How did you know I tasted it?"

Martha laughed. "Because you were gone slightly longer than was necessary to drop it off on the kitchen table and return. And it's what I would have done myself."

CHAPTER TWENTY-NINE

Martine

"Look, since we're stuck here for a while—" Edgar started.

"Don't remind me," Martine said.

At one time, she would have relished the chance to be alone with Edgar. In the beginning, there were stolen moments when they couldn't get enough of each other but now, in all honesty, she didn't want to wait out the time at this stuffy motel time seemed to have forgotten.

"Can I finish my sentence without you interrupting with a sarcastic comment?" he said tightly.

Martine looked at him. The heat and this place in the middle of nowhere and her general surliness must finally be getting to good-natured Edgar. He stood there with his hands on his hips, looking annoyed. She arched an eyebrow in his direction.

But Edgar was the least of her worries. Her main concern right now was her two children, who were at opposite sides of the country with neither parent with them.

"I was thinking," he said quietly. He leaned forward in the upholstered chair with the chipped wood frame, his hands dangling between his knees. He stared down at the floor. "Maybe we should use this time to air our grievances." He straightened up and used air quotes to emphasize the word "grievances."

She stared at him. They were stuck here, and he wanted a little impromptu do-it-yourself marriage counseling? Where had he been the last six months when she'd been telling him how unhappy she was?

"I'm worried about Mimi," she said. "My mother. Micah. Do you think I'd be engaged enough for this kind of conversation?" She was unable to keep the disbelief out of her voice.

"How would I tell the difference? You haven't been engaged for the last year of our marriage," he said gruffly.

It sounded like she wasn't the only one who was unsatisfied.

Finally, she asked him, "Edgar, are you happy?"

"I was until you told me you wanted a divorce."

"Can you honestly say things have been good between us?" she asked, incredulous that they viewed their relationship through two such different lenses.

"I thought they were. I knew you were struggling with something, but you've been so remote lately."

"It's because I'm unhappy," she cried. How many ways did she have to spell it out? Every time they started to discuss things, it turned into a circular argument, like an awful ride at the fair you couldn't get off of.

"Are you unhappy with me and our marriage, or are you unhappy with yourself? Because if it's the latter, then you need to work on you," he said.

Tired, hot, and sweaty, she put her head in her hands and said, "I don't know."

"Maybe you need to figure that out before you ask me for a divorce," he snapped.

She lifted her head. "You don't need to turn nasty, Edgar."

"Pardon me for being fed up. I'm tooling along for almost twenty years now, thinking we're pretty solid, and you come out of left field and tell me you want out. How do you want me to react? Either you've been lying or you're a pretty damn good actress. Because you had me convinced that you loved me."

"I did love you," she said.

"Nice use of the past tense there, Martine," he said smartly.

"I'm sorry but I'm going for truthful," she said. "Just because I'm not in love with you anymore doesn't mean I don't care for you."

"Well, thanks, that helps." He stood from his chair and said, "I'm going to get a beer."

"You've been drinking a lot of beer since we arrived," she said.

He stopped to look at her. "Really? I wonder why that is." And he took a few strides, patting his back pocket to check for his wallet. He stopped at the door. "While I'm gone, why don't you try and figure out why you're unhappy. Can you at least do that? Because I can't nail down these vague statements of yours."

She didn't respond, and he closed the door behind him.

Martine stared at the closed door for a long time, weary. She collapsed on the bed, no longer caring about the suspect bedspread, and stared at the ceiling. Finally, she forced herself off the bed and headed to the grungy bathroom to take a shower.

Chapter Thirty

Mimi

"Come on in," Kyle said, appearing at the screen door of his house. "Everyone's gone, so we can work at the kitchen table."

Mimi nodded and stepped inside, luxuriating in the coolness of the air-conditioned house. It was almost chilly, but it felt good. The last few nights had been still and hot with not even a gentle breeze coming in off the lake. The upstairs at her grandmother's house was stifling at night.

She followed him down a short hall that was lit from sunlight coming in through a kitchen window. The house was quiet, but there was evidence that other people lived here. Backpacks hung on hooks in the hallway. A baseball bat and a skateboard leaned in the corner near the front door. And when she stepped through into the kitchen, she spotted a little girl's pink bathing suit and a pink beach towel draped over a chair outside in the backyard.

The kitchen table was round, dark, and had chairs whose seats were stained a dark mahogany but whose legs and ladder-backs were painted black.

"Take a seat," Kyle said. "Do you want something to drink? Iced tea? Coke?"

"Coke is fine," Mimi said, slipping her backpack off her shoulders and setting it on the tiled floor.

She eyed the pool out back, the water the color of turquoise, thinking it must be sweet to be able to go swimming every day. If she had a pool, she'd never get out of it. But as it was, she couldn't even get to the lake across the street.

Kyle pulled two cans of Coke off the inside of the fridge door and carried them over to the table. He'd gotten a haircut. She could see his eyes now. He should wear his hair short; he had a handsome face.

He set the cans down on the table, returned to the counter and carried over a plate of brownies and took the chair next to her.

"Alice sent over salted caramel brownies, they're her specialty," he said.

"Play your cards right and maybe your father will marry Isabelle, and then you'll get tons of desserts," she teased.

Kyle paled, and she realized she'd gone too far.

"Let's not get carried away," he muttered.

She reached out and laid her hand on his arm. "I'm sorry, I didn't mean . . ."

He looked at her hand on his arm, then abruptly pulled away, moving his laptop into a better position so they both could see. "Never mind. Come on, let's find this Ned Lindahl."

They settled in side by side, hunched over Kyle's laptop.

Kyle reached over, picked a brownie off the plate, and bit half of it off, chewing thoughtfully.

"I don't know where to begin to look for him," Mimi admitted. She debated helping herself to a brownie. They looked good. As she debated, she took a sip from the can of pop.

"Let's try this," he said. He shoved the last bit of brownie into his mouth, chomped on it, and began typing across the keyboard. The words "Edward Lindahl" and "Canada" appeared across the browser search bar. Mimi held her breath as he hit the "enter" button. The list was short, showing various Eds, Eddies, Teds, and Teddys in Canada.

Kyle scrolled to the bottom of the page, but the entries morphed into something more obscure, variations on the name or spelling.

"At least there's not too many of them," Mimi said.

He nodded. "It won't take too long to go through them."

"It's also possible that he's dead," she said glumly.

"Don't give up hope yet, we've only just started the search," Kyle said. "Let's look at all the Edward Lindahls here, and it wouldn't be a bad idea to do a search for Ned Lindahl as well. We should also look through the obituaries, just in case." He stood and retrieved his backpack, unzipping it and pulling out a spiral-bound notebook.

"Here, start copying down all the names and the towns. After we do that, we'll figure out how to contact them," he suggested.

"Is Canada considered long-distance?" she asked.

They stared at one another as they contemplated this.

"Probably," Kyle said, his expression dour. "That would be the kind of luck we'd have."

Playfully, she punched him on the arm. "Come on, don't be negative."

"Okay, you're right. We'll figure that part out later," he said.

"We probably should look for him in Ohio too. He might have gone home after the war."

Kyle nodded, picked up his can, tilted his head back, and gulped it down, his Adam's apple bobbing. Mimi reached for a brownie and took a bite out of it. It was gooey, and a string of caramel hung off of it, which she pulled off with her finger.

"Okay, let's get to work," Kyle said, leaning over the keyboard. "Ready for the first name?"

Mimi threw the remainder of the brownie in her mouth and licked her fingers and nodded. "I am now." She retrieved her favorite pen from her backpack. It had a small plume of pink feathers at the tip of it. It was a little outrageous, but that's what she liked about it.

"Edward Lindahl, Alberta, here's the address," Kyle said, repeating the information twice.

"Okay, slow down," Mimi said. "I'm not a speed writer."

"Oh, okay," he said.

She was aware of his eyes on her and her notebook, and she was determined to be a little neater with her note-taking. She didn't know why she cared about what he thought, but she did.

CHAPTER THIRTY-ONE

Martine

"WE *HAD TO GET* married," Martine pointed out. Just out of the shower, she sat down in one of the questionable chairs, tilted her head to one side, and dried her hair with a towel.

After Edgar had finished his beer, he suggested again that they "clear the air." When Martine responded that she didn't know how, he told her, "Start at the beginning."

"Our marriage started out because we had to get married," she said again.

"I'm aware of that," Edgar said. He uncapped two beers and handed her one.

"It bothers me." She rummaged through her overnight bag in search of a comb.

"In what way?" he asked.

"If I hadn't gotten pregnant, would you have married me? Or did you do it out of a sense of duty?"

Edgar leaned forward, shaking his head. "I'm so sick of having this argument. We'd been going out for a while. You got pregnant. We got married. End of."

"But did you marry me because it was the right thing to do?" she pushed.

He let out a long, exasperated groan.

"Yes, the pregnancy was the motivating factor for me asking you to marry me. We hadn't been going out that long when you got pregnant. I thought I was doing the right thing," he yelled, startling her. "Things happen. It's called life. Sometimes it's best to go with the flow. In the end, I thought it turned out all right."

Martine would need to think about this later. Comb in hand, she ran it through her hair.

The room felt muggy. She stood and turned the window air conditioner up to high. It was as loud as a jet engine.

"Why can't you put a positive spin on it?" he said. "We got married because we had to, so what? Do you think we're the first couple in the world to have to get married? It went on a lot more than you think; they were just discreet about it in the old days. We ended up with two beautiful children I wouldn't trade for anything in the world. Not to mention, we've had a pretty good marriage up until this point. It makes me wonder—and I hate to ask but I feel I have to—is there someone else?"

Martine looked at him with wide eyes, gape-jawed, and asked, "How can you even think that?"

He shrugged, crossed one leg over his other knee, and took a pull off his beer bottle. "What am I supposed to think, Martine?"

"There is no one else," she said. Although she'd been daydreaming these past months about moving out with the kids and getting a dog.

"I'm relieved to hear that," he said.

"Do you believe me?"

He frowned. "Of course I do. It's trust built on almost twenty years of marriage."

She thought about this, how he blindly trusted her.

As if answering her thoughts, he added, "But that's a two-way street. Do you trust me?"

She tipped her head and let out a slow "Yes."

He scoffed. "You had to think about that."

She inhaled and exhaled a deep breath, not knowing what to say. A thought popped into her head, and she verbalized it. "Growing up, I did not have the best examples of married couples. My parents were miserable together and according to my mother, her own parents' marriage wasn't ideal. Apparently, my grandfather could be a bully."

"I know that, Martine," Edgar said, his expression softening. "But I did have a good example, and I thought the life we created together helped you to break that pattern."

Had she ever thought that too? She wasn't sure. Had she escaped the unhappy marriage legacy? Was she going through a phase? Although she hated that term because it sounded dismissive, like she was being silly.

"Look, all marriages go through ups and downs," he said. "That's one thing I've learned. But I think you have to ride out the rough spots. Do you remember when we were first married?"

"Which part?" she asked, narrowing her eyes.

"Remember when we were in our first home and we had no money and instead of going out, we'd have a couple of cocktails out on the back patio and listen to music? Those were some of the happiest days of my life."

She did remember that. At the time, after Mimi was born, she'd wanted to go out. She'd wanted to go to the nightclubs and go dancing. She was still young, but going out wasn't in the budget. Extra money was non-existent. Those years were hard but looking back, they'd been happy.

When Martine had grown tired of sitting in on a Saturday night, Edgar had surprised her with their very own beer garden. He'd strung Christmas lights around their patio, set up the CD player, and bought a blender and learned how to make piña coladas and margaritas. At the time, Martine had thought it was wonderful that her new husband had been so attentive to her needs.

What had happened in the intervening years?

CHAPTER THIRTY-TWO

Mimi

IT HAD ONLY TAKEN a couple of searching sessions, but they'd located an Edward Lindahl in Ohio. Excitement coursed through Mimi's veins.

"How are you going to contact him?" Kyle asked.

They sat out on the front porch of her grandmother's house. Earlier, she'd helped Gram upstairs to take a nap, and then she and Kyle had walked to the Pink Parlor and back. Kyle was digging into a banana split with extra chocolate sauce, and Mimi held a large pistachio ice cream on a waffle cone in her hand.

"I'm going to call him," she said, quickly licking a drip making its way down the side of her cone. "I thought there was an off chance he might still have a telephone in his house, and I found his number in the phone book or whatever you call it," she explained.

"Good thinking," he said, picking the cherry off the top of his banana split and tossing it into his mouth.

"I'm going to call him tonight," she said. "During dinnertime."

"Why not call him now?" he asked.

She shrugged. "What if he works during the day?"

Kyle snorted. "Isn't he your grandmother's age? Wouldn't he be home?"

"Not necessarily," she said. "He might have hobbies or something."

"But why dinnertime?"

"Did you ever notice older people are slaves to routine? My other grandma used to eat her lunch every day at noon and her dinner every day at five, whether she was hungry or not."

Kyle appeared thoughtful. "I think my grandparents are the same way. I'll have to watch them."

"I don't understand that myself. I mean, what if you're not hungry at that time? Are you still supposed to eat, or have they trained their bodies to be hungry at those times? It's a mystery to me. Someday when I'm older, I'm going to eat whenever I want to. Maybe I'll eat my breakfast late and skip lunch and eat dinner when I feel like it," she mused.

Kyle looked at her with a frown. "What if you've got a lot a kids? You all can't be eating whenever you feel like it, you'd never get out of the kitchen."

She hadn't thought of that but quickly dismissed it, thinking the solution to that was simply not to get married or have kids.

"Does your grandmother know you're trying to track Ned down?"

Mimi's eyes widened. "Oh, God no! I want to surprise her. Better to find him first and tell her then. I didn't want to get her hopes up if we couldn't find him."

"Then what?"

"I think she should go see him," she said, although she hadn't worked out the logistics yet. Gram's old yellow Cadillac ran great, but was she in any shape to make a long journey? Probably not. And as much as Mimi would love to drive her grandmother out to see him, she did not have a license yet, only a permit. She didn't think her grandmother would be keen on Mimi driving. But she couldn't worry about that now, she'd figure it out when the time came.

"What if this isn't the right guy? Or what if it is but he doesn't want to see your grandmother?" Kyle asked.

Mimi scowled. She hadn't thought of those what-if scenarios. In her mind, her grandmother and Ned were going to be reunited, and she'd settle for nothing less.

"That won't happen," she said with conviction.

"Hello, I'm looking for Edward Lindahl," Mimi said into the phone when it was answered on the third ring. In theory, it had been a good idea to make this call. But in reality, Mimi's heart rate had increased, and her mouth had gone dry.

"That's me," said a masculine voice. It didn't sound froggy the way old people sometimes sounded.

"I've been looking for you," she started, realizing she should have thought about a better execution as that didn't sound right.

"Who is this?" There was a faint trace of suspicion in the man's voice.

"My name is Mimi Duchene, I'm the granddaughter of Martha Cot—er, Hahn, Martha Hahn," she explained hurriedly before he could hang up on her.

"I'm sorry, but that name doesn't mean anything to me."

"Do you go by the name of Ned?" she asked, her hopes sinking.

"No, I'm Edward," he said but added quickly, "My dad is Ned."

Mimi sat up straighter with this information. "Ned Lindahl? Was he here in Hideaway Bay, New York in 1966?"

"Hideaway Bay?" the younger Edward Lindahl repeated. "I know he spent one summer there helping out relatives, but I'm not sure if it was '65 or '66."

"Is your father there? Could I speak to him?"

There was hesitation on the other end of the line. "My father is an elderly widower and lives in a nursing home," he finally said. "His health isn't the best. Can I ask what this is about?"

Mimi swallowed hard, unable to decide how much she should divulge, and decided to go for total transparency. She relayed the story of the summer romance between Martha and Ned, his decision to go to Canada to avoid being drafted, and how her grandmother was going to go with him until the plan went wrong.

When she finished he said, "This is all news to me. I've never heard this story before or of a Martha Hahn. I never knew my dad dated anyone else seriously other than my mother. Dad never spoke too much about Hideaway Bay."

Mimi's heart sunk. Maybe his father hadn't loved her grandmother the way her grandmother had loved him, to the point where it had affected her health when she realized it was a lost opportunity.

Mimi was at a loss for words. Was this as far as her journey would take her?

"My grandmother isn't in the best of health, and she wanted to see him one more time," she said in a half-lie.

"Why now? It's been a long time," he said.

Mimi rolled her eyes. What was it with all the questions. "Because she didn't know Ned had sent the note, it got lost. She spent her life thinking—no, believing that Ned chose to leave Hideaway Bay without her."

"Hmm," was all he said.

Mimi crossed her fingers.

"Well, Mimi, you've dropped a lot in my lap. Let me talk to my dad and I'll call you back."

That was hopeful.

"But I make no promises. Dad's been sick, and he may not be up for this. Can I reach you at this number?"

Afraid her grandmother might intercept, she said, "Can I give you my cell phone number? In case I'm not here. There's no answering machine," she said. That was the truth. She'd questioned her grandmother on why she had no answering machine and her pert response had been "if it's important, they'll call back."

"Sure, hold on, let me get a pen and paper," he said. It took a few moments before he came back on the line and said, "Okay. And you said your name is Mimi . . . ?"

"Yes, Mimi Duchene."

"And your number is?"

Mimi recited her number from memory.

"Thanks, I'll talk to him and call you back."

Going forward, Mimi checked her phone nonstop. Even her grandmother noticed it and asked brusquely, "Who are you waiting to hear from?"

"No one," Mimi lied.

"You must be waiting for someone to call you, or you wouldn't keep checking your phone."

Mimi shrugged and didn't elaborate, and she was relieved when her grandmother didn't press her.

Chapter Thirty-Three

Martha

"I KNOW YOU'RE THERE, Mimi, no need to be quiet," Martha said, opening her eyes.

She'd only been dozing anyway. There was no dinner to get that evening; Mimi had talked her into trying Chinese, and she rather liked the idea of not having to drag out pots and pans, letting someone else do the cooking for a change. Plus, she'd grown tired of beef barley and chicken noodle soup from Mimi's limited repertoire.

"I'm glad you're awake, Gram, because I wanted to talk to you about something," Mimi said, coming fully into the room.

The teenaged girl did not sit on the embroidered stool next to Martha's chair as she was keen to. Instead, she sat on the sofa in front of the fireplace, hugging the arm as if her life depended on it. She stared at Martha. There was an excitement in her that was palpable.

This made Martha sit up and pay more attention. Something was wrong.

"What's the matter?" Martha asked.

"I have some good news," Mimi started. She sat up straight.

Martha narrowed her eyes at her granddaughter. Her voice was a little too high-pitched and affected, as if she was trying to convince herself of something. As if somehow, doubt had crept in between the time she entered the room and now.

Martha braced herself.

"We've found Ned," Mimi announced.

What?

Martha tilted her head, not sure she'd heard correctly. "What do you mean you've found Ned? And who's 'we'?" Panic took hold of her. What did all this mean? Ned? After all these years? What was she supposed to do with this information? What did Mimi *expect* her to do with it?

"Me and Kyle. Anyway, we found Ned Lindahl and spoke to his son—"

Martha put up her hand and tried to control her anger, but she realized she was shaking. "Who told you to look for him?" she demanded. Who did this girl think she was, meddling in her affairs? And with this boy named Kyle—did everybody in Hideaway Bay now know her business?

"I thought it would be a good idea if you were reunited," Mimi said, her voice wavering.

"*You thought,*" Martha repeated. "Did you ask my permission?"

"No," Mimi said.

"Did your mother not teach you not to interfere in other people's business?"

Mimi said nothing and Martha continued. "It never occurred to you to consult me about this?"

Mimi looked at Martha. "I didn't want to get your hopes up in case we didn't locate him or in case he was dead or something."

Ned was alive. And her granddaughter knew where he was. Martha was glad she was sitting down as she could feel her knees getting weak.

Mimi continued to speak, but Martha was only half-listening.

"— this was so romantic, and I thought you'd want to find out what happened to him," Mimi said.

"Did you now? How do you know what I think? We hardly know each other," Martha said.

Mimi flinched as if she'd been slapped, but Martha was too angry to care about the girl's feelings. It beggared belief that the girl would think she could just dredge up the past like that. Start an excavation without Martha's permission.

As her fury rose, so did her voice. "How dare you presume to know what I want?"

"Don't you want to know what happened to him?" Mimi interrupted.

"If I wanted to know, I would have looked for him myself!"

She resisted the desire to ask Mimi about Ned. Where was he? How was he? It took all her self-control to tamp down that urge. Instead, she focused on being angry, on being furious. This was a huge violation of her privacy.

Mimi shrank into the corner of the sofa and lowered her head. From where she sat, Martha could see the girl's chin quivering.

Roughly, she reached for her purse at the side of her chair and set it in her lap. She opened the clasp and dug through it until she laid her hand on her wallet. She retrieved it and pulled a twenty-dollar bill from it.

She set the purse back down and waved the twenty toward Mimi. "Here, Mimi, go on and take this money and go pick up the food."

Slowly, Mimi stood and looked at her grandmother. Martha noted her eyes were shiny, but she ignored that too. There had to be consequences to actions. Especially egregious ones.

"But it's only four o'clock," Mimi protested.

"I don't care. I'm hungry and I want to go upstairs early tonight," Martha said.

"What did you want to order?" Mimi asked, hesitant, looking as if she might bolt.

Martha had no idea what the menu entailed; she'd never eaten Chinese before. "I don't care. Just get me something. Nothing too adventurous."

Mimi took the twenty but didn't move. She stood there and lowered her head again.

"I'm really sorry, Gram, I thought you'd be happy," Mimi said quietly.

"I don't want to discuss it anymore, young lady," Martha said brusquely. "Go on now and we'll talk about it later."

Without another word, Mimi turned and walked hurriedly from the room, her hair swinging behind her.

Martha sagged in her chair, closed her eyes, and groaned. It hadn't taken long to alienate her granddaughter. Even less time than it had taken to alienate her own daughter.

Maybe she should just go back to avoiding people at all costs. Especially those she loved.

The following morning, Martha was downstairs before Mimi woke. She'd been awake early, and the thought of a breakfast of eggs and bacon appealed to her.

The Chinese food had been delicious. Mimi'd chosen beef and broccoli with rice for Martha, and she'd ended up eating half of it, saving the rest for her lunch today, which she was looking forward to. They'd eaten in silence and when Martha was finished, she retired upstairs for the night.

She was in the middle of cracking eggs into a frying pan when Mimi appeared in the doorway of the kitchen, sleepy-eyed and with her hair tousled. She wore an oversized T-shirt for a nightgown. What passed for bedclothes these days made Martha raise an eyebrow.

Mimi stood there, unsure. She folded her arms over her chest and eyed her grandmother.

"Did you want some eggs and bacon? Sit down," Martha said, turning back to the stove to keep an eye on the cast-iron skillet. Breakfast sizzled, and the delicious smell of bacon filled the air.

"Gram—" Mimi started.

Martha held up her hand but did not turn her attention away from the frying pan. "Start making the toast, please, and put the butter and jam on the table."

They operated in tandem, getting the breakfast ready. Plates of eggs and bacon arrived on the table at the same time as the stack of toast. They sat down together, but Mimi kept her head down and ate speedily as if she wanted to be done and out of the room.

As she'd expected, Martha had not slept well. The thought that Ned was out there somewhere and still alive had overwhelmed her. For most of the night, she debated what she was supposed to do with this information. Was it foolish to want to see him after all this time? She hadn't seen him in more than five decades.

The kettle boiled, and Mimi made tea in the cups and set them on the table.

"Thank you," Martha said when the teacup was set down in front of her.

Mimi slugged her tea down, set her empty cup aside, and stood.

"Hold on a minute, I'd like to talk to you," Martha said.

Slowly, Mimi sank back into her seat as if she were facing the gallows. Martha didn't want this either. But how to re-establish the equilibrium and the goodwill they'd achieved? She sighed. Interpersonal relationships weren't her strong suit, but she supposed it wasn't too late to try and learn. Even at her age.

"I know you meant well, and we'll go with that for right now," she said, finishing off her piece of toast with a final bite.

Mimi looked at her but remained silent.

"But in the future, please don't do anything of this magnitude without consulting me first," Martha said.

Mimi nodded quickly and appeared to relax a little bit.

Martha pushed her plate aside and rested her clasped hands on the table. "Now, you said you've found Ned."

"Yes, we did," Mimi said.

"Can I ask how you found him?" Martha asked, curious.

"Searching some databases on the Internet."

The nebulous Internet and all things online. These things were beyond Martha. The fact that anyone could be found by some nosy teenagers would almost be appalling if she didn't have a personal stake in this herself.

"And what have you found?" she asked.

"He's living in a nursing home in Ohio," Mimi replied.

Martha sagged slightly in her seat. He wasn't far from her. She wondered if he ever made it to Canada. She had so many questions.

"And you said he had a son?"

"Edward. I spoke to him on the phone."

Ned had at least one child. That made Martha happy. She didn't know why, but it did. The time for wishing it had been their child was long gone.

"And Ned is in a nursing home? Where in Ohio?" Martha asked.

"I have the name of the place and the address written down," Mimi said.

Martha processed all this. Such new and exciting information, but what to do with it and how to slot it into her life. Had too much time elapsed?

"Does Ned know about all this? Or has his son not told him?"

Mimi nodded enthusiastically. "I told Edward about the lost note, and he told his father."

Martha was able to draw some conclusions from that. The fact that the information had been passed on to Ned indicated that maybe he was all right, at least mentally, even if he did reside in a nursing home.

"What did he say?" Martha asked, her heart rate increasing.

"He said he wants to see you," Mimi said with a smile.

Martha said nothing. She couldn't quite find the words to respond.

"I looked it up on Google Maps," Mimi said. "It's only about four hours if we take the 90. Are you up for a road trip?"

Things were moving too fast. Drive to Ohio? See the love of her life again, a man she hadn't seen since 1966? Yesterday at this time, Martha hadn't even known Ned was still alive.

"I need time to think about this," she finally said.

"He seems keen to see you," Mimi added.

"How do you know that?" Martha eyed Mimi suspiciously, wondering if she was just saying that to make it sound more enticing and to eliminate her doubt.

"Because Edward told me. He said his father would love to see you," Mimi explained.

Martha leaned back in her chair, one arm resting on the table. Did she want to see Ned? Did she want to admit to him that her life after him hadn't turned out like she'd wanted it to? That she'd made a spectacular mess of things? He'd obviously been able to get on with his life and probably made the best of it, might even have been happy. Did she want to see him and tell him that not only had she been *un*happy, but she'd dragged Cal into her turmoil?

"I'll go with you and then you won't have to drive alone. I don't have a driver's license, but I could be the navigator," Mimi said enthusiastically.

Her granddaughter was enjoying this way too much.

"I don't think I'd be able to drive that long distance," Martha said. "I'm only used to local driving."

"We could stop for lots of breaks. I love coffee, and we could take our time," Mimi suggested.

Martha laughed. The girl had it all figured out.

"I don't know. I'll have to think about this."

"Come on, Gram, it'll be fun!" Mimi said. Her earlier reticence and discomposure had seemingly evaporated.

"Fun isn't the word that comes to mind," Martha said. A lot of other words did. Fear. Foolishness. Curiosity. Yes, there was a gamut of words.

Before Mimi could run with it, Martha said, "There's no way the two of us can go by ourselves. I can't drive that far, and you can't drive at all."

"Don't worry about it, I'll figure something out," Mimi said brightly.

Martha envied her her self-confidence. "That's what I'm worried about."

Mimi laughed. "And he wants to talk to you on the phone."

"He does?" Martha said, her courage wavering.

"Yes. You should call him."

"Remember I haven't said 'yes' yet to this whole idea," Martha reminded her.

"I know." Mimi smiled. "But you haven't said no either, so there is that."

Martha must have studied the orange Post-It note a hundred times. On it was scribbled the cell phone number of Ned Lindahl. Her heartbeat drummed so loudly she could hear it in her ears. She fingered the scrap of paper, picked up her phone, set it down. She did this multiple times. Now would be the time to call him as Mimi had gone over to Kyle's for dinner and a movie.

Finally, she dialed the number and held her breath.

It rang four times before it was picked up.

"Hello?"

Martha closed her eyes and sagged in her chair.

Ned.

"Hello?" he asked again.

"Ned?" she managed to get out.

"Yes?" his voice was a little croaky, but she recognized it nonetheless.

Her respiratory rate picked up and she felt as if she might hyperventilate.

"Ned, it's me. Martha," she said. "Martha Hahn."

"Oh, Martha," was all he said.

Panicking that he might not want to talk to her, she said, "Is it a good time to talk? I can call back later."

"No, this is the perfect time. I just got back from having my dinner in the dining room."

She didn't know what to say first. She had a million questions but didn't know which one to start with.

He saved her the trouble. "When Edward told me your granddaughter called and you were still alive and living in Hideaway Bay, well, you could have knocked me over with a feather," he said.

"Same here."

It was like ghosts from the past. That's what they were, the two of them.

"My note got lost," Ned said. She could practically see his grin.

"Can you believe it?" Martha asked. She still couldn't quite believe it herself.

"No," he sighed. He sounded tired and weary over the phone, and Martha wondered about his health. They certainly weren't spring chickens.

There was a pause and then they both spoke at once.

"You go ahead with what you were going to say," Martha said.

"That lost note certainly changed the course of my life," Ned said.

"Mine too," Martha said quietly.

"We can beat ourselves up for it, but maybe our lives turned out the way they were supposed to," he said.

God, she hoped not, thinking of her estranged daughter and the grandchildren she didn't know.

"Did you go to Canada?" she asked.

"I did. After I dropped the note off, I went to the train station, purchased two tickets to Buffalo, and waited all night for you to show up."

"Oh, Ned," Martha said, guilt stabbing her.

"What is it the youngsters say these days? 'It is what it is,'" he said. "At the time, I figured you came to your senses and decided not to run away with me."

"And I thought you decided to leave me and go to Canada alone," Martha said.

"What a mess."

Martha laughed. "That's for sure."

"I went on to Buffalo that night and then three days later, I crossed the Peace Bridge into Canada with some help from the anti-war movement there in Buffalo."

Martha was glad to hear Ned had got away. That he'd remained intact and that the war hadn't touched him the way it had touched so many. She didn't fault him for going to Canada, especially after having seen the aftereffects firsthand, living with Cal.

"I'm glad to hear that. When did you come back to the States?"

"I came back in '81. President Carter had pardoned the draft dodgers in '77, and we made our way back to Ohio with the kids."

She'd known that he'd married.

"Was it a good marriage?" she asked.

He hesitated. "It was. I grew to love Linda, very much, although it wasn't the same way I loved you. We had a happy marriage. We had three children and seven grandchildren," he said proudly.

She smiled, relieved that he'd had a happy life with someone else. A life and a family. But that was Ned; his capacity for love was just too great to have spent it on one girl.

"I'm glad to hear you had a good marriage."

"What about you? You married? Children?"

Martha nodded. "Yes. I married Cal Cotter." She waited for his reaction.

Ned did not disappoint her. "Cal? Cal Cotter? He was a good guy. Were you happy?"

Martha decided not to lie. "No. We married after he came back from the war. The war changed him. He had too many demons and I . . . I had my own problems," she admitted, clearing her throat. There was no sense in telling him she'd never recovered from his departure from Hideaway Bay.

"How is he now?" Ned asked, his voice faltering.

Martha dragged in a deep breath and said, "Cal's been dead for over thirty years."

"Oh, Martha, I'm sorry. You had children?"

"Yes, we had one, Martine, but she lives on the west coast. I have two grandchildren, Mimi and Micah."

"Grandchildren are wonderful. Everything we did wrong with our kids we can make right with them."

That's the plan.

"It was Mimi who found me, wasn't it?" Ned asked.

"Yes, it was. She's a hopeless romantic, I think," Martha said with a laugh.

"Well, good for her. We were hopeless romantics once, as I recall," he said.

"We certainly were," she said.

It was funny to her how as they continued to chat, the years slipped away and it felt like it was yesterday. Was it just that way with some people? With some relationships?

"Look, Martha, would you think of coming to see me sometime? I'm in a nursing home just outside of Cleveland," he said.

Martha hesitated, unsure.

"I'd come up to see you, but my health isn't the best," he admitted.

"It's nothing serious, is it?" she asked, feeling the lines on her forehead deepen with concern.

He laughed. "Everything at our age is serious."

"That's true," she agreed.

"Would you drive down to see me?" he asked again. His voice faltered over the line. He sounded elderly, and she wondered if he thought the same of her. She reminded herself that they were elderly.

"I'll drive down to see you, Ned," she promised.

The feeling was reminiscent of when she used to meet him in the middle of the night at that old house before the Reynolds bought it. Somehow, she'd make the arrangements, figure out the logistics later. But she was going to Ohio to see Ned. It felt like such an opportunity, and there were so few of those in life that she figured she better grab onto it with both hands while she still had life left in her.

"That makes me happy, Martha," Ned said.

"I'm glad."

They spoke of generalities for another half hour and before they hung up, Martha promised that as soon as she had arrangements made, she'd call him and let him know.

When she hung up the phone, she was smiling from ear to ear.

Chapter Thirty-Four

Martine

"It's a nice area," Edgar said, driving slowly around Hideaway Bay.

It was no lie that it had been one long, interminable week. It was hard to believe they'd finally made it to Martine's hometown. The air was hot, and there was no breeze. Martine had rolled down her window and had her arm resting on it. She preferred the fresh air and the breeze to the air conditioner.

She wasn't ready to face either her mother or her daughter just yet, and had suggested that he turn left onto Main Street at the end of Erie instead of turning right and landing at her mother's house on the corner of Erie and Star Shine Drive. She only had to turn her head a fraction of an inch and she'd see the house she grew up in, the house her mother still lived in.

As she looked around at everything, she realized not much had changed. She eyed the lake, thinking it most likely looked exactly the same as it did when her great-grandparents first laid eyes on it. Maybe there was comfort in that.

There were new shops on Main Street, but the five-and-dime was still there. The grocery store was gone, and in its place was an olive oil shop. Martine smiled at this. Hideaway Bay was becoming quite metropolitan. The Old Red Top was still boarded up, which Martine thought was kind of sad. They'd had the best Texas hots she'd ever had.

"You never told me Hideaway Bay was this nice," Edgar enthused, driving down Main Street. He drove slowly as he tried to look at everything on both sides of the street, his head swinging from left to right.

Martine remained silent. She supposed it was nice to outsiders and even to those people who lived there. But all she remembered was growing up in a household where her parents existed in some kind of uneasy truce. Her mother had been guarded, and her father appeared to exist in the shadows. After her father's death, her mother became more emotionally remote if that was even possible. There were a lot of unanswered questions about her father's death. She'd been eleven when he died, and her life had been split into two: before his death and the painful aftermath.

It had never occurred to her to tell Edgar or Mimi or Micah anything about Hideaway Bay. When they asked her what her childhood was like, she'd either brushed them off or been vague in her answers. Maybe she was just as remote as her mother. Maybe it was a genetic thing.

"There wasn't much to tell," she said, continuing to stare out the window. She moved her arm, making her bracelets jangle.

"Martine, this would have been worth mentioning," he said, glancing over at her.

"Not when you grew up here like I did," she said.

"I suppose not," he finally admitted.

In their early years together, she'd told him what it had been like to grow up in *that* house as the daughter of Martha and Cal Cotter. He'd been lucky and had had a somewhat normal childhood in Southern California. His father went to work, and his mother stayed home and raised Edgar and his siblings. After meeting his parents, she'd envied him. Maybe there had always been an undercurrent of resentment in their relationship, and maybe it could be traced back to the beginning.

"It's such a sleepy, quaint little town," he said.

Martine had to agree that outside of the house she grew up in, it was all of those things. It was picture-postcard perfect with the beach right there and all the little shops that lined Main Street with their colorful awnings.

Her eyes widened when she spotted Mr. Lime outside his shop, Lime's Five-and-Dime. He had to be in his nineties. She'd assumed he'd died years ago. Thoughts of saltwater taffy filled her mind, and she wondered if he still sold it. Cherry had been her favorite flavor.

When they reached the end of Main Street, she said, "Circle around the green and we'll head back up Main Street to my mother's house." She would have preferred to continue driving around town. She was in no hurry to reunite with her mother. Mimi, yes, but not her mother. It's not that she dreaded it; it was just that she didn't know what to expect or how it would go and as a result, her stomach was in knots. She tapped her knuckles against her teeth.

Edgar drove off Main Street and went around the green with its war memorial and gazebo. The gazebo had a fresh coat of white paint, and the giant oak trees that surrounded it were even bigger than she remembered. She noted the war memorial, a shiny black granite square with all the names of Hideaway Bay's fallen from foreign wars. Ancestors of hers had their names etched in the granite. It was funny how the name of a long-dead relative was just that: a name. She knew her grandfather's brother had been killed in Guadalcanal and although she thought it was a terrible thing, there was no feeling attached to it. Was it this way for everyone? Maybe it was because she'd never met him or her grandfather. She didn't know and was too tired to try and figure it out.

Edgar continued to drive slowly, taking in all the sights, commenting on everything he saw. When he finally turned onto Star Shine Drive, Martine pointed at the house on the corner and said, "That's it there." She felt uneasy as it came into view.

The house looked more or less the same. It was still the largest house in town. It was still painted in the same colors it had been when she was living in it. It had been kept up well. She knew her mother had hired people to paint, cut the grass, run a snake through a bathroom drain, whatever the house needed. Her mother, as her grandparents before her, simply hired people out to do the manual labor. There'd be no rolling up the sleeves of its inhabitants. It had always been like that.

Seeing the house now, she felt mixed emotions. Although her relationship with her mother had all but ended in a big blowout and their little family of three was not ideal, there were some happy memories. Her grandmother had lived there until her death, and she'd been the retreat for Martine from her parents and their marriage. When she was younger, she thought she'd never have a marriage like her parents, and yet here she was on the verge of divorce.

"You can pull in the driveway," Martine said as Edgar slowed the car near the curb.

He stopped and looked at Lake Erie. "You never said you lived right across the street from the beach."

"I must have taken it for granted," she said casually. She blew out a breath.

Edgar pulled the car into the driveway, put it in park, and shut off the engine.

Martine didn't move at first. She didn't know what was waiting for her behind that front door: a rebellious teenage daughter or an unforgiving mother or both.

"Come on, let's go," Edgar encouraged. "It might not be as bad as you think."

Martine laughed but it was hollow. "No, it'll probably be worse."

"I, for one, want to see Mimi," Edgar said, and he was first to get out of the car, leaving Martine no choice but to follow.

He stood in the driveway, hands in his pockets, looking up at the house. "Boy, that's a grand house."

"Several generations lived here all together. My grandfather died before I was born, but my grandmother lived here when I was growing up and when my mother was young, her grandparents lived in the house," Martine explained.

"Nice, all that extended family together," he said.

It was nice, she had to admit. Deciding she wanted to get the initial meeting over with, she climbed the front steps with Edgar following her. She wanted to collect her daughter and head back home.

She rang the doorbell, taking in the brand-new door. The chairs on the porch were old; she remembered them from her own childhood when she'd sit out here with her grandmother.

She pressed on the doorbell again, hearing its familiar chime ring through the house, transporting her back in time. Goosebumps rose on her arms despite the mid-afternoon heat. Her heart pounded as she waited.

The sound of hurried footsteps alerted her to the fact that someone, most likely Mimi, was on their way. Through the window, she spotted her teenage daughter, her nut-brown hair scraped back into a loose ponytail, and her heart melted.

When Mimi opened the door, she eyed her mother warily.

But Martine was overcome with emotion as Edgar cried out, "There she is! Our favorite runaway!" And even she had to laugh. She stepped over the threshold and pulled her daughter into her arms, breathing in the scent of her.

"Thank God you're safe," Martine said, and she thought she might cry but she fought it off. "Don't ever do that to me again, Mimi," she whispered into her ear. She held onto her for a minute longer, squeezing her, and then abruptly let go, stepping back and wiping her eyes.

Edgar hugged his daughter. "How are you, sweet pea?"

Another cutesie nickname, which Martine ignored. Her gaze swept around the interior—the front parlor, the staircase—and not much had changed since she left all those years ago. It was like being caught in a time warp. There were still ferns on pedestals in the front parlor. The house looked like just that: a house. She never considered it to be a home.

Martine dug through her purse and pulled out a glasses case and handed it to Mimi. "I brought your glasses. I found them on your nightstand."

"Thanks, but Gram bought me a new pair."

"And where are they? Certainly not on your face where they belong."

Mimi looked sheepish and shrugged. "They're upstairs."

"How can you see without your glasses?" Martine asked.

"I manage."

"Maybe we can discuss the glasses another time," Edgar said. They both looked at him.

Finally, feeling as if she couldn't put it off anymore, Martine drew in a deep breath through her nose and asked, "Where's your grandmother?"

Mimi half turned and said, "She's in the back room."

Stalling, Martine asked, "How has it been going?"

Mimi nodded hurriedly and said, "It's been going great."

Martine regarded that answer with great skepticism. No doubt Mimi had her bags ready and standing at the door, anxious to return home to the west coast. It was most likely a hard lesson learned. Not all grandmothers were grandmotherly.

"Come on, let's say hello to your mother," Edgar suggested.

Martine nodded and led Edgar to the back of the house, aware that behind her, her husband couldn't look at things fast enough.

"You never mentioned that you grew up in such a large house," Edgar said.

Martine shrugged. She certainly hadn't thought of it as grand when she'd lived there.

The house still smelled the same: Lemon Pledge and the smell of an older house, something fusty, something that needed to be aired out, maybe curtains or wallpaper that needed to come down. Or old books that needed to be binned.

Nothing had changed. It was as she remembered it. Didn't people get tired of looking at the same wallpaper? The same carpet? The same pictures on the wall? She did and was always changing things up in their own home. It used to be a running joke between her and Edgar that sometimes he walked in and wasn't sure he was in the right house.

She was as opposite in taste to her mother as was possible. Their own house back in Washington State was all clean lines and had a contemporary look with abstract art prints on the wall. No fussy floral or striped wallpaper. No heavy, dark woodwork or sepia-colored photographs of long-dead or unknown ancestors lining the walls.

Martine pulled up short just outside the doorframe of the back room that had once been her grandfather's study.

It, too, still looked the same, as if the whole house were in a time capsule. Three of the four walls were lined with bookshelves, which were crammed with books, books that had been there for as long as she could remember. Books that she could never remember anyone reading. The back wall housed a long window that looked out on the backyard. The fireplace was still not in use, and the back of a leather sofa was parked up against it. At the far end of the room was a large antique walnut desk with a green leather inlay. Apparently, this had also been her grandfather's, but she never saw anyone sitting at it while she lived there. Her mother occupied a wing chair in front of the desk, the back of the chair up against the front of the desk.

Martine was aware that her mother's eyes were on her.

The sight of her mother leaning to one side in her chair with her cheek against her hand should have softened Martine's heart. Should have made her feel something, but she was too busy bracing herself against the anticipated blowback of the reception she'd receive from her mother.

"Hello, Mother," she said from the doorway.

"Hello, Martine," Martha said quietly.

For a moment neither said anything; they stared at each other, sizing each other up, deciding how much the other had changed in the intervening years and whether the changes were positive or not.

Her mother had not changed much. She looked the same except her hair was whiter and her skin was grayer and more translucent. She appeared like a faded photograph that had been left in a drawer too long and whose colors had become muted.

"Don't stand in the doorway, come in," Martha finally said with a quick wave of her hand.

Martine hesitated for a fraction of a second before stepping into the room and closer to her mother. She'd forgotten Edgar was with her. He stepped out from behind her and approached Martha, extending his hand.

"Hello, Martha, we've never met but I'm Edgar Duchene," he said.

Martha's expression was unreadable. She shook his hand.

"This is a fine house you have here," Edgar said.

Martine hoped he wasn't going to make small talk. She didn't think she could stand it.

"Thank you. My great-grandfather built it at the turn of the last century," Martha told him.

Edgar nodded and looked around, taking it all in. His hands were thrust into his pockets, and he jangled the keys in his pocket, something he did when he was nervous. Martine narrowed her eyes at him. *What is he so nervous about?* A small, infinitesimal part of her suddenly felt protective of him.

"Sorry to hear you had health problems," he said to Martha.

"Comes with age. There's no future in getting old."

"I suppose not."

"Car trouble on the way in?" she quizzed.

"Yeah," he said, rubbing the back of his head.

An awkward silence ensued. Martine looked at everything but her mother. Edgar looked up at the ceiling, studying the coving. And Mimi looked as if she were going to burst. Martine frowned at her.

"I didn't know what you wanted to do for dinner," Martha said. "I thought we could order something from one of the restaurants in town. I'll pay for it if you don't mind picking it up."

Martine exaggerated the action of glancing at her watch. "We won't be staying. We're just here to pick up Mimi and head back on the road." She did not make eye contact with her mother.

Suddenly a silence descended as if no one knew what to say. Martha looked at something just behind Martine. Edgar continued to jangle his keys in his pockets, and Martine kept her focus on the backyard beyond the window.

Martine broke the silence by looking pointedly at Edgar. "We should probably get on the road. We've got a long trip cross-country."

Edgar could not hide his surprise. Surely, he hadn't expected to stay in Hideaway Bay for any length of time. Had he expected to stay overnight? Her plan had been to get on the road and find a hotel later that evening. A hotel room would be much safer than her mother's house. There'd be no triggers. She realized she probably should have told him her plan before they arrived. It exasperated her to think that he actually thought she'd want to spend the night in Hideaway Bay.

She widened her eyes and raised her eyebrows as if to impart, *Jump in here any time and back me up.*

But it was Mimi who spoke up and gave the dissenting opinion. "We're leaving right now? I don't want to leave yet!"

"Your father and I just spent the last week driving cross-country to get here to pick you up."

"But I'm not ready to go," Mimi said.

"Too bad," Martine snapped. "Next time, run away closer to home. That way, you can stay longer."

A heavy, voluminous silence descended. Martine sighed and crossed her arms over her chest. Why was she always made to be the bad guy.

"I can't leave, because Gram and I have plans. We need to do something," Mimi said.

"Do what?" Martine asked.

Neither said anything, and Martine felt like they were keeping something from her.

"Mimi, it's all right," Martha said quietly from her chair. "Let it go."

Mimi turned to her grandmother and said, "Gram, I can't. This is too important."

"What is so urgent that you need to do?" Martine asked, her patience thinning.

Now her daughter mirrored her, crossing her arms over her chest. Martha and Edgar both spoke at once.

"I thought we'd stay the night before we started back," Edgar said.

"Why don't you stay here overnight, and you can leave in the morning," Martha suggested. "I've got plenty of room."

"Come on, Mom," Mimi pleaded.

Martine felt outnumbered.

"As enticing as that sounds," Martine said sarcastically, "We've got a long trip ahead of us, and let's not forget about Micah."

"He's at my sister's and he's in good hands. He probably doesn't even miss us," Edgar joked.

"I miss him," Martine said tightly. She changed the subject and asked her mother, "How are you feeling?"

"Since when? The last time I saw you, almost twenty years ago?"

Martine refused to be baited. "Mimi mentioned you haven't been well."

"Oh, that was nothing. I'm fine now."

Looking at her, Martine was also doubtful of that.

"Look, we won't keep you any longer," Martine said, anxious to leave. "I want to thank you for letting Mimi stay with you until we got here." Taking a deep breath, she said, "I appreciate it."

Martha tilted her head slightly to one side in acknowledgment. "It was my pleasure."

Martine searched her mother's face for any signs of sarcasm but found none. She didn't know what to make of her mother's behavior. Did people mellow with age? She didn't really believe that.

"Do you need anything before we leave?" Martine asked, moving her stack of bracelets up her arm and then letting them fall back to her wrist.

"Mom, we can't leave," Mimi said.

"You're going to have to tell me more than that, Mimi," Martine said, her patience thinning. She was unable to imagine what the two of them could have to do. And that it could be important.

"It's a long story and we planned on telling you over dinner," Mimi said.

"All these secrets," Martine huffed. Nothing had changed.

"Why don't we order dinner, and we can sit down and talk about things," Martha said.

All sorts of red flags went off in Martine's head. What was going on?

"You must be hungry," Martha said. "Mimi can show you the restaurant."

Martine shook her head, but Edgar spoke up. "Thanks, Martha. I'm not looking forward to that long drive back."

"Then a good night's sleep will be of great benefit," Martha said.

Martine shot a daggered look at her husband, who ignored her.

To try and move things along, Martine said to Mimi, "Let's go get the dinner."

"We can walk, Mom, it isn't that far," Mimi said.

"I know nothing in town is very far. I grew up here, remember?" Martine pointed out.

"Sorry," Mimi mumbled.

"Here, pay with this, Mimi," Martha said, handing her her credit card.

Her daughter hadn't even been here a week and she was already using her grandmother's credit card to purchase things? Martine didn't know how comfortable she felt with this arrangement. Before she could say anything, Edgar spoke up.

"Martha, we'll pay for dinner."

Martha put up her hand. "No, you just spent a lot of money on gas and repairs, please let this be my treat."

"All right then. We appreciate it."

"Now Mimi, you know what I like, so go on and take your mother to the restaurant," Martha said.

"Okay, Gram," Mimi said.

Martine was envious of the easy rapport between her mother and daughter. They behaved as if they'd known each other all of Mimi's life. There was a pang of jealousy within Martine. Why couldn't her mother have been like that with her?

"Edgar, would you humor an old woman and stay here with me? I'd like to get to know you better," Martha said.

"Of course," Edgar said amiably.

Martine's eyes widened at the woman sitting in her mother's chair. Who was she? And what was she up to?

Martine headed out of the room, looking at her watch, wondering how much longer she'd have to spend there before they got on the road. The cross-country trip with all its problems and worries had shredded her nerves and more than anything, she wanted to be in the comfort of her own home. And she missed Micah.

"Come on, Mom, let's go," Mimi said, taking the lead and heading out the door.

Martine hesitated, thinking she should say something, but she didn't, and she followed Mimi outside.

CHAPTER THIRTY-FIVE

Martine

It was disconcerting to be walking around her hometown with her daughter. The area that had been once as familiar to her as the back of her hand, her own daughter now navigated with ease. Mimi didn't hesitate, she headed toward Main Street as if she'd lived there her whole life.

Her daughter was different. There'd been a subtle shift in her demeanor. Her posture was straight, and she held her head high. A slight smile had transformed her features. She appeared almost happy. *Was that possible?* Usually, back home, she slouched and hung her head. Could one week effect that kind of change in a person?

"Well, what do you think of my mother?" Martine asked.

Mimi smiled. "Well, she can be spiky at times. And she has an opinion on just about everything. And she certainly is set in her ways..." She paused and looked both ways before stepping off the curb to cross Erie Street. "But I like her a lot."

"She's not like Grandma Duchene," Martine said, "showering her grandchildren with love and homemade baked goods."

"No, of course not," Mimi said, frowning. "I don't expect her to be."

Martine didn't know how she felt about this easy alliance between her mother and daughter. She swallowed hard and looked ahead, taking in the scenery, making note of the things that had and hadn't changed.

"How do you like Hideaway Bay?"

Mimi didn't hesitate. Her expression bloomed as she declared, "I love it. I love everything about it."

Her words were like a sharp stab to Martine's heart. It hurt that the place they'd chosen to raise their children had been an unhappy place for their daughter. Maybe home wasn't her place of belonging.

"I wish we could live here," Mimi said.

There was no way that was going to happen. Under no circumstances was Martine returning to Hideaway Bay to live. Ever. Her life was out on the west coast. No matter what happened between her and Edgar.

Mimi stopped at the Chinese restaurant, and Martine noted that this was a new addition to Hideaway Bay.

"Does your grandmother know you're getting Chinese?" Martine asked.

Mimi looked at her. "Of course. She had it the other night and she liked it."

They stepped inside and studied the lit-up menu board overhead.

Once they ordered—Martine chose something she thought Edgar would like—Mimi paid for it with Martha's credit card. They took a seat on the vinyl bench against the front window and waited for their order. Neither said anything.

The door opened and a teenaged boy stepped inside. His expression changed to one of recognition when he spotted Mimi.

"Hey, Mimi!" he said brightly.

Martine looked at her daughter, whose cheeks held a faint pink blush. She lifted her hand in a little wave. "Hey, Kyle, what's up?"

"Just picking up takeout," he said with a smile.

He was young like Mimi, but he was cute, Martine thought.

Kyle glanced at Martine, who smiled at him.

"Um, this is my mother, Martine Duchene," Mimi said, gesturing to Martine with her palm up. She turned to Martine and said, "This is Kyle Koch. He lives here in Hideaway Bay."

Kyle nodded. "Hi."

"Nice to meet you, Kyle," Martine said.

"I better get our dinner," Kyle said with a wave of his hand toward the counter but not taking his eyes off of Mimi.

He stepped up to the counter and waited while his order was put together in a large brown paper bag. After he paid for it with cash, he shoved the change into the pocket of his shorts, picked up the bag, and turned around, heading toward the exit.

"I'll call you later, Mimi?" he asked, his voice tentative.

"Okay," Mimi said brightly.

After he exited, Martine turned to Mimi and asked, "Who is that?"

Mimi shrugged, trying to appear casual, but she couldn't hide the smile on her face. "Kyle? He's just a friend."

Her daughter had a friend.

And that made Martine happy.

Chapter Thirty-Six

Martha

THE THING THAT HAD surprised Martha most about her daughter was how angry she was. It was palpable. It rolled off her in waves. And sadly, Martha surmised that her daughter's anger was either because of her or directed at her or maybe both.

She liked Edgar. He was easy to talk to, and it was almost a relief to be able to talk to someone about the mundane of life without every statement or question feeling loaded. And she'd concluded that if Mimi was anything to go by, Edgar couldn't be all that bad. After all, he was Mimi's father.

She stood up from her chair and paused a minute to get her bearings. Edgar immediately stood and put his hand out to her. She wondered why people did that, put their hand out when an elderly person stood. She knew it to be a solicitous gesture; after all, she'd done it with her own grandparents and then with her own mother as she aged, and now it was being done to her.

"We should set the table," she said.

"I can help with that," Edgar volunteered.

Martha smiled. "All right, then, come on."

Edgar followed her out to the kitchen, and she stood at the counter, pulled out silverware and plates and glasses, and handed them to Edgar, who placed them on the table.

"Does it matter where we sit? Where's your place, Martha?" Edgar asked.

"I sit there, and Mimi usually sits across from me," Martha said, pointing to the chair nearest the sink.

When the table was set, they both sat down, and a silence descended between them that threatened to make it awkward.

"Would you like to see some pictures of Micah?" Edgar asked.

"I'd love to," Martha said.

He pulled out his phone and set it down in front of Martha. "Just scroll to the right."

The screen was filled with the image of a cherubic boy with nut-brown hair and wide-set hazel eyes. There was a splash of freckles across the bridge of his nose. His smile was sunny, and he wore a baseball uniform.

"He looks just like Martine when she was a little girl," Martha said as a rush of memories of Martine as a young girl came flooding back.

The thoughts clutched at her heart. She couldn't help but smile at the photo. Edgar showed her how to scroll through the phone to look at the rest of his photos. It was hard to believe that these lovely people were her family, her legacy, when she didn't really know them. She shook off the sadness that threatened to weigh her down.

When Martine and Mimi returned laden with bags of Chinese food, Martha heard them before she saw them. Their chatter was natural, and she regretted that it had never been like that between her and Martine. But she had only herself to blame.

When all the cartons were placed on the table and then identified as to whose was whose, all four of them sat around the kitchen table.

Martha had another plate of beef and broccoli, and it was delicious. After they all returned to the west coast, she could see herself ordering Chinese for dinner some evenings.

"What's this long story about, now?" Martine started.

Martha's fork froze mid-air. The intended trip to see Ned had been a good idea; she'd let Mimi convince her of that. But now with Martine sitting next to her and staring at her expectantly, she realized that there might be some unintended consequences. And not of the positive variety. Here she was, going forward, about to admit to her estranged daughter that she hadn't loved Cal the way she should have. That there had been someone else. That there had always been someone else and now, at her advanced age, she wanted to meet with him for what would probably be the last time.

Martha didn't know where to start. Did you go back and start there, or did you stay grounded in the present and begin there? It seemed complicated. From the pocket of her tabard, she pulled out the note and slid it across the table to Martine.

Martine took the aged, yellowed note, flipped it open, and read it, her lips moving in silence. She frowned. Finally, she raised her head and looked at her mother.

"I don't understand what this is," she said.

"That note was from a man named Ned Lindahl," her mother explained. "Asking me to meet him at the train station so we could run away to Canada together."

Martha's voice shook when she spoke, but she didn't care. Her emotions regarding this whole affair, which had been buried deep for so long, had burst forth to the surface with the discovery of the lost note.

"When was this?" Martine asked, fingering the note, reading it again before handing it to Edgar, who scanned it while he chewed his dinner, before sliding it across the table to Martha.

Martha slipped the note back into her pocket, where it would be safe and near.

"1966."

Martine appeared to think about this. Martha could practically read her daughter's mind: before she was born, before Martha's marriage to her father.

"Were you in love with him?" Martine asked.

"Yes."

"Then why didn't you go with him?" Martine asked.

Martha told her the story and when she finished, Martine stared at her and said nothing. Martha was aware that Mimi and Edgar were taking everything in but choosing to remain silent.

"Would you have gone with him?"

Without hesitation, her mother said, "In a heartbeat." She didn't want to hurt Martine, but she also didn't want to lie. It was time for the truth to be out there, no matter how painful it was or how it might feel.

"It explains a lot," Martine said with a sigh.

"What do you mean?"

"Your relationship with Dad," Martine said pointedly, raising her eyebrows to add emphasis. "This revelation is sobering for sure."

"It is not my intent to hurt you with this information," Martha said quietly.

"The good news is that Ned Lindahl is still alive. He lives in a nursing home in Ohio, and I want to take Gram there to see him," Mimi piped in.

"What?" Martine said, turning her focus onto Mimi.

"Gram spoke to Ned on the phone. He wants to see her. We're going to Ohio," Mimi said enthusiastically.

When she and Mimi had spoken about it earlier, it had seemed like a good idea. But now, verbalized out loud to other people, Martha could immediately see there were problems with their plan. And Martine was only too happy to voice them.

"I don't see how that can happen when the three of us are leaving first thing in the morning," Martine said.

Martha was glad to hear that Martine had at least decided to stay overnight.

"Aw, Mom, come on," Mimi pleaded. "I told Gram I'd go with her."

"You should have checked with me first before you made these plans," Martine said sharply.

Martha decided it was best to remain silent. She studied her meal, unable to lift her eyes. She noticed Edgar continued to eat, either oblivious or unwilling to engage. She suspected the latter.

Martine turned her attention to Martha. "And I don't know much about your health, Mother, but it seems a considerable distance to drive by yourself."

"I suppose it is," Martha said.

"And you say this Ned wants to see you?" Martine asked. "After all this time?"

"Yes," Martha answered. She could understand how her daughter viewed with skepticism the strong desire between two people to see each other after fifty years. But love had no limits.

"I've got an idea!" Mimi said, her eyes sparkling. "Mom, why don't you drive? The three of us could go together. It'll be like a road trip!"

Martine pushed her food around on her plate with her fork and said, "It wouldn't be much of a road trip, it's only four hours down the thruway."

"So we could do the trip and be back the same day," Mimi said.

"I think it's a great idea," Edgar said.

Martine looked at him as if she'd forgotten he was there. She narrowed her eyes at him and pressed her lips together. "*That* is not helpful, Edgar," she muttered.

"At least think about it," he suggested. He helped himself to more rice from one of the containers. "Martha hasn't seen Ned in over fifty years. No time like the present."

Not as oblivious as he'd appeared.

"To meet a man she wanted to run away with who was not my father," Martine hissed.

That was the crux of it then. Her loyalty to her father was commendable.

Even though she hadn't seen her daughter in years, Martha did not miss how unhappy she was. So angry. Martha sighed.

"Gram?" Mimi looked to Martha for help.

Martha shook her head. "Do as your mother wishes, Mimi."

"But what about Ned?" Mimi asked.

She didn't know why her granddaughter was so adamant that she meet Ned after all these years, but she was touched by the teenager's gesture nonetheless.

"Don't worry about that," Martha said.

There was no reason she couldn't drive herself down to Ohio, as long as she took her time. She'd have to purchase a GPS for her car as she wouldn't be able to read a map to save her life. She would have liked to go with Mimi. She had kind of looked forward to it. But maybe it wasn't meant to be.

"We're leaving in the morning," Martine said with finality.

Mimi jumped up from the table. "You ruin everything! Just because you're miserable you want everyone else to be just as unhappy." She bolted from the room, and the three of them stared after her at the empty space she left behind.

If Martine was stunned, she didn't let on.

"Well, that went well," Edgar said, and helped himself to more General Tso's chicken.

CHAPTER THIRTY-SEVEN

Martine

"You know, your mother doesn't seem that bad," Edgar said later that evening as they got ready for bed. As Mimi currently occupied her old bedroom, Martine and Edgar had been relegated to the bedroom that had once been Martine's grandmother's.

She snorted. "You don't know her like I do."

"She's nice," Edgar pushed.

"She wasn't always sweetness and light," Martine said sharply.

"People change. It happens," Edgar said, pulling on a T-shirt and a pair of old shorts for bed.

Martine wasn't sure she believed that.

"This house was toxic when I was growing up in it," she said. She pulled her pajamas from her overnight bag. "Between my father and his drinking and my mother. When she was engaged, she was critical. When she wasn't, she was remote and aloof." Martine zipped the bag closed. "I'll tell you, every morning when I went downstairs, I had no idea what faced me for the day. But I quickly learned to adjust."

"It doesn't sound ideal," Edgar said with a sigh. He pulled back the bedcovers. "Which side do you want?"

"I don't care," she said, pulling her pajama top over her head and slipping her arms through the short sleeves.

"Then I'll sleep by the window, I want to listen to the surf," he said, climbing into bed. He'd left the window open.

"I haven't seen her for almost twenty years, and now I'm expected to drive her to Ohio!" Martine shook her head as she slipped on her pajama shorts.

Edgar didn't say anything.

Martine stared at him. He lay on his back with his hands clasped behind his head, staring up at the ceiling.

"You think I should drive her to Ohio?" she asked.

"She's an old woman, she wants to see the love of her life one more time," he said.

"The love of her life who wasn't my father! It explains a lot, let me tell you," Martine ranted. "No wonder my father was a drinker."

"You don't know the reasons he drank," Edgar said.

"Do you always have to play devil's advocate?" she asked. "Just once, be on my side."

"Martine, grow up, it's not about sides. We're not back in grammar school," Edgar said, exasperation evident in his voice.

Martine went around to her side of the bed and slipped beneath the covers, only realizing how exhausted she was when her head hit the pillow. She rolled onto her side, reached over, and turned off the bedside light.

As they lay there in the darkness, Martine asked, "If I were to go to Ohio, what would you do?"

"I'd stay here. You'd be back in a day. I wouldn't mind taking a break before we drive back. And I like the look and the feel of this town. I'd like to check it out."

She was aware that he could have flown here on his own to pick up Mimi, but because she had insisted on coming along, that meant they had to drive. He always drove them everywhere and never complained.

"I don't know if my mother would feel comfortable with you staying here in the house," Martine said.

"No problem. I could stay at a hotel or a B & B if there's one around," Edgar suggested.

Neither said anything for a while. The only sound was the crashing of the surf against the beach across the street.

"That's music to my ears," Edgar said.

She'd forgotten what it was like, the briny smell in the air and the sound of the surf. It was nice.

"Maybe it would be a good idea for you to spend some time with your mother before we head back. She's not getting any younger."

"I don't know if our relationship can be patched up."

"Maybe not. But at least try. You know how I feel about family members not speaking to one another. It's wrong," he said firmly.

There were disagreements in Edgar's family, but no one ever fell out over it. How many times had he prompted her to call her mother at Christmas over the years, but she'd always refused out of a combination of stubbornness and fear. Fear that her mother might not want to hear from her.

Martine sighed loudly in the dark. "I'll sleep on it."

The following morning, Martine woke up and blinked, looking around the room, momentarily forgetting where she was. The clock on the bedside table read nine, and she rolled over to face the window, noting that Edgar was no longer in bed. She felt his vacated space. The bed was no longer warm, which indicated he'd been up for a while. She stared at the white lace curtains on the windows. They didn't move, so there was no breeze, but she could hear the lake crashing against the shore.

She rolled on her back, thinking she should get up. She yawned and stretched her arms over her head before flipping back the bedcovers.

Once out of bed, she took a quick shower, brushed her teeth, and got dressed before heading downstairs.

The house was quiet, with no sign of Mimi or Edgar anywhere. She wondered if her mother was still in bed; she wasn't familiar with her daily habits. But she found her in the back room.

"Good morning," she said, standing in the doorway.

Martha nodded. "Good morning." She sat in her chair with the morning newspaper open on her lap. There was a cup of tea on the table beside her, and she wore reading glasses.

Tentatively, Martine stepped forward into the room. "Where are Edgar and Mimi?"

"They had breakfast, and then Mimi wanted to show him around Hideaway Bay. They were heading to the beach and then to town." Martha folded up the paper, then removed her reading glasses and set them aside.

"You and Mimi seem to be getting on well," Martine remarked, folding her arms across her chest.

"She's a lovely girl," Martha said. "Would you stop being ridiculous and sit down, Martine. You look like you're about to bolt any minute."

Martine sat on the sofa that backed up against the disused fireplace. She did not look at her mother, instead choosing to look down at her hands in her lap, not quite sure what to say.

"Hideaway Bay hasn't changed much," Martine said, anxious to fill in the awkward gaps and silences.

"You don't need to make small talk with me, Martine," Martha said.

Martine snorted. "I can never get it right. You're always ready with a criticism."

"It wasn't a criticism. I was trying to put you at ease," Martha said.

"That'd be a first."

Martha pressed her lips together. "You seem anxious—no, agitated—to be here."

"We haven't spoken in twenty years, how should I be?" Martine asked.

"That was your choice."

"My choice?" Martine repeated, her voice shrill. "When's the last time you called me? Or came out to see me or my children? To even meet them."

Martha paled and sagged in her chair. "You made it very clear when you left that you never wanted to see me again."

"But I sent you birth announcements of the kids," Martine wailed.

"And they were just that, announcements," Martha said, leaning forward. "Never was there an invitation to come out and visit you. Did you think I was just going to show up on your doorstep, uninvited and unwanted? I don't go where I'm not wanted."

There was a flash of anger behind Martha's eyes, and shades of the mother Martine used to know began to surface.

"You left and you never looked back," Martha said.

There was truth in that. As soon as Martine turned eighteen, she left, went to a college on the west coast to get as far away as possible from Hideaway Bay and her mother, and made a life for herself out there.

Before Martine could respond, Mimi swept into the room, holding a white paper bag. "Dad and I picked up pastries in town. He's in the kitchen making tea and coffee." She held up the bag. "We've got Danishes. Cheese and apricot and almond."

Martha and Martine said nothing.

"Gram, you okay?" Mimi asked, the bag dropping to her side.

"I'm fine, honey," Martha said.

Honey?

"Did you want tea or coffee?" Mimi asked.

"I've got a cup, but I'll take a cheese Danish," Martha said.

"Mom, Dad is making you a cup of coffee, and he said you'd like the apricot Danish," Mimi said.

Martine nodded.

"I'll get the plates, Gram," Mimi said, and she disappeared from the room.

"Edgar makes your coffee for you?" Martha asked. She thought it was a sweet gesture.

Martine shrugged. "Yes, probably because he's making himself one."

"That's very thoughtful of him."

She supposed it was; she'd never really thought about it.

"It's easy to take people for granted," Martha said.

"You're not going to start doling out marriage advice now, are you?" Martine asked.

Mimi entered with Edgar behind her. She carried in a tray laden with plates of pastries and set it on the coffee table in front of Martine. Edgar handed Martine a cup of coffee and sat down next to her on the sofa. Mimi took it upon herself to pass the plates of pastries, then seated herself on the embroidered stool near Martha, taking a bite out of her own pastry.

"This is a great little town, Martha, I love it," Edgar said enthusiastically. He took a sip of his coffee, set it down, and picked up his plate.

Martine shot him a look that said *tone it down*.

For a few moments, they made small talk as Edgar asked Martha questions about the town and the house. When a natural lull appeared, Mimi asked, "Mom, can we please go to Ohio?"

Three pairs of eyes stared at Martine. She realized she held a lot of power in her hands. Even her mother seemed to wait, expectant.

Martine finished her pastry and licked her lips, setting her plate down. "I suppose I have no choice but to go on this trip."

Mimi jumped up from her stool, which startled Martha, who put her hand to her chest.

"Settle down, Mimi," Martine said. "We'll go. But let's do it sooner rather than later. Can you get a hold of Ned and see if tomorrow's good?"

"I'll call him," Martha said.

"I'll drive," Martine said. "We can take our car."

"I'd rather take the Caddy," Martha said.

"You still have that old car?" Martine said in disbelief.

"I do indeed, and it's in perfectly good running condition," Martha said with an air of finality that suggested the decision had been made.

"What about Dad?" Mimi asked.

"Don't worry about me. I'll hang out in Hideaway Bay and explore the area. Is there a hotel around?"

Martha frowned at him. "What do you need that for? You can stay here in the house."

"I didn't know how comfortable you'd feel about me staying here," he said.

"Nonsense. It'll be good to have someone here while we're gone."

"We might want to stay overnight," Martine suggested. If the reunion was emotional after the long drive, then returning that same day might not be in her mother's best interest.

"Whatever you think is best," Martha said. "Book a hotel and I'll pay for it."

"I can pay for it," Martine said.

"No, you're doing all the driving. I'll pay for the motel."

"Now, girls, don't fight, we're going on a road trip!" Mimi teased.

Everyone laughed.

After they finished their pastry and coffee and tea, the three of them left Martha alone to call Ned and make the arrangements. She reported to them that it was all set for the next day, and that Ned's son would meet them at the nursing home.

Chapter Thirty-Eight

Martha

The four of them stood in the driveway with three overnight bags at their feet. It was a glorious day for a drive. The sun shone, and the sky was deep blue without a cloud in it.

Martha had packed an overnight bag the previous day and had checked and rechecked the contents. It had been a long time since she'd gone anywhere, and she wasn't sure exactly what she'd need other than a change of clothes and a toothbrush. Just to be sure, she packed extra underwear and a couple of adult undergarments, even though she despised them.

She hadn't slept much the previous night, tossing and turning, on one hand, excited to be seeing Ned and on the other hand, wondering if it was too late.

She leaned on her walker and stared at the driveway. The asphalt was faded, and she reminded herself to call the paver to have it redone next spring.

"Mimi, would you open the garage door?" Martha asked.

"Sure, Gram," Mimi said and ran to the garage to hit the button. The door lifted slowly to reveal the pale-yellow Cadillac.

"I can't believe you still have this car," Martine said.

"Of course I do," Martha replied. "It doesn't even have one hundred thousand miles on it."

Other than Martine, it was the one thing she and Cal had loved. It had brought them both pleasure. On rare occasions they would go for a drive in it and get lunch or dinner or take Martine somewhere. The three of them would tool around Hideaway Bay, and in that car with Cal behind the wheel, sober, and herself happy with the novelty of being out of the house, Martha felt like they were a happy, *normal* family. But then they always had to return home.

She couldn't part with it. Wouldn't part with it. She'd decided that long ago. Her mechanic had promised he'd keep it going for her.

"It's a boat of a car, Martha," Edgar said, admiring it.

"Edgar, would you back it out of the garage, please."

With some satisfaction, Martha noted that the car started on the first try without so much as a hiccup. She glanced sideways at her daughter, who raised an eyebrow as Edgar slowly backed it out of the garage.

When Edgar got out of the car, he enthused, "She purrs like a kitten."

"I don't know. I still think we should take our car," Martine said.

"If Martha says she's been keeping it up, then she's been keeping it up," Edgar said. "It'll be fine."

Martine still appeared doubtful.

"You'll be back tomorrow."

"I think we should get on the road," Martha said.

"Okay, Mother, let's go," Martine said.

As Edgar loaded their bags into the trunk, a cell phone rang. It was Mimi's. She glanced at the screen and said, "Oh, it's Kyle. I'll just be a minute." And she stepped away and stood on the sidewalk in front of the house for some privacy.

"I've met Kyle but who is he? Is he from around here? Is he local?" Martine asked.

"Kyle Koch. He's the same age as Mimi. His father teaches at the elementary school, and his mother died from cancer. I believe his father sees one of the Monroe girls. Isabelle, I think," Martha said.

"Have you met him?"

"Just in passing. He seems like a nice boy," Martha said. She glanced at her wristwatch, anxious to get going.

"What is he, like a boyfriend or something?" Edgar asked, his enthusiasm for the Cadillac having dwindled.

"No, I think they're just friends," Martha said.

Martine and Edgar exchanged a glance that Martha did not miss.

"Why? What's wrong?" Martha asked.

Martine looked at her husband and then her mother. "High school has been a struggle for Mimi."

"A struggle? In what way?" Martha wondered if it had something to do with academics. Mimi appeared to be quite intelligent.

"She hasn't made any friends since she started the ninth grade," Martine admitted. She crossed her arms over her chest and stared at the ground.

Martha could not believe this. "What do you mean? Mimi's a lovely girl. I thought she would have a lot of friends back home."

Martine shook her head and Edgar said, "Nope, I'm afraid not. For whatever reason, things haven't gelled. We think she's a lovely girl too."

"The first year did not go well, she never settled in," Martine said. Martha did not miss the pain in her daughter's voice. This news upset her to no end.

"Is she being bullied?"

"Not that we know of," Edgar said.

"We've asked her about this, but she says no," Martine said. "She just hasn't made any friends."

"People used to say that high school was supposed to be the best time of your life. They don't still spout that garbage, do they?" Martha asked.

"No, thank goodness," Martine answered. "She just seems to have drifted apart from her friends from elementary school."

"That's normal," Martha said.

"I guess so."

"What can I do to help?" Martha asked. The thought of Mimi suffering anything distressed her.

Before anything further could be said, Mimi ran up the driveway, all smiles. "That was Kyle, he wanted to wish us luck."

This made Martha smile. Maybe Mimi didn't have friends back home, but she had one friend in Hideaway Bay. And that was a start.

"Let's get going," Martha said, making her way to the passenger side of the vehicle.

"Ohio, here we come!" Mimi said.

She hugged Edgar goodbye and climbed into the back seat.

Martha noticed that Martine did not hug or kiss Edgar goodbye, and this concerned her.

Edgar put Martha's walker in the trunk and came around to the driver-side door. Martine rolled down the window and

Edgar leaned in, resting his arms on the door. "If there's any problems, call me."

"I will," Martine said.

Once they were all in and buckled up, Martine reversed the car onto the road. Edgar stood in the driveway, one hand in his pocket and the other waving them off.

When they got on the highway, Martine looked in the rearview mirror and asked, "Where are your glasses?"

Mimi answered sheepishly, "Oh, I forgot them."

Martha couldn't remember the last time she'd left the house to go traveling. Most likely when Cal was alive. Was it Saratoga Springs? Or was it West Palm Beach? No, it was most definitely Saratoga Springs as they'd had that big blowout and left early, cutting short their week's vacation. At the encouragement of her mother, they'd left Martine with her and gone away by themselves, just the two of them. They'd only stayed two days—or was it three?—before they checked out and drove home in their yellow Cadillac in tense silence. They never went on a vacation again after that.

"Mother, just let me know when you want to stop and use the bathroom," Martine said, glancing over at her from the driver's seat.

"I will," she said. From her handbag, she pulled out her sunglasses and put them on.

Mimi slouched in the back seat, earbuds in, and scrolled on her phone.

Martine didn't say much, and Martha was surprised at how much her daughter resembled her late mother.

Martha didn't require any conversation; she was happy enough to enjoy the drive. There was a lot of greenery along the thruway, and she watched deer eating at the edge of the green, awfully close to the road.

As they drove along the 90-West, Martha leaned her elbow on the window and wondered what they would find at the end of their journey. She couldn't believe Ned had even agreed to it. She wondered if he had ended up as bitter as she had. She hoped not; that would kill her. He'd been so sweet and pure back then. But he hadn't sounded bitter when she spoke to him on the phone.

If someone had told her a year ago, even six months ago, that she'd be taking a road trip with her daughter and her granddaughter, she would have told them they were nuts. And yet here she was, like she'd been a part of their lives every day for the past eighteen years.

The sun shone through her window and eventually, it made Martha sleepy enough to lower her head in the seat and doze off, dreaming about spending time with her daughter and grandchildren.

Chapter Thirty-Nine

Martha

Carefully and slowly, Martha pushed her walker toward the entrance of the nursing home. The automatic doors slid open with a whoosh. Martine and Mimi flanked her, their pace adjusted to Martha's slower gait.

She had a crick in her neck from dozing off in an awkward position. The drive had been uneventful. There'd been no palpable tension between Martine and Mimi, and she was grateful. She knew she could rely on her Caddy.

The arrangement was that Ned's son Edward would meet them in the lobby. All she knew was that Ned was in room 329. The thought that she was in the same building as Ned after all this time made her skin prickly and put knots in her stomach. She cursed her age and infirmity; it slowed her down in getting to him.

Her heart beat so fast that it felt more like a steady rhythm of thuds. She hoped this meeting—as monumental as it was—wouldn't kill her. But she supposed if it did, it wouldn't be the worst thing that could happen to her, to die after seeing Ned one last time. No, she'd brook no argument with that.

The nursing home was standard fare, with walls painted a pale green that reminded her of pistachio ice cream. The wood trim was also pale, maybe oak. The floor beneath her feet was industrial tile. Along the walls of the lobby, residents sat in wheelchairs. The scent of disinfectant tainted with the smell of bodily secretions seemed typical for all such institutions. Nursing homes were no place for people. She understood their purpose, but institutionalized living was not optimal in her view. Aside from her mother who had died in the hospital, her father and grandparents had remained in the house on Star Shine Drive until their deaths. The thought of Ned in a place such as this burned an ache in her heart. She refused to go down the road of thinking that had Ned married her, he'd be spending his final days in the house on Star Shine Drive.

It was depressing.

But Martha straightened up as much as her back would allow and lifted her chin, unwilling to cave in to defeat.

As they approached the reception desk, Martha spotted Edward Lindahl, recognizing him because he so strongly resembled Ned. She took in the younger Lindahl for a moment, imagining what Ned would have looked like in middle age. She couldn't help but smile. She turned her walker toward him, and he broke into a smile as he met her halfway.

"Martha Cotter?"

Martha nodded. "You must be Edward."

He was a replica of Ned, right down to the timbre of his voice. It was unnerving; it was like hurtling back into the past. She felt momentarily light-headed.

He put forth his hand. "Edward Lindahl, Mrs. Cotter."

"It's nice to meet you," she said. She tried to suppress the thought, but it formed itself anyway: *This could have been my son.* She'd promised herself she wouldn't think along those lines. Remembering she wasn't alone, she said, "This is my daughter, Martine Duchene, and my granddaughter, Mimi Duchene."

After the introductions were made, Edward said, "Mrs. Cotter, it's a long walk. My dad's room is at the end of the corridor on the third floor. Would you like me to get you a wheelchair?"

"No, thank you," Martha said. She was determined to walk in of her own accord.

"Mother, maybe it would be better." Martine stood beside her with her purse slung over her shoulder and her arms crossed.

She knew Martine meant well. They all did, but she wanted to walk. She'd take her time. They'd waited this long to see each other; an extra ten minutes wasn't going to make any difference.

As they walked along with Edward at Martha's side, leading the way, Martha asked, "How long has Ned lived here?"

They'd reached the elevator, and Edward pushed the "up" button.

"For the last year. He's had some health problems."

The elevator arrived and when the doors slid open, all of them had to step back to allow an employee to step out of it, pushing a metal cart as tall as she was. Once she cleared them, Edward held the door open and Martha stepped inside, followed by Martine and Mimi.

The doors opened onto the third floor, which seemed busier and louder than the sedate lobby area.

"His room is at the end of the hall," Edward indicated.

Politely, he asked Martine about the drive down, and he and Martine made small talk as they walked. Mimi brought up the rear.

Martha looked in each room as she passed. Most of the residents were sitting up in chairs, and some had their televisions blaring. There were a few who occupied their beds and appeared to be sleeping, or at least she hoped they were sleeping.

She swallowed hard. She wanted no part of a place like this when it was no longer possible for her to live alone. But she might not have any choice. There was no one to take care of her. She pushed that thought as far as possible out of her mind.

She asked Edward, "What did Ned do after he returned from Canada?" She realized there were huge gaps in what she knew of him. Oh, she had imagined down through the years what he might be doing, but now she was starting to get the pieces to the puzzle, and she wanted to fit them all together.

"When he came back to the States with Mom, he worked for Dutch Boy paints, which is now Sherwin-Williams, and he went to college at night. He got his degree in civil engineering. It took him years to get it, but he finished it," Edward said with a smile. "He'd be helping us with our homework while he did his own."

Martha was proud of him. He'd done it. He did it his way, but he got his degree.

"So you were born in Canada?" she asked.

"My brother and I were born there, but our sister was born in Ohio."

Martha stopped and leaned on her walker, trying to compose herself and catch her breath. She tried to straighten up, but her back was giving her some grief; it was the ride in the car. She looked up at Edward and asked, "And your mother?"

A shadow passed across Edward Lindahl's face. "Mom died eight years ago. Breast cancer."

"I am sorry to hear that," she said truthfully. Her death must surely have caused all of them pain, and that sobered her.

Mimi put her hand on Martha's arm. "Are you all right, Gram?" she asked, a crease furrowing the unblemished skin between the dark arches of her eyebrows. "We're almost there."

Martha gave her a reassuring smile. "I'm good." Her breaths came in short gasps, and she feared she might hyperventilate as her excitement was building. She was glad they were both here with her. She didn't think she could have done this alone.

"It's okay, Mother," Martine said. She laid her hand on her back and moved it in slow, circular motions. "If it's too much, you don't have to do this."

Unexpectedly, tears filled Martha's eyes with Martine's touch. When was the last time another human being had touched her with tenderness? She couldn't remember. What a mess she'd made of things. Buoyed by so many things recently, she was determined to start making things right.

"No," she said more sharply than she intended. "I want to see Ned. It's just that it's been a long time. Almost sixty years."

"I know," Martine said. "Get your bearings and we'll soldier on."

Her and Martine getting along? Trying to accomplish a common goal? Why couldn't it have always been like this? Why did they waste so much time?

At the doorway of room 329, she stopped and peered in. It was a private room with a large window. Along the windowsill stood framed photos of what she supposed was Ned's family. In front of the window was a hospital bed that no amount of nice cozy bedding could disguise. A collection of watercolors hung on the wall, depicting various country scenes: birds, ducks, and horses. On the other half of the room, there was a high-backed armchair, a large flat-screen television on a long stand, and a recliner, in which sat a frail old man.

Her heart lurched at the sight of him. She'd recognize that face anywhere. But immediately, she became concerned. A cane rested against his left leg, and he looked beyond frail; he was emaciated and bald. This was not a man with health problems, this was a dying man. His eyes were closed as he dozed.

She cursed the walker; it was an impediment that slowed her down from getting to the love of her life. Her breathing came faster, and her eyes filled with tears. *Dammit, I will not cry. At least not yet.*

Martine and Mimi walked in behind her. She could feel the slight, reassuring pressure of her daughter's hand on her back.

Edward sidestepped the three women and made his way to the side of his father's chair. "Dad, Martha is here."

Ned's eyes opened and widened, and a big grin appeared on his face when he spotted Martha. He struggled to get to his feet and on the third try, with his son's help, he managed it. He wasn't as tall as Martha remembered. He appeared to have shrunk, his back a little crooked. It didn't matter. He was still as handsome as the day she first saw him as she sat in the gazebo all those years ago in Hideaway Bay.

"Martha, Martha!" he cried. The skin of his face crinkled with his broad, generous smile, the crevices deep.

"Ned," she sobbed.

She pushed the walker aside and was relieved when Mimi took it from her. Martha and Ned, their arms extended, reached out for each other at the same time. Martha stepped into his embrace. She reached up, her heart expanding and blooming within her as she rested her hand against his cheek.

Ned wrapped two thin arms around her, and Martha laid her head on his chest, right next to his heart.

He pulled her tighter and rested his chin on the top of her head, and Martha was transported back to 1966. It was as if all the time in between had simply disintegrated, as if five decades had been a blip on a radar screen.

She began to wobble as a pain shot through her hip, and Ned listed toward her.

Both Martine and Edward spoke at once.

"Mother, you should sit down."

"Easy does it, Dad."

Martine gently prised Martha from Ned's arms and guided her to the armchair Edward had placed right next to his father's recliner.

With some shakiness, Ned shuffled back to his recliner, leaning on his cane.

Concerned, Martha automatically reached out for him with both hands as if to steady him as he sat down.

Ned winked at her, and she burst out laughing, leaning back in her chair and clapping her hands.

Once Ned was settled in his recliner, he looked at his other visitors.

"You must be Martine and Mimi," he said with a smile.

Both answered him with a smile and a nod.

To Mimi, he said, "And you're the young lady who found me! Well done."

Martha beamed proudly at her granddaughter.

He pointed toward Edward. "That's my firstborn and namesake. He kind of runs the show around here, or at least that's what we let him think." His eyes twinkled in merriment.

"And do your other son and your daughter live around here?" Martha asked.

"John lives in Nebraska, and Denise lives in Florida."

"They're spread out," Martha remarked.

"Unfortunately, yes, but they have to live their own lives," Ned said softly.

Martha nodded in agreement, her own daughter and grandchildren living on the other coast of the country.

Ned tore his eyes away from Martha and said, "Son, why don't you take Martine and Mimi to that restaurant at the corner. I'd like to spend some time alone with Martha and catch up."

"Sure, Dad," Edward said. He looked to Martine and Mimi and asked, "Are you hungry?"

"Starving, to be honest," Martine said. "Mother, what about you? Do you want something to eat or drink?"

Martha shook her head. "No, not right now. I don't think I could eat a thing."

"We'll be back shortly," Martine said.

"Great, let's go," Edward said. He looked to his father. "Dad, do you need anything before I go?"

Ned did not take his eyes off of Martha. "No, I have everything I need right here."

"Okay, then. We won't be long," Edward said, waving his hand and indicating that Martine and Mimi should go out the door ahead of him.

"Take your time," Ned called out after him, his voice feeble.

Once Edward, Martine, and Mimi were out of sight and earshot, Martha inched her chair closer to Ned's until the arms of both chairs touched. She laid her hand on the armrest of his chair and he immediately covered it with his.

"So, my letter got lost," he said.

"Can you believe it?" Martha asked, incredulity lacing her voice.

"No, I can't, but at this point in my life, nothing surprises me anymore."

"How've you been?" Martha said.

"I'm okay, although they tell me I've got lung cancer," he said. When her mouth fell open, he shrugged. "What are you going to do? We all have to die sometime."

"What about treatment?" she asked, concern filling her. She didn't want to find him only to lose him yet again.

"I had treatment. Chemo and radiation, but the cancer didn't respond to it," he said. He did not seem sad about it. Just stating the facts.

"Oh, Ned, I'm sorry to hear that," Martha said, rubbing her other hand over his.

"Don't be, Martha, I've had a good life. It didn't go as originally planned, but it turned out all right," he said, looking knowingly at her.

"No, it did not go as planned."

There was silence and Ned asked, "Tell me about your life, Martha?"

A week ago, Martha would have said no. But now with all that had transpired in the past few days, her answer was profoundly different.

"My life has been bumpy, but I'm in a better place now," she said truthfully. The arrival of Mimi on her doorstep had been a blessing; she realized that now. That girl had somehow managed to worm her way into Martha's heart in a short span of time, and Martha planned on keeping her there. There was a chance of reconciliation with Martine, something she hadn't thought possible only a short time ago. And this visit with Ned, it dawned on her, meant that she didn't have to romanticize him anymore. They were no longer the young lovers they once had been. She would always love him, but that lost love would not dictate the rest of her life. For better or for worse, they'd gone on to live and have families and create a life without the other. Maybe Ned had been more successful in that regard, but Martha was optimistic about her own chances given the recent change in her circumstances.

Actually, she realized, she was filled with gratitude. Gratitude toward Mimi, who'd found Ned and pushed for this meeting. Gratitude to Martine for driving her here despite her initial reluctance. And gratitude for this meeting with Ned because she could finally see that it was time to let go and move on.

"And what about Cal?" he asked gently.

She was thoughtful for a moment. Even her recollection of this had changed. "It wasn't the best marriage, though it was no one's fault."

"I'm sorry to hear that," he said.

"Cal returned home from the war, and he was a different person. I married him knowing he was different, yet waiting for the old Cal to return. But he never did. That man died over there."

Ned shook his head. "He was a good guy."

"Yes, he was." And that's how Martha was going to try to remember him, as he was before the war.

She paused, thinking this was not the time or the place to do a post-mortem on her marriage with Cal. There was nothing she could do about that now. But she still had a daughter and grandchildren. She had family of her own. All was not lost. There was so much hope ahead of her that it made her dizzy.

She stared at Ned, trying to memorize everything about him. The lines on his face, his baldness, the age spots, the translucent skin. She didn't want to forget the changes time had made.

"I've thought about you often over the years," he said, brushing his hand across the top of hers. He stared down at their clasped hands. "Wondered what you were doing, who you were with, that sort of thing. I always pictured you in Hideaway Bay."

"You'll be glad to know I never left Hideaway Bay," she said with a laugh. "You won't be disappointed."

"You could never disappoint me, Martha," he said.

She laughed. "I'm glad to hear that." There was still someone in the world whom she hadn't disappointed.

"I've often thought about how it all turned out," he said quietly, narrowing his eyes. "And I think it worked out the way it was supposed to. For whatever reason, we were not meant to be with one another."

"I guess not," she said. For the first time in her life, she was okay with how things had turned out. 1966 was a long time ago, in the past. It was time to rejoin the land of the living.

She looked up at him and grinned. "We've become quite the philosophers."

"We all become great philosophers with age; we've got a lot of time on our hands and not much else to do but think."

Chapter Forty

Martine

Martine didn't remember much about the restaurant or even what was on her plate in front of her, as she was anxious to return to the nursing home to find out how her mother was getting on with Ned.

During the journey down from Hideaway Bay to the suburbs of Cleveland, Martine had done a lot of thinking, and things were beginning to slot into place. All her life she'd had one idea of her mother and her personality: abrasive. It was a belief firmly held in place, but now it felt as if everything had been turned on its head.

Had her mother just been unhappy all this time? Could anyone be that unhappy for that long, so miserable that the people who lived with them, the people who were supposed to love them, needed to distance themselves from them? Had her mother been a victim of fate? And what did it say about her and her father that her mother's love and allegiance lay elsewhere? Especially since her father had been so troubled. Martine wasn't sure she was ready to go there just yet. Had Cal and Martine simply been second best? Had Martha felt she'd settled when she looked at Martine and her father?

And her poor father. Had simply not being Ned Lindahl been the cause of his suffering? From an early age, Martine had suspected her parents were not in a happy marriage. Her father's constant companion had been a bottle of booze. He was rarely sober.

Her heart ached for him. To have been trapped in a loveless marriage with her mother for the rest of his life must have been purgatorial. He certainly deserved better. Maybe they all did.

And even at her age, she couldn't help but wonder if she was unwanted. When her mother looked at her, was she constantly reminded that Martine was the child of another man and not the product of the man she loved? The thoughts were sobering, and a weariness began to settle deep within Martine's bones. Her immediate urge was to get back home to put distance between her mother and herself. But that was no great shakes either, as her own marriage was coming to a grinding halt and the marital home wasn't the safe refuge it had once been.

On the short walk back to the nursing home, Martine was quiet, lost in her own thoughts, the chatter between Mimi and Edward a low buzz in the background, like white noise.

She was first to arrive back at Ned Lindahl's room. For a second, she didn't announce her presence, wanting to observe the two former lovers in situ to see if she could glean any information about her own mother.

Her mother and Ned leaned toward each other in chairs that had been placed right next to one another. They'd turned their bodies so that their arms were entwined and their foreheads rested together. Their eyes were closed, and Martine wasn't sure if they had fallen asleep. Somehow, she doubted it.

She took a step back to allow them some privacy and bumped right into Edward.

"Ah, maybe they need a moment," she said.

Edward glanced over her head and said to her, "Come on, I'll show you the grounds. They have some beautiful flower gardens."

Martine went along silently. When Mimi looped her arm through hers and looked at her beseechingly, Martine tried to give her daughter a look of reassurance. But all this newfound information had left her on even less stable ground than before.

They'd found a hotel and stayed the night and left shortly after breakfast. Once they checked out, they got on the road.

"Did you ever love Dad?" Martine asked, unable to keep the pain out of her voice.

In the rearview mirror, she'd seen that Mimi had fallen asleep in the back seat, leaning against the door. Martine had wanted to wait until they returned to Hideaway Bay, but she was impatient to get answers to her questions.

"I was very grateful to your father," Martha answered. "He rescued me from a dark period in my life and of course, he gave me you."

"That's not what I asked, Mother," Martine said tightly.

She'd seen her mother with Ned Lindahl, and not once could she ever remember her looking at her father the way she'd looked at Ned. Never with such a soft, adoring expression.

Martha sighed. "I loved him, but I was never *in love* with him. If that makes any sense."

Martine looked skyward, exasperated. "I'm a grown woman, you don't have to spare my feelings. If you didn't love him, you didn't love him."

Martha seemed to consider her words carefully. "Like I said, I was grateful to your father, and I cared about him very much."

Martine made a sound of disgust. "Did Dad know you didn't love him?"

Martha hesitated and then squirmed in her seat. "He knew that I had at one time loved Ned. That was no secret. We got married thinking our friendship was a good foundation for marriage, which sometimes is true, but there were too many cracks."

"Poor Dad."

She'd known her parents were unhappy; she'd never been able to figure out why, but maybe they didn't love each other. She'd grown up never questioning whether they loved each other, only knowing they didn't get along.

"I regret that," Martha said quietly.

"Do you?"

Martha nodded slowly. "I do."

"Why did you marry him?"

"Because I thought he could help me recover from Ned. I realize now that was a mistake. That it was too much of a burden to put on your father's shoulders."

"Is that why Dad killed himself?" Martine asked.

Martha's head spun toward her daughter. "Oh my goodness, of course not! Why would you think that?"

"What am I supposed to think? You loved another man. Dad loved you. His heart was broken over it."

Martha let out a heavy sigh. "It wasn't as dramatic as that. Your father and I were good friends before he went off to Vietnam. When he returned, he was a changed man. A haunted man. He couldn't exorcise his demons."

"Did he get help?" Martine asked.

Martha shook her head. "Remember this was the early seventies. There wasn't all this talk about mental health issues. It just wasn't discussed."

"Have you ever loved anyone besides Ned?" Martine asked. She had to know.

"Of course I have," her mother said with a frown. "I love you."

Martine snorted in disbelief.

Martha tilted her head slightly. "Just because I wasn't loving didn't mean I didn't or don't love you."

"You were a terrible mother," Martine said.

Martha flinched and went pale. "I suppose I was."

There was silence for a few miles before Martha spoke again. "There's nothing I can do about the past. It happened. It's over. I'm sorry."

Martine listened, choosing not to respond.

"But I don't want to spend the rest of my life estranged from my only child," Martha said. Her voice wobbled as she spoke.

"You want us all to be one big happy family?" Martine asked in disbelief.

"Well, we're not big, and maybe happy isn't a goalpost yet, but 'together' is a start," Martha said.

Martine was tired. "I don't know, Mother. It might be too late."

"Don't say that," Martha said. "It's not too late."

Mimi stirred in the back seat.

Martine sighed. "Let me think about it."

CHAPTER FORTY-ONE

Martha

THEY'D ARRIVED HOME NEAR lunchtime. Martha had immediately gone upstairs for a nap as the journey had taken a lot out of her. But there was a sense of satisfaction with the trip. And the lost note she'd carried around with her on her person, she tucked away in one of the drawers of her wardrobe. She and Ned had agreed to keep in touch with a phone call once a week. It had been good to see him. But now she needed to concentrate on her own family. It was high time. She needed to start being the mother Martine needed her to be. Hopefully, it wasn't too late.

Edgar and Mimi had already gone up to bed. Mimi had been quiet, most likely brooding over the fact that the three of them were departing the following day.

It was late, almost eleven, but Martine had remained downstairs with Martha in the back room. Using the remote, Martha turned off the television. The sound of crickets could be heard through the open back window. In the distance was the faint sound of a siren.

"I think we should clear the air," Martha said evenly. "Once and for all."

Martine blew a strong breath out through her nose. "You sound just like Edgar." There was an edge to her tone.

"What do you mean?" Martha asked. Sometimes, Martine talked in circles.

"Never mind."

"All right. I'll start, then," Martha said. "You've said I was a terrible mother."

"Yes, you were," Martine said with a lift of her chin.

Martha couldn't argue with her. Couldn't protest. Couldn't justify or explain or even defend. She put an elbow on the arm of the chair and pressed her forehead against her hand. She didn't know where to start.

"You never spoke about Dad," Martine said. It sounded like an accusation.

"What do you want to know?" Martha asked. How did she talk about Cal? How did she tell her that Cal before the war was a beautiful person but the Cal that came home from Vietnam was no longer that man? That after his return from Vietnam, red flags had popped up about some of his behavior, especially his drinking, but she'd chosen to ignore them, thinking the old Cal would return soon.

"What was he like?"

Martha bristled. Some parts of the past she did not want to return to. No matter what. How did you sort through all the pieces, take out the important ones to show a cohesive whole? How did one decide what was important? Could you distill your life into moments or pivotal events? Didn't it all matter?

She gasped, not from surprise but from breathlessness, as if the task would require too much physical energy.

She lifted up her head. "I knew your father for as long as I can recall. I can't remember when I first met him. It seems he was always there, right from the beginning."

Martine pulled her legs up beneath her on the sofa.

"He used to have a crush on me when we were teenagers," Martha said, smiling at the memory of it. Of simpler times. Before everything else.

"Was it reciprocated?" Martine asked.

Martha shook her head slowly and said quietly, "No."

"Poor Dad."

Martha could say she wished she had felt about Cal the way he'd felt about her. But the way things had turned out, even if she had loved him like that, she still wouldn't have been able to save him. Or them.

"Are you that selfish that you have no regret for marrying a man you didn't love?" Martine demanded.

"You want yes-and-no answers, and it isn't that simple—or that easy," Martha said.

"How could you marry him knowing you didn't love him?" Martine asked again.

"I cared very deeply for your father, and I thought I could grow to love him in time," Martha explained. "And had he stayed the same Cal, I'm confident we could have been happy together."

"But of course, you couldn't," Martine said.

"I tried, I did," Martha said, her voice trailing off. When she'd married Cal, she'd been hopeful, almost optimistic about their future. But over the years, she'd asked herself if she'd tried hard enough. Had she? Would it have made a difference if she'd tried harder? Loved him more? Would the outcome have changed? Somehow, she doubted it.

"Was I a constant reminder that you didn't get what you wanted?"

Martha stared at her daughter, her mouth hanging open. She began to shake. "How could you think that? That I didn't love you because you were Cal's daughter and not Ned's?"

"What am I to think, Mother?" Martine demanded. "I saw how you interacted with Ned in the nursing home. It was like I didn't even know who you were."

Martha closed her eyes for a moment. Things were such a mess. How did she explain to her only child that the person she'd witnessed in the nursing home was the real Martha, excavated and dusted off after fifty years. It couldn't be explained. There were no words.

"As your mother, I love you very much," Martha said. It sounded weak and inconsequential, but she had to say something. And at least it was the truth.

Martine snorted.

"Is this what we're going to do now? Rip each other apart? Because if that's it, I want no part of it."

Martine ignored her.

"What is it you need to know, exactly, Martine?" Martha asked.

Martine burst into tears. "I want to know why I wasn't good enough for my father to stick around and see me grow up!"

And now the tears transformed into big, ugly sobs. Martine leaned forward on the sofa, put her head in her hands, and continued to sob.

Martha recognized her daughter for what she was: a wounded child. Her heart filled with pain at her daughter's suffering.

"Martine, if you don't understand anything else, then understand this: your father's decision to take his own life had nothing to do with your worth," Martha said. "Quite the opposite, in fact."

Martine slowly lifted her head, her eyes and nose red. "What do you mean?"

"The war in Vietnam ruined your father. All the good that was Cal was left over in Southeast Asia. He continued to fight that war in his head every day for the rest of his life."

Martine sniffled and looked around for a tissue. Martha took the box off the table beside her, leaned forward, and handed it to her daughter. She often thought that if Cal had come home now, things would have been different. Maybe not resolved, but maybe healed. There was so much more help available now.

"Did he ever talk about it?"

Martha shook her head. "Not willingly, no." She pulled in a deep breath. "Sometimes he had nightmares, and there'd be a lot of shouting and tossing and turning as if he were reliving the moment." She did not tell Martine that it led to Martha moving out of the bedroom at night.

There was one more thing Martha needed to say. "Your father was a tortured, lost soul after the war. I wish you could have known him before the war, the way I did, when he was a good and decent man."

"Me too," Martine said quietly.

"And he did love you," Martha said. "There was still goodness and kindness in Cal, it was just buried beneath all the leftover debris of the horrible things he'd witnessed. More than anything, he wanted to be a good father to you."

"If that's true, then why did he leave me?"

"He never told me he was thinking about committing suicide, so I don't know if it was planned or if it was a spontaneous thing," Martha said. "But he used to say that he didn't want you to grow up with that kind of father." He'd say that off the cuff from time to time, and Martha had tried to reassure him.

All the talk of Cal's death sent her back to that day, a day she'd rather not remember. It had been a beautiful summer day. She could still remember the cloudless blue sky and the way the sun glinted off the lake.

"Did you feel bad at all?"

"His death devastated me. I was overwhelmed with twin feelings of grief and guilt. All my life I have wondered if I could have prevented it. Could have done more."

There was a stretch of silence as the truth settled down around them.

She realized she was failing in getting across what she was trying to say. It only seemed to be making Martine angrier. Maybe she should have left things the way they were. But it also seemed that it was too late to turn back, and she should soldier on.

"When you're fighting with Edgar or not getting along, does it affect how you love your children?" Martha asked.

"I may not be in the best mood," Martine started.

"That's not what I mean," Martha said. "Do you love your children more or less because you have marital problems?"

"Of course not," Martine asked, sounding irritated.

"When Mimi or Micah are annoying you, do you love them less?"

"No."

"How about when you're in a bad mood? You're angry, depressed, or sad? Do you love your children less?"

"No, because I'm able to separate those things. My love for my children is automatic."

Martha said no more, deciding to let all that sink in.

"I'm not proud of what I've done or how I mothered you and if you want to know the truth, I'd give anything to go back and do it all over again," Martha said.

Although her eyes were on Martine, she looked inward. "I realize it's probably too late for us and I take full responsibility for it, but with Mimi I'm hoping to restore some kind of equilibrium to the family. And eventually, Micah."

Martine looked at her. "You're not using my daughter for your own personal redemption. You will not play the martyr in this relationship."

Exasperated, Martha said, "I'm not trying to play anything! I'm trying to make amends for the past."

Martine snorted. "It's a little late for that, Mom."

"Would you like our relationship to be different than what it is now?" Martha asked.

The expression on Martine's face appeared pained.

Martha felt as if she wasn't able to reach her daughter. She tried a different tack. "Just because our marriage was a failure doesn't mean your father and I didn't love you," Martha said. "I can assure you, we both loved you very much. When we found out we were having a baby, we couldn't have been more excited."

Martha swallowed hard. The core of her daughter's anguish was not only feeling unloved but believing it as well. She prayed she had enough time left in her life to fix this.

Martine regarded her with an expression that could only be described as disbelief. She rubbed her wrist, her stacked bracelets jangling.

"I take full responsibility for how you feel and what you believe," Martha said. "If you let me, I'll try my best to be a better mother."

Martine nodded, her eyes shiny, but she didn't say anything.

Suddenly, Martha was overwhelmed with exhaustion and thought if she didn't get upstairs to bed soon, she might not be able to make it up. The last few days had run high on emotions.

Shakily, she stood. Martine jumped up from the sofa.

"I'm sorry, but I have to go to bed," Martha said. "Would you close that window before you come up?"

"Do you want me to go up with you?"

"No, I think I can make it." Martha gripped her walker and made her way out of the room.

She stopped in front of Martine, leaning on her walker for support. She had to ask a question. Needed an answer. "When you left all those years ago, you said you never wanted to see me again, and I'll be the first to admit that my reaction to your pregnancy was wrong," she conceded. She wished she could go back and change or fix a lot of things. But she couldn't. She could only move forward.

"I'll say. All you kept saying was how stupid I was to let that happen. That I was irresponsible. Do you know what it feels like to be a grown woman and to have your mother berate you? What I needed from you at the time was support. But you just couldn't help me," Martine cried.

"I am so sorry, Martine," Martha whispered.

Martine crossed her arms over her chest.

"Is it still true," Martha asked, "that you never want to see me again? Do you still feel that way?"

Martine lowered her head and whispered, "I don't know anymore."

She hadn't said yes, hadn't said she no longer wanted anything to do with her. Martha clung to that small piece of hope. "I'll admit I don't know what I'm doing here. With you. But I'm willing to try. I'd even go to counseling myself if I thought it would help."

Martine regarded her but said nothing. She followed her mother out of the room.

"I'd like to fix what is wrong between us. I don't know how to do that, but as I've said, I'm willing to try," Martha said. She stopped and looked over her shoulder at her daughter. "But I also understand if you can't get beyond our past. I won't force you. I'll leave it up to you."

When she reached the doorway, she said over her shoulder, "Goodnight, Martine."

"Goodnight, Mother."

Martha pulled the bedcovers up to her chest and sighed. Clearing the air had left her exhausted down to her bones. The night was still, and her windows were wide open but there was no relief. In the darkness, she stared at the ceiling, trying not to think about the fact that they were all leaving the next day and she would go back to being alone.

There was a knock at her door. Martha peered through the darkness. There was another knock, this time slightly louder.

She lifted her head off the pillow and said, "Come in."

The door opened, and the hall light illuminated Mimi in silhouette in her oversized T-shirt.

"Mimi?"

"Gram, can I ask you something?"

"It can't wait until morning?" Martha asked.

"No, it can't. It's important," Mimi said, still standing in the doorway.

"Then you better come in," Martha said, reaching over and turning on the bedside lamp. With some effort, she sat up and leaned against her pillow.

Mimi closed the door behind her and came and stood at the end of Martha's bed.

"Is everything all right?" Martha asked. She knew it wasn't. The girl had barely said two words all evening.

"No, it isn't. I don't want to leave tomorrow."

Martha had already guessed that. "And?"

"I've had an idea," Mimi said.

Martha was so tired that she wanted to laugh but she said good-humoredly, "Not all ideas are good."

"Just hear me out, Gram," Mimi said.

"I'm listening."

"I want to know if I can stay here with you in Hideaway Bay and do my senior year at the high school here."

This was a lot to unpack. It was almost midnight and Martha was exhausted. She didn't know what to say. The girl's gaze remained fixed on Martha's face.

"Sit down. I can't talk to you properly with you standing there like that," Martha said curtly.

Mimi sat on the edge of the bed near Martha's blanketed feet and folded one leg beneath her.

"Why don't you want to go home?" Martha asked.

Mimi shrugged. "I hate my high school there. And I love Hideaway Bay. I don't ever want to leave." Despite it being so late at night, her voice was filled with excitement and enthusiasm.

Although Martha was aware of Mimi's difficulties at home and would love to have her stay, at the back of her mind, she knew this would present other problems. "Have you talked to your parents about this?" she asked.

Mimi shook her head. "Not yet."

If there was one thing that could distance Martine from Martha further, this might possibly be it. She'd think she'd coerced the girl into staying. Martha had to proceed with caution. Mimi's mental health was a concern for her, but she also did not want to further alienate Martine.

"In my experience, if you're having problems in your life, moving does not necessarily solve them. You only seem to bring your problems with you." She paused and added, "Wherever you go."

"I suppose."

"Your mother will not be happy about this," Martha said. "And she'll blame me."

Mimi's eyes widened. "Oh, no, I would tell her it was all my idea. That I roped you into it."

"'Roped into' being the key words," Martha said with a smirk.

The smile on Mimi's face disappeared as she appeared to consider something. "Do you not want me to stay in Hideaway Bay and live with you, Gram?" Her voice was anxious.

Martha was quick to reassure her. "Of course I want you to stay. But I don't want to cause trouble with your mother."

"Oh, it won't be any trouble," Mimi said.

Martha did not share the girl's confidence.

"We'll talk to your parents at breakfast," Martha said. "But if they are totally against this, I will not go against their wishes." She was making a tiny bit of progress with Martine, and she wasn't going to jeopardize it.

Mimi's shoulders sagged. "All right."

Martha yawned. "Now, go on off to bed because it's getting late."

Mimi unfolded herself from her position and hopped off the bed. "Goodnight, Gram," she said, making her way to the door.

"Goodnight, Mimi."

As she opened the door, Martha called out after her. "If you do stay, Mimi, we've got to get you some proper pajamas," she said, eyeing the offending nightwear of choice.

Mimi laughed and her eyes twinkled. "Okay, Gram." And she disappeared out the door, closing it softly behind her.

Chapter Forty-Two

Martine

"Why do I feel like I'm being sandbagged, Mother?" Martine demanded.

Edgar had taken the car up to the grocery store off the main highway to do some shopping for Martha.

Martine sat at the kitchen table with her mother. They were getting ready to eat a breakfast of grapefruit halves, using the serrated spoons her mother kept in the drawer just for that purpose, and toast. Mimi manned the toaster on the counter, and in the middle of the table was the butter dish, the butter now soft, and two jars of homemade jam: sour cherry and apricot. Martine had already decided she'd have two pieces of toast so she could try each one.

But now her mother and her daughter had dropped this little bombshell into her lap, and she was gathering her thoughts before she responded.

"We're not sandbagging you, Martine," Martha said, sprinkling a little bit of sugar over her grapefruit. "Mimi only asked me last night after I went upstairs to bed if she could stay and finish her last year of high school in Hideaway Bay."

Martine didn't know what surprised her more: the fact that her daughter wanted to change schools and remain in Hideaway Bay, or that her mother was willing to house her for the next year.

She could see holes in both aspects of the plan. Big, gaping ones. But she knew of her daughter's unhappiness back home and how much she hated school and her lack of friends. It was an awful feeling for a mother knowing her child was sitting alone at the lunch table at school. Then there was Mimi's burgeoning friendship with Kyle Koch. She was grateful for that, but she was also selfish in that she wanted her children near her. Admittedly, she was torn.

"And how would this work out?" Martine pressed. There was an undercurrent of panic in her voice as they were all set to leave after breakfast.

Mimi handed her a plate of two slices of toast, and she took it and set it down in front of her. She picked up her knife and sliced off a bit of butter, spreading it over the toast before reaching for the two jars of jam.

"This would be her residence," Martha said, still working on her grapefruit. "We need to call the school and see what she needs to do to register for the start of school in September and transfer her records from her high school in Washington. She could walk to school; it isn't that far."

Martine leveled a glance at her mother. "And how do you feel about Mimi living with you for the next year?" Out of the corner of her eye, she could see that Mimi had gone quiet at the counter, waiting for the next round of toast. "You've lived alone for a long time, Mother."

Martha shrugged. "I know that. But Mimi knows she can live here with me. We get on pretty well." She half turned in her chair to look at Mimi and asked, "Don't you think we get on pretty well? You don't mind living here, do you?"

Mimi nodded her head vigorously. "I love living in this house."

"Spoken like a true Hahn," Martha said triumphantly.

Martine narrowed her eyes at her mother. "Is this your way of re-establishing contact with me? Through Mimi?"

Martha set her grapefruit spoon down and appeared to wilt. "I can have a relationship with my granddaughter, and you don't need to be a part of it if that is what you wish. However, just to be clear, whatever your final decision, Martine, I will support it."

A little ribbon of jealousy wound through Martine. Why couldn't she have had the relationship with her mother that Mimi so obviously did? But there was also a part of her that was a little joyful that the two of them seemed to have forged a bond. Her mother's offer of an olive branch the previous night still weighed on her mind. But it was up to her, and she would need to think about it. Maybe there was hope.

Edgar arrived, whistling, carrying a canvas bag of groceries in each hand. Through his thinning hair she could see his scalp had some sunburn. He'd told her he'd spent the day enjoying the beach and walking around Hideaway Bay while they were in Ohio.

"Edgar, you're just in time, we're having some grapefruit and toast. Would you care to join us?" Martha asked.

"Let me put these groceries away first and I'll have some toast," he said. Still whistling, he emptied the bags and laid everything out on the counter.

"Mimi, put some toast down for your father," Martha said, finishing the grapefruit and squeezing the rind until juice dribbled onto her spoon.

"Where will I put all this stuff?" Edgar asked.

"I'll do it, Dad, sit down," Mimi said.

"You're just in time for something else, too," Martine said. "Mom and Mimi have cooked up a plan."

"Should I be worried?" Edgar asked.

Martine said, "It depends."

Martha shrugged and said, "Of course not."

Edgar pulled up a chair, sat down, and looked to his wife and then to his mother-in-law. "Well, what's this plan?"

Martine opened her mouth, but Martha put up a hand. "One moment, Martine." She looked at Edgar and said, "Mimi would like to live with me and finish out high school here in Hideaway Bay."

Martine watched the expression on her husband's face as it crumpled. They may be in the midst of marital trouble, but the one thing she could never fault Edgar on was fatherhood. He was a good father. Actually, he was a great one.

"Stay here? And not go back home with us?" he asked. He blanched, and the lines on his forehead deepened. Martine knew he would struggle with this idea and wouldn't be surprised if he vetoed it outright. She said nothing, choosing to spread jam on her piece of toast.

"Yes, that's right. She'd stay with me," Martha continued. "And whatever she needed during the course of the year, whether it be books or clothes or spending money, I would take care of that."

"Martha, that's a very gracious offer, but I—we'll have to think about it," Edgar said soberly. He glanced quickly at Martine, who shrugged and took a bite of her toast with the apricot jam on it.

Mimi laid a plate of toast in front of him, and he stared at it as if unsure what to do. He looked over at his daughter, who sat in the chair opposite him. Mimi gave him a tentative smile.

"And you want to do this, Mimi?" he said. His toast lay in front of him, getting cold.

Martine took his plate and spread butter on his toast for him and then slid it back in front of him. He looked at her quickly and said, "Thanks."

"Very much," Mimi responded.

"But it's so far away," he protested, and his voice trailed off. "And it's your last year before you go away to college. I had all sorts of plans for the four of us."

Mimi snorted. "Three of us."

Martha raised an eyebrow, but Martine ignored them, slathering jam on her second piece of toast. Let Edgar do the heavy lifting and say no. She only wanted to enjoy her breakfast.

"Sweet pea, I'm unsure about this," he said honestly.

"Come on, Dad, you know I hate that high school, and I have no friends," she said quietly.

Edgar winced at this. It hurt him just as much as it hurt Martine that high school had been such a nightmare for Mimi.

"You can change schools out there. Our Lady of the Sacred Heart is a great school," he said.

"Yuck," Mimi said, making a face. "Uniforms, no boys, and we're not even Catholic."

"It's the 'no boys' part I like best," Edgar said.

Martha chuckled at that.

"I like Hideaway Bay. A lot," she pushed. "I could be happy here."

"You haven't been here long enough to be sure," Edgar pointed out. "We all love vacation places but stuck in any place for too long of a time and it would grow old. And you'd miss home."

Poor Edgar, Martine thought. He was grasping at straws.

"If I decide I don't like it, I could always come home," Mimi said.

"Oh, just like that?" Edgar said. "Just transfer back to your old school?"

"I'm sure it's been done before, Dad," Mimi said, her voice weary as if she was growing tired of the subject.

"I don't like the idea of you living so far away from us," he said again. "You're only seventeen!"

"But I'll be eighteen in the spring."

He regarded her for a moment, broke eye contact, looked at the two jars of jam, and finally decided on the sour cherry. "You've got an answer for everything."

She smiled.

Edgar turned to Martine. "What do you think?"

Martine shrugged. "I don't know what to think anymore," she muttered.

Everything was different. Everything she'd encountered since arriving in Hideaway Bay had turned all her preconceived beliefs and ideas onto their heads. She couldn't begin to venture a guess about anything anymore.

Edgar turned to Martha. "And you don't mind a teenager living under your roof? They're a handful. She doesn't keep her room clean, and we have to constantly remind her to get the wet towels off the floor."

"There'll be some rules, but I'm sure we'll manage," Martha replied.

"I've got to think about this some more. But if she stays, we'll pay for her clothes and food and school supplies."

Martha waved him away. "Not necessary."

"You'll have to think about it in a hurry, Edgar," Martine said. "We're supposed to leave after breakfast."

Edgar looked at Martine and appeared crestfallen. She felt sorry for him.

"And what about Christmas?" he said. His face went pale. Edgar loved Christmas. Although he was mindful of their budget during the year, he'd insisted they have a special savings account just for the holidays, and he went all out. Martine had enjoyed Christmas with him down through the years.

"What about it?" Martha asked.

"I like to spend the holidays with my family," Edgar said. "And I can't do that if Mimi is here."

"She'll just have to fly home for it," Martine said.

"I used to like to spend it with my family too," Martha said softly.

A loaded silence drifted down and began to settle around them.

"You could all come here for Christmas," Martha said. "The house is certainly big enough. And maybe you'd like to see Hideaway Bay in the winter."

Edgar looked at her as if she'd just grown a second head, and Martine regarded her thoughtfully over the rim of her teacup.

"Don't you think it's time I met Micah?" Martha said.

"Well, you've given us plenty to think about," Edgar said.

Mimi jumped out of her chair and threw her arms around her father's neck. "Dad, thank you!"

Edgar disentangled himself from her arms and put his hands up. "I haven't said yes yet, Mimi."

But it felt like a foregone conclusion.

Well, that's settled then, Martine thought.

Chapter Forty-Three

Martine

"You keep saying that we had to get married," Edgar said tightly.

After breakfast, Martine had accompanied Mimi to the local high school and filled out all the necessary paperwork. A part of her couldn't believe that this was really happening, that Mimi was leaving the nest.

Despite their daughter's jubilant mood, she and Edgar were still a little stunned over Mimi's decision to remain in Hideaway Bay, and the two of them had retreated to the backyard to be alone. Martine had found an old blanket in one of the upstairs closets and had spread it out over the grass. Due to lack of rain, the grass was turning brown, and crunched beneath them when they lowered themselves onto the blanket.

She wondered if Edgar had brought up this painful topic as a way of not having to deal with the idea that his daughter was leaving the nest prematurely.

"Well, we did," Martine replied.

"But it wasn't like we were eighteen and nineteen and just out of high school. We were almost thirty with well-established careers," Edgar said. He'd stretched out beside her, his hands clasped beneath his head. He stared up at the sky. White puffy clouds sailed lazily past them.

"But you didn't want to get married at that time," Martine said. "You wanted to travel as I remember."

"Did you, Martine? Did you want to get married at that time? We'd only been going out for a few months, we had sex, we weren't careful, but we took responsibility for our actions," Edgar huffed.

Martine was unsure of what she wanted. Or what she wanted him to say. All she knew was she felt a little tender and raw.

"I feel as if we started off wrong," Martine said.

"It wasn't ideal, but I wouldn't label it as wrong or bad," he said. "I wouldn't label it as anything."

"But you didn't want to marry me," she said, pained.

"Always this. We always come back to this!"

"But it's true!"

"How do you know how I felt back then? What makes you think you were privy to my thoughts?"

"Because one night when you had too much to drink, you admitted that to me," Martine cried.

They hadn't even been married a year at the time. Mimi wasn't even Mimi yet; she was still Martha and still an infant. After a night at home of homemade cocktails, Edgar had admitted that he had had a lot of plans, plans that had included solo traveling, plans that did not include her or their baby. When he spoke of his plans—his former plans—his face had lit up. It had been both a soul-crushing moment and a stark realization for Martine. Throughout the course of their marriage, she'd always wondered about it, if she'd held him back. She wondered if he felt he'd settled.

"The key phrase being 'had too much to drink,'" Edgar pointed out.

"*In vino veritas*," Martine said softly.

"I can't go back and change the past, but I've tried to make it better," Edgar said. Frustration tainted his voice. "Eighteen years and I'm still here. It's still me, no matter how we started out. Why doesn't that count for anything? Can you tell me that, Martine?"

"I don't know," she said honestly. And she didn't. Why did she always go back to the beginning? Why couldn't she move on?

"Isn't the staying power and the fact that I've tried to be a good husband and father redemptive of the beginning?"

"I guess it should be," Martine said.

"Can we be honest?" Edgar asked, lowering his voice.

"I would appreciate it," Martine said. Even if it hurt. Even if it wasn't what she wanted to hear.

"Getting married hadn't been in my plans, as you know," Edgar said, his voice rising slightly and enunciating every word. "But as the years rolled on and we raised Mimi and then Micah came along, I can honestly say I wouldn't have traded any of that for any kind of traveling. It has been a marvelous adventure."

Despite the fact that she believed him, she was still filled with doubt.

"But would you have chosen me? If I weren't pregnant and you weren't forced—" she started, her voice anxious. She didn't know why she needed these answers. Or even if she had the answers, that it would be enough.

"Stop saying 'forced.' Nobody forced me to do anything. I made my own decision. You make it sound like I had to marry you under the threat of death! It was a choice I made, one I don't regret!" he said.

Martine didn't say anything. Could you be almost fifty years old and still be filled with loads of self-doubt? She reached past the edge of the blanket and picked at a blade of grass.

Edgar looked back up at her childhood home. "I get that your childhood wasn't ideal. Your father suffered from PTSD and your mother . . . had her own issues," he said. "But I came from a home where there was a good marriage, so I have a template we can work off of."

Martine burst out laughing.

Edgar scowled. "What is so funny?"

Tears rolled out of the sides of her eyes. It wasn't really that funny. Maybe she was just tired. "It was your use of the word 'template.' I don't know why, but it sounded funny. Like if we follow a template, fill in the blanks, then maybe everything will be all right. Everything will be perfect."

"It doesn't have to be perfect. But maybe it will be all right. Have a little faith," Edgar said. "We've made it this far." He picked off a dandelion head and threw it at her playfully.

Martine caught it and twirled it between her hands. "My impressions of my father, such as they are, are that he was a good father when he was sober. The few memories I have of him are good ones."

"I'm happy to hear that, Martine."

"But then growing up and learning that he committed suicide left me with this feeling that I wasn't good enough. Not good enough for him to stick around."

"I get how you would think that, but that probably is far from the truth. Your father likely wasn't even thinking about you and the effect taking his own life would have on you."

"I'll say he didn't think about me," Martine said, trying to sound funny, but it fell flat.

"I didn't mean it like that. I mean he was wrestling with inner demons that prevented him from seeing anything or anyone else besides his own pain," Edgar said quietly.

"Mom was guarded growing up. It was hard to be close to her, she had so many walls up and kept me at arm's length." She rubbed her forehead. More than anything, she'd wanted to be close to her mother, but it had been impossible. Martine had done all sorts of things trying to please her, thinking that now, maybe now, she'd love her, and they'd be close. But it had never happened. Straight A's in school, nothing. Salutatorian of her class, still nothing. Graduated from college, again no change. The hurt was always there. The hurt of the subpar relationship with her mother. She wondered if that feeling would ever go away. Again, the nagging feeling that she didn't measure up. That she wasn't good enough. She relayed all these thoughts to Edgar.

"That couldn't have been ideal," Edgar said, turning his head slightly to face her.

"It was not."

"Why do you want a divorce?" Edgar asked, shifting gears.

"Because I'm unhappy."

"I've guessed that."

Both remained quiet, each lost in their own thoughts. But it was Edgar who spoke first.

"Look, Martine, I'm no psychologist, but this way you feel—sad, depressed—I don't know, will you feel better if we get divorced? Or will you still be feeling the same way you do now?"

"I honestly don't know," she admitted.

"Whether we stay together or we get divorced, I think you might still be unhappy either way."

"Well, thanks for that," she huffed.

"Your feelings will not go away with a divorce."

"I suppose not," she admitted. Maybe she was looking for relief.

"You're stuck on our beginning, looking way back in the past, and you can't see all that we've done since then, or how deeply I have fallen in love with you along the way," Edgar said. "You can't see what's right in front of you. Now."

Martine turned her head slightly and shielded her eyes from the bright midday sun overhead to look at her husband. Over the years, he'd said he loved her, might not have said it all the time, but he did say it here and there. Could that be enough? To maybe not have loved her in the beginning but to have discovered love with her along the way.

"May I make a suggestion?" he asked.

She nodded.

"Martine, I love you, but you need help. Help I cannot give you and that you're not going to find on your own. I think you should see a therapist when we get back home. I'll support you—hell, I'll even drive you to the appointments. But I want you to be happy, more than anything. And then after six months, a year, if you decide you can only be happy by divorcing me, then I'll understand and I won't fight you on it," he said quietly.

She didn't know why she burst into tears. It was as if the sadness had welled up in her and overflowed. Edgar scooted closer to her and pulled her next to him so that her hand rested on his chest and her head lay in the crook of his shoulder. Her body shook as she cried.

"Come on, Martine, it'll be all right, no matter what happens," he said. "And just for the record, you'll always be good enough for me."

Martha

"We really need to get going," Edgar said, glancing at his watch for the fourth or fifth time. He kept saying it but then made no real move to leave. Their suitcase had stood at the front door all morning and hadn't even been put into the trunk of their car. Martha suspected they were dragging their feet about leaving Mimi behind. She couldn't blame them.

"Okay, Edgar, let's do this," Martine said, taking a deep breath.

The four of them stood in the front hall but Martha stayed back a bit, leaning on her walker, giving them some privacy.

"I've got your list, and we'll mail you some of your belongings when we get home," Martine said to her daughter.

"Thanks, Mom."

"Also, could you please wear your glasses from time to time? Until you get contacts?"

"Okay, I will."

Martine turned to Martha. "Mother, are you sure about this? Mimi staying with you? It's a lot to take on." There was a deep furrow between her eyebrows.

"I'm positive. She'll be fine and so will I," Martha said, reassuring her.

"Will you promise me that if it doesn't work out or if it's too much for you, you'll let us know?" Martine said.

"Mom!" Mimi protested.

"Yes, I promise," Martha said.

"Are we ready?" Edgar asked.

"I don't know if I'll ever be ready," Martine said, and her eyes welled up as she pulled Mimi into a hug. She held on to her for a few moments and when she pulled away, she sniffled. "If it doesn't work out and you're not happy here, call us anytime and we'll come get you."

"Okay, Mom," Mimi said, her chin quivering. Her eyes were bright with tears. She tucked a strand of hair behind her ear.

"Everything your mother says, sweet pea," Edgar said, hugging his daughter. When he pulled away, he asked, "Did you put that money in a safe place?"

"Yes, Dad."

"And do exactly as your grandmother says."

"I will," Mimi said, annoyed.

Martine hugged Mimi again, and Edgar turned to Martha. "Martha, thank you for everything." He shook her hand and leaned in and kissed her cheek. "And we'll make plans for Christmas."

"Good," Martha responded.

Martine stared at her mother. Edgar looked from Martha to Martine and back to Martha. "Come on, Mimi, help me load up the car."

He picked up the suitcase, gave Martha a final wave, and slipped out through the front door, followed by Mimi.

"Well, Mother, this is it," Martine said, but she appeared to hesitate.

Unsure, Martha pushed her walker a few steps forward. "Have a safe trip, Martine."

"I'm not looking forward to it," Martine said.

"It's a long drive."

Each of them regarded the other.

"Can I call you?" Martha asked.

"I'm not ready for that yet," Martine replied. Upon seeing her mother's downcast expression, she said, "But I will call you when I am."

"Fair enough."

Martine pointed her thumb over her shoulder. "I better go."

Martha nodded, a huge lump in her throat.

Martine closed the gap between them, leaned over the walker, and put her arms around her mother. Surprised, Martha quickly wrapped her arms around her daughter. Martine let go and slipped through the front door.

The hug was brief, stiff, and awkward, but Martha thought if that was all Martine could give right then, she would gladly take it.

Chapter Forty-Four

Mimi

The sky was largely pink, with a fireball-orange sun just above the horizon. The lake was turbulent in colors of purple, gray, and green. Mimi thought the whole color scheme was pretty. She didn't think she'd ever tire of watching the sun set over Lake Erie.

It had been a long time since she'd felt this good. She was so happy her parents had agreed to her remaining in Hideaway Bay, even if it was on a trial basis. She had three months, and if things weren't going well at the end of that time, then she was to return to Washington State. They also stipulated that she had to text both parents every day and talk on the phone several times a week. There was only one stern warning from her mother: she had to answer her texts.

She and Kyle headed out of the Pink Parlor, ice cream cones in hand. Kyle had gotten his usual: chocolate marshmallow, and Mimi—who was determined to try all the flavors—had chosen caramel swirl, which she'd put in her top five.

They stood on Main Street for a moment, enjoying their cones and looking around.

"Where do you want to go?" Kyle asked.

Mimi shrugged, not caring. She'd tapped into a thick vein of caramel with her tongue and was lost in the moment, enjoying it. A warm, gentle breeze blew through, and she liked the way it felt across the bare skin of her shoulders.

"Do you want to go to the beach or head up toward the highway?" Kyle pressed.

For the past ten or twelve days she'd been in Hideaway Bay, she had hung out a lot with Kyle. They liked to walk up Erie Street to the main highway, sometimes stopping at the Anderson Farm stand to get a piece of fruit. Mimi always bought a peach, but Kyle would pick something different every time.

Other times, they hung out at the beach or walked over to the gazebo in the village square. And as Kyle always seemed to be hungry, they usually made their way to one of the eateries on Main Street to get a bite to eat, whether it be an ice cream cone or salty fries in a white paper bag or saltwater taffy from the five-and-dime.

Mimi thought for a moment. "Why don't we walk up to the highway and then turn back and go to the beach?"

"Okay," Kyle said good-naturedly.

They walked to the end of Main Street and turned right, heading east onto Erie. Mimi glanced at her grandmother's house on the corner. Gram was sitting on the porch, and lifted her hand in a wave when she spotted them.

It was good to see her out on the porch, she thought. It was a magnificent porch that was meant for sitting and enjoying. Mimi planned on making the most of it until the snow fell and forced her inside. She imagined herself sitting out there in a big, bulky sweater and jeans, warming her hands on a cup of pumpkin spice latte. Sometimes, she even pictured Kyle alongside of her.

They walked along Erie Street, moving in toward the curb when a car passed them. They didn't talk, just concentrated on finishing their ice cream cones. When Mimi was finished with hers, she wiped her hands on the napkin and crumpled it up and stuffed it into the pocket of her jeans.

She hadn't seen Kyle in a few days. He'd been to some amusement park in Cedar Point, Ohio with his father and brother and sister, and Isabelle Monroe had gone as well. When Mimi asked him how it went, he'd rolled his eyes. "Just about what you'd expect. Dad and Isabelle are all smiley and laughing all the time. It's kind of gross. Not that I'm against love or anything, but at their age, come on!"

Mimi chuckled at his feigned outrage.

They crossed the railroad tracks and made their way to the main highway. Kyle stared at it and said casually, "When are you heading home?"

She looked at him. She'd been waiting for the right moment to tell him her news. "Actually, I'm going to stay here for the school year. My mother took me to the high school to register for classes before they left."

She pressed her lips together and waited. Although she was hopeful, she was unsure as to what his reaction would be.

But Kyle didn't disappoint. He broke into a big grin and said, "That's awesome!"

Mimi lowered her head so he couldn't see her blush. She didn't know why, but it made her happy that he was pleased. She kicked at a stone.

Kyle lifted his shoulders and glanced at the highway, then pivoted on his foot and looked back toward the lake behind them.

Through the dense foliage of the town's trees, there were glimpses of the bright orange sun. The air was cooler now at nighttime. It was beginning to feel like autumn.

"Come on, let's go to the beach," he said, heading back in the direction they'd come from.

"All right," she said.

As they walked along, he said, "Hey, maybe we'll have some classes together."

She could only hope.

"And if you want, I could maybe show you around and give you the lowdown on the teachers," he said. He looked over at her beside him and added quickly, "But only if you want."

Pleased, Mimi said, "I would like that very much." Maybe they could even sit together at lunch so there'd be no more sitting alone at the lunchroom table.

She lifted her chin and looked toward the lake, unable to hide her smile.

It was going to be a great year.

Chapter Forty-Five

October

"Hello?" Martha said, picking up the handset of the rotary phone in the back room.

"Mother?"

"Hello, Martine," Martha said. It was the first time she'd heard her voice since she'd left. Her heart beat faster with excitement.

"Is this a bad time?" Martine asked nervously.

"Not at all," Martha said. "I'm just sitting here reading the newspaper."

"How's it going with Mimi?"

"Great, she's a good girl," Martha said truthfully. She knew that Mimi spoke to her parents a few times a week and she knew that the girl had settled in and seemed to be happy. She appeared to like school and regaled her with tales every evening at dinner. Along with Kyle, she'd gotten a job at the stand at

Anderson Farms at the corner of the highway and Erie Street. Right now they were busy selling pumpkins and squash.

"How are you, Mother?"

"I'm fine," she said. "I've been going to physical therapy for my hip, and that seems to help."

"I'm glad to hear it."

"And how are Edgar and Micah?" Martha asked.

"They're good. We're adjusting without Mimi here but we're carrying on," Martine said.

"How are things going with you?" Martha asked.

"I'm in a better place."

Martha closed her eyes with relief. "I'm glad to hear that."

"I'm going to therapy and after Christmas, Edgar and I are going to couples' therapy."

"That's wonderful news."

There was a long stretch of silence that quickly turned awkward.

Martine cleared her throat and said, "I have something to ask. And it's kind of trivial."

"Go ahead," Martha said. She could not imagine what it would be.

"Remember how Gram used to make the best pies? Strawberry-rhubarb, blueberry?"

"I do."

"What I remember is how flaky her pie crusts were. My own crusts are not as flaky, and I don't know what I'm doing wrong."

"I'll tell you the secret: ice-cold water," Martha said. She beamed. So this was what it was like to have a normal conversation with your daughter.

"Really? Huh. I'll try that. I wonder, would you share her recipes with me?" Martine asked nervously.

"Of course I would. Her recipes are still here in the house, and I can send them to you," Martha said. This made her happy. Martine should have her grandmother's recipes.

"You don't mind?"

"Of course not, they should be passed down and as you know, I was never much of a baker," Martha said.

Martine laughed. "I do remember that."

There was silence again and Martine said in a shaky voice, "Okay, Mother, thanks. I'll be talking to you."

"I'll look forward to that."

"Have you decided if you're going to the semi-formal?" Martha asked.

She was in a good mood. The phone call from Martine had buoyed her and filled her with hope.

Mimi had mentioned the dance to her the previous week, and she thought she sensed excitement within the girl. She'd like to see her all dressed up with her hair done. She was a beautiful girl.

Mimi sat on the small embroidered footstool at the side of her grandmother's chair, sipping her tea. No matter how many times Martha urged her to sit in a more comfortable chair or on the sofa, she always chose the stool next to Martha.

"I am. Kyle and I are going as friends." When Martha raised an inquisitive eyebrow, Mimi added hurriedly, "He's my best friend, and it seemed like the way to go."

"Of course," Martha said.

She was glad Mimi had a date, and she liked Kyle. He was a mannerly boy, and maybe she had a soft spot for him because he lost his mother so young. That couldn't have been easy. "We'll need to get you a dress and shoes."

Mimi perked up at that.

"And maybe get your hair and nails done," Martha added. She might be old, but she remembered what it was like to be a young woman.

Before Mimi could reply, the phone rang, interrupting their conversation. Mimi jumped up and lifted the receiver from the cradle.

"Oh, hello, Edward, sure, she's right here. I'll get her. Just a minute." She lifted the heavy old-fashioned phone off the desk and carried it over to her grandmother, handing her the receiver.

"It's Edward Lindahl, Ned's son," she whispered.

Martha's heart sank. With a shaking hand, she took the phone from Mimi, said hello, and listened to what Edward had to say on the other end of the line. Nodding intermittently, she finally said, "I see. Thank you for letting me know, Edward."

She handed the phone back to Mimi, who placed it in its cradle.

Martha couldn't help that she began to cry. She and Ned spoke on the phone every Sunday night, but the last few times, she'd noticed his voice was getting weaker, and he tired easily.

"Gram, what is it?" Mimi asked, her voice a horrified whisper.

Martha pulled a tissue out of the box next to her and wiped her eyes and blew her nose. "Ned passed away this morning." She swallowed hard, blew her nose again, and tossed the crumpled-up tissue into the small wastebasket at her feet.

"Gram, I'm sorry," Mimi said. She pulled her stool closer until her knees touched her grandmother's shins. Tentatively she placed her hand over her grandmother's folded ones.

"Edward said he developed pneumonia on Monday night, and his wish was not to be resuscitated," Martha explained. Tears filled her eyes again and she dabbed them away. For the second time in her life, she'd lost him. But this time for good.

"Did you want a cup of tea?"

Martha shook her head and gave Mimi a smile, thinking that seemed to be the girl's solution to everything: a cup of tea. She supposed she was too young to be knowledgeable in all areas of comforting people, but she had a good heart and the rest of it would come with time. She was a natural at making people feel better.

"Your company is enough right now for me," Martha finally said.

Mimi gave her a tentative smile. She swallowed hard and asked, "Do you regret not marrying Ned?"

Martha gave her a reassuring pat on the hand. Aware the girl's eyes were fixed on her, she said, "I've given this a lot of thought. No, I don't regret not marrying Ned. It was just one of those things." She appeared thoughtful for a moment. "Besides, if I'd married Ned, I wouldn't have you."

And her granddaughter broke into a wide smile that was beautiful for its earnestness.

"Gram, do you want me to go in with you?" Mimi asked as they waited in the reception area of the doctor's office.

"Of course not!" Martha said, feigning annoyance.

Mimi laughed.

"It's hard to offend you, young lady," Martha said with a grin.

"Because I know you too well, Gram," Mimi said.

"I'll have to try harder. I must be losing my touch," Martha said. She leaned forward and picked up the latest issue of *People* magazine and began to leaf through it.

It had been a week since Ned died. Martha had decided against going to Ohio for the funeral. She didn't think she was up for it. She and Ned had been given a little more time, and that was what she was going to remember.

The door to the back room opened and a nurse stepped out and called, "Martha Cotter."

"That's me," Martha said, standing and placing her hands on her walker.

"I'll be right here if you need me," Mimi said.

The nurse smiled at her. "It's nice to see you, Mrs. Cotter. We haven't seen you in a long time."

"Mm."

"I'm going to get your weight and take you to an exam room."

With the nurse's assistance, Martha stepped on the scale and once her weight was recorded, the nurse helped her off and directed her to exam room three, where she recorded her temperature, heart rate, and blood pressure. She helped Martha up onto the exam table that was covered in a paper sheet.

She didn't have to wait long before Dr. Morrison appeared.

"Well, Mrs. Cotter, this is a pleasant surprise," he said, smiling.

Yes, she definitely liked him. His expression was warm and open, and his smile reached his eyes. His face was lined in the corners of the eyes and around his mouth, suggesting a lot of time spent outside and a lot of time laughing and smiling. The world needed more people like him and Mimi.

"I like keeping people on their toes," she said evenly with a hint of a smile.

He looked at her and there was mischief in his eyes. "I bet you do." He pulled the wheeled stool out, took a seat, and glanced at the computer screen. "Your vitals are good. Have you had any more spells?"

She shook her head. "No, not once. Like I said at the time, I had a shock that day. But things are all right now."

"I'm glad to hear it. Martha, you haven't had bloodwork in a while. I'm going to give you a script to take to the lab, you know the one on the highway in the same plaza as the supermarket?"

Martha nodded. "I knew you'd sucker me in for other things."

He slapped his knee and let out a hearty laugh. "Just doing my job."

She smiled along with him.

Chapter Forty-Six

Martha

"There's a lot to remember when driving in snow," Martha said from the passenger seat in the yellow Caddy.

In the driver's seat, Mimi looked quickly over to her grandmother before returning her attention to the snow-covered road in front of her. She had just backed out of the driveway and now headed toward town.

She'd gotten her New York State permit to drive. Martha took her out practicing a few times a week. But Hideaway Bay had had its first snowfall of the season, and everything looked pretty covered in snow. Martha felt as there wasn't a lot of accumulation, this was the perfect time to learn how to drive in inclement weather. The girl would have to learn sooner or later.

"First, don't speed," Martha said, putting up a gloved finger. "Because if you hit a patch of ice, you'll go sailing in the air."

Mimi nodded but kept her eyes on the road. She wore a lavender-colored parka with fur trim on the hood. Around her head, she wore a snood. And most importantly, she was wearing her glasses.

"Second, don't slam on the breaks if you do hit a patch of ice because you'll go sliding all over the place. With the Caddy, you'll need to pump the brakes, but I don't think that's necessary with these newer cars."

Christmas was only three weeks away and Martine, Edgar, and Micah were flying in for ten days. Martha couldn't remember the last time she'd been so excited. She was looking into all sorts of activities for Micah. She had purchased a Christmas tree from the Anderson Farm stand, where Mimi and Kyle continued to enjoy their part-time jobs. With Mimi's help, she'd pulled down all the boxed Christmas decorations from the attic, things she hadn't seen in decades. Some items were beyond saving and had to be tossed, but there was still a good number of vintage decorations. In the meantime, Mimi and Kyle had been baking up a storm of Christmas cookies and bars in Martha's kitchen. Alice Monroe had given them some recipes to start with. They'd made a deal: Martha would buy their ingredients, and they would do the baking and the cleanup. Everyone was happy.

"Also, if you go into a spin, don't slam on the brakes, let your foot gently off the gas pedal and steer in the direction of the spin," Martha advised.

Martha looked at all the shops along Main Street and studied their decorations. There were giant wreaths with red ribbons, every store window had Christmas lights on it, and the braver ones had opted for sprayed-on snow, which would require a blowtorch to get off after the holidays were over.

"I hope I remember all this," Mimi said. She drove to the end of Main Street, circled around the space that held the gazebo and war memorial, and headed back down through town.

"You will."

Martha made a mental note to put together an emergency kit for when Mimi had a car of her own. She'd need a blanket, a flashlight, a pair of jumper cables, and a bottle of water.

"Okay, where to, Gram?" Mimi asked when she arrived at the end of Main Street.

Martha was aware of the line of cars that had built up behind them as Mimi was driving slowly. But they would just have to wait. Mimi needed to take her time. She was not to be rushed.

"Why don't we stop at the Monroe house and see if Lily has any beach-glass crafts we could buy as gifts or decorate the house with."

Mimi looked over at her, eyes wide. "Really?"

"Yes, really."

Mimi smiled, turned on her indicator, and made a right-hand turn onto Star Shine Drive.

Martha glanced at the beach. The lake was gray and turbulent, with heavy, foamy whitecaps hitting the shore. The beach itself was covered in snow. Even when it appeared bleak, it was still beautiful.

She still thought about Ned sometimes, and every once in a while he would visit her in her dreams, looking the way he had when she'd first met him: his blue-eyed gaze intense and his blond hair shining in the sun. But it was no use dwelling on the past. Christmas was coming and so was the rest of her family. She smiled to herself, content. There was so much to look forward to.

To stay up to date with new releases and to receive the exclusive novella, *Escape to Hideaway Bay*, sign up for my newsletter at www.michelebrouder.com

ALSO BY MICHELE BROUDER

The Hideaway Bay Series

Coming Home to Hideaway Bay

Meet Me at Sunrise

Moonlight and Promises

When We Were Young

Once Last Thing Before I Go

Escape to Ireland Series

A Match Made in Ireland

Her Fake Irish Husband

Her Irish Inheritance

A Match for the Matchmaker

Home, Sweet Irish Home

An Irish Christmas

Happy Holidays Series

A Whyte Christmas

This Christmas

A Wish for Christmas

One Kiss for Christmas

A Wedding for Christmas

Printed in Great Britain
by Amazon